Just Went Out For Milk

TOMMY COTTON

Photo copyright © Mariya Mova

Tommy Cotton is a quirky writer from Melbourne, Australia.

CONTACT TOMMY:
www.facebook.com/TommyCottonAuthor
Twitter @tommycotton
Instagram @tommycotton
www.tommycotton.com

JUST WENT OUT FOR MILK

ISBN:
978-0-9925927-1-4 (Paperback)
978-0-9925927-2-1 (Ebook)

Book design by Scarlett Rugers Design
www.scarlettrugers.com

*For my mother, Elizabeth. I hope I'm making you proud.
And for Pauli. My father, best friend and hero.*

The most beautiful people are not those thought to be ideal.
They are the ones who have suffered, endured and overcome pain.
They are scarred and imperfect.
But they are strong and stand out for their spirit,
their smiles brighter for the darkness they've experienced.
They are real.

LEAVING HOME

It was on the first day of Grade Three that I received two pieces of conflicting advice, which would shape my course of action whenever trouble found me from this point on.

I stood at the school gates. My older brother, Stevie, knelt down in front of me, his blonde fringe dipped below his eye.

'You're twins, Dane; you know he's got a short fuse.' He nodded toward Josh, who sat by the swing set with his arms crossed, sulking because he had been bullied at lunch. 'I'm not going to be there all the time, so you need to stand up for him.'

'But what if one of the big kids tries to fight me when I do?'

'Never back down for what you believe in, and especially not for the people you love.'

He faked a slow motion punch to my jaw. I took his fist in my palms and kicked him in the shin. 'Like that?'

'Yep, just like that,' he chuckled as he rubbed his leg.

That afternoon Josh and I walked up our driveway, scuffing our feet in the dirt. Before we could touch foot on the first rickety wooden step Mum flung open the screen door. Behind her came the smash of glass.

'Boys, take your school bags and go into the paddock.' She was panicking in a way I had never seen her do before. 'Run!'

I didn't think about what was happening; just followed impulse and my mother's instruction.

Since then I have known what it's like to feel a rush. I've always lived on a whim. Well, mostly. If I had followed every urge I've ever had, I would have had much more sex and killed a lot more people.

Although I often met conflict head on, it was my impetuousness and an echo of my mother's advice that found me at Tullamarine airport on an overcast November day in 1986, with only a backpack, about to board a plane to Los Angeles. Any plans I had for a life in Australia had been crushed in the preceding days.

It was on the Melbourne waterfront that a friend and fellow docker, Teddy Fitzpatrick, first told me about life in America. Bear, as we called him, was a gentle giant who towered over me and dwarfed my six-foot-four frame, whose voice hit octaves so low they made Barry White sound like a Chipmunk. Teddy had been on a university exchange to the States as part of his medical degree.

For years I roamed North America. The travel and encounters along the way bred new life into me. The quiet nights I slept under stars in Texas, the noisy nights at bars in Brooklyn, the days I strode along deserted Midwestern highways. The endlessness of the Grand Canyon and wandering through misty woods in the outskirts of Minnesota.

It didn't matter how much I journeyed, though, the urge to move on remained. As soon as an adventure was done, I needed a new one. Another chance to start over.

The constant throughout my life was always the beach. I would find myself there when I became lost and needed to feel at home. I'd sit on sand and rocks, in sun and rain, and listen to the waves wash into the shore and whisper, 'Life always carries on.'

I stopped on the shore one scorching-hot afternoon in California, 1988.

I lay on the sand of Venice Beach. A lonely cloud floated across the blue summer sky. A gentle sea breeze massaged my skin and soothed the heat of the sun's rays. Water ebbed and flowed on the shoreline like the slow swinging arm of a pendulum. The place was alive with vibrant sounds. From the boardwalk behind me, local merchants hollered, drum circles pattered African beats, street performers turned out tunes, impassioned street-ballers trash-talked and metal clunked from Muscle Beach Gym. On the sand children played, narrated only by their unaffected laughter. The bikinis, bronzed skin and bodies: it was amazing. For a boy who had grown up in a small country town some hours out of Melbourne, it felt like a movie set.

An old man with leather for skin plucked the notes of *Hotel California* on an acoustic guitar. At the moment he hit the second G, something walked across my line of vision.

The girl wasn't obsessed like everyone else – checking to see who admired them. She seemed to notice very little, alone in her own world. She was about the only girl on the beach not in a bikini, but with her sun-blessed skin and the way her light, white summer dress clung to her body, there was every reason to suggest she would have shamed them all. She passed no more than a few metres in front of me, brushing her wavy brown hair from her face. I cleaned my Wayfarers. 'If her personality is half as good as how she looks, then wow,' I thought. 'I need to know.'

With my backpack still attached, I ran after her and left the sun bakers behind me with a shower of sand. The bottom of her dress ruffled in the breeze like the sail of a yacht. She crossed her feet as she walked, hips swaying side to side ever so slightly. Every few steps she made a small skip forward as if to dodge imaginary cracks in the ground.

I slowed as I caught her. 'Excuse me,' I said. She was tiny, so perfectly feminine. I touched her shoulder. 'Hi ...'

That was as far as I got.

Before I could finish any introduction she spun and kicked me in the nuts. 'Don't touch me you fucking creep.'

I fell to the ground and held on.

I went to talk but the pain increased, as it does with a firm kick to the crown jewels. I gasped for air. She had taken my breath away, in every sense, but for some strange reason I felt more alive than ever.

I coughed and spluttered, and finally wheezed out, 'Hello would have been nicer.'

The corner of her lip curled upward and sunshine glazed her cheek. I was captivated by a smile that would spawn a thousand happy memories.

'Hello,' said Kayla, and she had me.

CHAPTER 1

It was one of those nights when something eerie is in the air. Like the calm when haze covers a city sky and you can smell a bush fire burning thirty kilometres away.

For late October the heat was outrageous, even for California. It was as if autumn had jumped back to summer for the night, the way a scratched CD skips on a track. The kind of night when people sleep with windows open, bedrooms like oversized ovens, a gentle breeze and the cool side of the pillow the only fleeting respites.

Midnight had long expired when Kayla and I sneaked out of the apartment with a blanket and ran through the streets hand in hand. My ears rang and eyes, although burning, remained peeled and alert with the energy of over-tiredness.

On the beach, the tide rolled into the shore, the shhh of the water, a sound usually drowned by the eclectic resonances of Venice, heard from far away in the dead of night.

The day to come would mark five years since Kayla had kicked me in the nuts. Five crazy years. Every twist on our rollercoaster ridden with passion. The laughs we shared brought on stomach cramps, and Kayla made me smile so much my jaw ached.

Beside the pier, we stopped and held hands. Moonlight illuminated her face. I got lost in her emerald eyes, a place where I could see everything beautiful about this world. Kayla's effect on me was mystical, beyond what words can describe. I ran my hand through her hair and down her neck, then pulled her close and felt the curves of her waist, the smoothness of her skin beneath her tee, and let out a snigger. It was hard not to when the immensity of what I felt for her crashed over me in a wave of joy. I loved her more than I ever thought

I could love anything. In times like this, I wished I could lock it away to keep it safe, and perhaps one day express it properly. 'I'm so bloody lucky to have you, Babe,' I said.

'You're pretty awesome, Dane.'

One smirk from her, a flair in those eyes, and the joy inside me erupted like a volcano and spat passionate lava, energy surging from every muscle in my body. We broke into a rushed and urgent tango of tearing each other's clothes off.

Into the early hours of the morning, we lay atop the blanket under the pier and screwed like hormone-riddled fifteen-year-olds. Our bodies slid against one another, heat steaming in the glow of moonlight. Kayla's sweat filled my mouth as I massaged her neck with my tongue and lips, and then her nipples, down to her legs and back up to her pussy. Her thighs tightened around my head and she clawed my forearms as her body jolted to the movement of my tongue against her clitoris. Sand stuck to my knees as I came up for air and moved back to her neck and then mouth.

I'd been away on a breather for nine days. Kayla was wound up and so was I, which I discovered with powerful, body-clapping thrusts inside her. She rolled me over, off the rug and into the sand, and while she grinded on top of me she held my throat. I grasped her buttocks and drove her back and forth. I tossed her onto her back once again and pinned her down. My pubic bone pressed into her clitoris and she lost control, her fingernails breaking skin on my back as she came. We switched, slapped, clasped and took control of one another in turn, and as we faced each other on our sides Kayla's third climax brought me to explode in time with her.

Panting, we sprawled over the rug, exhausted, and covered in sweat and sand.

'I see you've missed me,' I said.

'Another day and I was buying a dildo and changing the locks to the apartment,' she said. 'Don't flatter yourself. You're replaceable.'

I wiped sand onto her naked breast. 'You're a bitch, you know.'

'And you're a jerk.' With a clump of sand in her palm she slapped me.

I left it there. With Kayla these play fights could go on forever, and would often escalate to the point where I feared for some part of my manhood.

Kayla rolled over and nestled into me. 'You remember the house I told you about?' she asked. 'The one up the coast, just out of San Francisco, the one on the cliff overlooking the ocean? The one with all the ghosts and all that stuff that supposedly happened there. It's beautiful. You know the one, right?'

I knew it well. Kayla crapped on about it constantly.

'Yeah, what about it?'

'We should buy it, tomorrow … we should just go. It's been for sale forever. They can't sell it because of the ghosts and the history and all that.'

'We don't have the cash, and I don't know if I want to move from here. I like LA. I've made friends. I'm comfortable here. This is our home.'

'You have no trouble leaving for ten days,'

'Nine.'

'Whatever. Fuck you.' Kayla sat up. 'Why can't you just relax and think about it? We'll figure out the money … Anyway, forget about it now. There's something I need to talk to you about.'

It was nearing sunup and I hadn't slept. I was crabby and needed coffee. 'This is our home – what don't you understand?'

'We won't buy the house. Screw it … Dane, I need to talk to you.'

I snapped. 'So talk!'

Kayla swung her arm out and hit me in the shoulder. 'Don't worry about it.' She lay down with her back to me.

I realised what a grump I was being. 'If you want to tell me something, I'd love to hear it,' I reassured her, but it was little use. Kayla's breathing had deepened to an opened-mouth snore.

As the sun rose across the water I shook her awake enough to dress. I slung the blanket over my shoulder, attached Kayla and piggy-backed her home.

'I love you, Rascal. You know that, right?' I said as I rounded the corner onto our street.

Kayla's mouth clacked with saliva. 'I know. I'm pretty fond of you, too.'

I bumped her arse and feet entering the apartment, which was met with a grumbled expletive. She slid off my back, stripped down to her knickers in a flash and passed out on the sofa.

I put on a pot of coffee. Although I fought against weights on my eyelids, my body clock was forever tuned to the early morning starts of Melbourne's waterfront, and a dependency on coffee.

The alphabet magnets on the refrigerator were arranged into **DANE EATS ASZ**. Beneath the Z was a picture of the house in San Francisco that Kayla had torn from a magazine. I opened the fridge door. An empty milk bottle. No milk meant no coffee, and I needed coffee.

I took a pad of Post-it notes and sat at the coffee table across from Kayla.

Her head was propped up on a throw cushion. Mouth open and snoring with the sound of a two-stroke motor, ever so elegant my girl, her breathing grew louder until she snorted and startled herself, wriggled and then reset her position. I enjoyed watching her sleep, as gross as it was. When you fall in love with someone, you treasure their quirks as much as anything else. Flaws become unique marks of character: things you'd miss if they weren't there.

The cream of the sofa showed through the gap in between her upper thighs, which ran all the way to her lace pink knickers. I grew hot as I surveyed her from toe to head: ticklish calves, tight little pussy, the indent of her waist, perky breasts, tanned skin, sex eyes (even when closed) and, despite drool seeping from her mouth, lips that drove me wild with what they could do.

I should've given into temptation …

I scribbled, 'Just went out for milk.'

I stuck the note to Kayla's cheek and kissed her forehead. She mumbled something about Colonel Clink and kicked out her leg.

The morning crowd was out on the footpath: drunkards stumbling home, dog walkers, joggers, the elderly aplenty. Three blocks over I entered the corner convenience store, the door jingling a familiar welcome.

'Good morning, Skippy.' George Hernandez tilted the straw hat that never left his head. His brother, Jose, who with tanned, wilted skin and deep brown, teddy-bear eyes looked close to a twin, uttered the same over his shoulder as he restacked the cigarette shelf.

Many years before, the exact date I'm not sure, the Hernandez brothers had come north from Mexico. They never said so, but, with certain intimations, made it known to me that rather than a Boeing they'd taken the Rio Grande. They had come with nothing other than wet clothes on their backs and a dream to make a life in the country that promised so much. Together they worked from the bottom and turned one convenience store into six, and took a bud of an idea and made it blossom into one of the largest funeral parlour chains in Greater Los Angeles, Ibis Funeral Homes. They still worked at the first store they'd opened.

'Is an extension of the night for me, I'm afraid,' I said and placed a bottle of milk on the counter, 'so I'm in need of a kick to make it a morning.'

'Coffee doesn't replace sleep, Amigo.' George took the coins and rather than slotting them inside the open cash register, dropped them into the jar marked with my name.

'You know, if I keep this up you will have to start taking my money.'

'Maybe,' he replied. 'Maybe you take what we owe you though.'

In turn, the three of us glanced to the half-moon of plaster on the ceiling some shades lighter than the surrounding paint. It was how we became friends, how we learned to trust each other.

The evening after I first met Kayla I wandered into the Hernandez's store. Had I not needed milk, had there not been a robbery about to take place, had I not tackled the gunman, had the bullet not shot into the roof: things may have been very different ...

After this the brothers wouldn't let me pay, but I wouldn't keep the money, and so a compromise was reached – the jar.

Through the window, rain now teemed down.

'I can find an umbrella if you want one, Amigo,' said George.

'I'll pass. A walk in the rain can do wonders for the soul.'

'Can do wonders for a cold,' added Jose.

I took the milk from the counter. 'I'll pass.'

'I hear a storm's coming, going to wash everything away,' said George. 'Everything just disappear.'

'This is Los Angeles, Fellas, think you've got your weather tuned to the tropics.'

'You don't get caught out in that storm, Hombre, you don't get swept up in that water and disappear now,' George called.

'Life's full of waves.' I winked at him. 'I learned to surf a long time ago.'

'Send me a postcard from your desert island, Skippy.'

The doorbell jingled and I waved goodbye.

✳ ✳ ✳

I had walked a block in the downpour. The throngs of early-morning folks had disappeared, and I was nearly alone. Over the road at the steps of an apartment building a man and woman cursed each other in screams and jagged hand movements. They were drug addicts, or alcoholics, or crazy – perhaps all.

The skeletally thin woman scrunched her face: the determined look girls get just before they jump on top of a man or slap them. She slapped him. Then, like a movie when someone sits on the remote control and bumps the fast-forward button, the man reeled back, cocked his fist and punched the woman square on the nose.

When I was a child I learned that it is never okay to strike a woman. Some men deserve to be beaten severely, some deserve to die, but no woman should be harmed. Blood poured from her nose. I was now only a couple of metres away.

In a flash, grey buildings, graffiti and sidewalks disappeared. There was no beach, no palm trees. A yellow expanse surrounded me – straw it might have been, or was it a kitchen with linoleum floor? Glass smashed, someone told me to run … I couldn't.

The man was on his back. His head bounced against the concrete as it was pounded fist by fist into a bloodied pulp. I was on top of him at one point. Then I watched from my knees. There was an awful lot of blood, so much blood … Beyond the puddles of blood, the milk bottle was smashed to pieces, milk dripping into the gutter.

The next thing I remember, my face was pushed onto the bonnet of a car. Red and blue lights. Loud talking. Cuffs.

LETTER 1

October 21 1993

Dane,

I need to tell you something.

Last night I tried but, like always, you got caught up and had to make a point. Next time I try, I will shut you up and make you listen.

I've rehearsed over and over again for the past week how I will tell you. You'll be fine with it, and I remind myself of this every time I go through the sit-down, speak-calm and comfort-each-other bits, but it's been eight days since I found out, and still I haven't told you, and I know I need to.

I'll treasure last night, regardless. I needed one more stupid night, one more sunset and sunrise unchained, and one more awkward, out-of-control round of sex on uneven terrain before I become a homebody by imposition.

How is it you finished school at sixteen and still have a higher education than me? It's funny, now I come to think of it, that this is almost the entire extent to which we've indulged each other in our respective histories. With what lies ahead maybe it's time for us to share where we came from. But I don't know how you would accept my past. I think it's a lot to ask.

'The past is the past for a reason, Babe,' you've always said when the topic creeps into conversation. 'There's a reason humans aren't built with rear-view mirrors – we aren't made to look back.'

I wonder if you have as many ugly monsters hidden in your closet. It would be easier if you did. One big disgusting monster party in our bedroom when the closet doors open sounds like fun.

The past is the past, you're right, and it is unchangeable, but maybe we can glance back sometimes just to know the road ahead is so much prettier for the bumpy ones we've already traveled.

I haven't written anything longer than a scribble for years – not since I traded a chewed pencil and knife for a handful of clay and a paintbrush – and after this I probably won't, because this is just another rehearsal. When you're home with some fattening milk for your coffee (and belly) I'll sit you down and tell you. I need to tell you.

I was at the studio Monday morning when I received the call. For as long I could, I continued to slosh paint onto the canvas but stopped eventually and stared at the children huddled into the corner. Where the hell are they now? When the air became thick I left and escaped to the foreshore to further delay the drive to the tall white-plastered building.

As I walked along the sand my legs felt like they could walk forever. The waves rolled in at ankle height and cooled my feet at water's edge. A Dalmatian bounded up to me and I petted its head before I tossed the chewed tennis ball for it to fetch. The dog bounced away after its prize. There was a family to my left with the porcelain-white skin of holiday makers from the north. The mom read a magazine under a sun umbrella, while the dad threw a football with the son and the daughter arranged a selection of seashells near her mother's perfectly painted toenails.

The far end of the foreshore was deserted. I could taste the ocean air on the back of my tongue. As I crossed toward the boardwalk, the sand became softer. I could imagine what it would feel like to have clouds underfoot. There was a moment before I stepped onto the boardwalk when I turned to see distant white cliffs and a house peering over the ocean, a man outside, tall and scruffy, statuesque and unaffected by the wind. His arms didn't move but he reached for me, clapped his little finger against his thumb, an invisible tear in his eye. I could've gone home. I didn't need to go and find out – I already knew – but I did.

I went to the hospital. I waited in the waiting room for a doctor who was running late, sat in a chair I couldn't quite get comfortable in, in a room of uniform and uninspired safety furniture. I listened to words I'd already heard from a doctor I'd already imagined with his hands clasped in the same way I'd already seen, and he told me the news I already knew.

Remember the lump, the one you couldn't feel?

'It's nothing to worry about,' you said. 'Come on Kayla, you're not a hypochondriac.'

You're somewhere out in the warming Cali rain as I write this. And once you return I might just drag you right back out there. We'll run around like children and laugh at the people as they flee indoors with papers on their heads.

At least one more occasion unchained before I settle into the shackles. Life is crazy, we're crazy and free, and we were born to run. But we can't run from this. I can't run from this. I don't need you here, but hell, I'd like it if you were. There're not too many people who I can be bothered with, but you are one of them.

It's cancer, Dane. The tumor is malignant, and they can't tell me the primary cause.

They won't operate on it, given the size and where the elephant sits on my inner thigh, so they will nuke it with chemotherapy first before radiation burns it up completely.

'We have to be cautious and do everything to stop it spreading,' said Dr Simms. 'We will work to determine the primary cause, but the area is sensitive. Right now we cannot give you a prognosis.'

There was a time when I thought death might be an escape, but now I dread to think of not being here. The thought of losing the things I have, like my art, the beach, and you, scares me the most.

I'll be glad to have you there in a white protective suit to bear the oncoming bomb and mushroom cloud with me.

We'll get through this, it's what we do, and then we'll take our cash: yours in the cookie jar and the stash of mine you don't know about in the mattress, and we'll get that house on the hill, and gaze over the sea every morning. You and me, Babe, that's how it's meant to be.

I know you'll be fine with me going bald and weak, and you'll take it in your stride, because that's what you do. And I hope you'll be fine with my dark past, because I see our future as bright.

Kayla

DIARY 1

February 14 1978

In the morning I got ready for school and did my hair in
pigtails so it was extra pretty. Mommy was still in bed when I
ate my breakfast. For breakfast I had a bowl of Cheerios and a
glass of juice. I packed my books, my lunch and my Leroy the
Lion in my bag and then I went to school. On the bus a girl
named Anna in Fourth Grade sat behind me and pulled on my
pigtails and said they looked stupid the whole way to school.

At lunch time I ate my sandwich in the back corner of the
yard, so there was no one else around. Leroy helped do a
celebration for my birthday and gave me a pretty pink flower.
He told me it made me look like a princess when I put it in my
hair. I felt like a real princess for the whole of lunch time, until
we had to go back into class. That's when Sophie in my class
stole the flower and ruined it. I didn't feel so good for the rest
of the day. When it was time to sing happy birthday to me, I
didn't want to hear it.

When I got home, Mommy had a friend over and I could
hear their noises, even when I put *Looney Tunes* on really loud
and covered my ears. Some noises you can't stop from hearing.

I've met four of Mommy's friends before: Mr Checker Suit,
Mr Policeman, Mr Gray Suit and Mr Black Suit.

Mommy's new friend is Mr Ignatius. The stairs creaked three
times when he and Mommy came downstairs – the second,

fourth and ninth. He said hello to me and told me I looked pretty with my hair in pigtails. He left and kissed Mommy on the cheek. 'Same time next week then Carol?'

Mommy nodded. As soon as she closed the door she hurried up to her room, and then came down in different clothes with new makeup and her hair done nicely. She had on black stockings and a black dress. Mommy is really pretty. I wish I'm as pretty as her someday.

She rushed around the house for a little bit and then fluffed her hair in the mirror near the entrance.

'Kayla, I've gotta head out. We will celebrate later, or tomorrow, okay? There is cake in the freezer if you want to take it out.' She kissed me on the cheek.

The door sounded like a boom of thunder when it closed behind her. The house was silent except for Bugs Bunny. I stood at the window and put my hands on the glass. I wanted to go outside, and walk next to Mommy and hold her hand, but I couldn't. I wasn't allowed to. Mommy's car drove away. It looked like the hedges at the start of our street ate her car. Sometimes it feels like Mommy's car won't come back and I get scared and don't know what to do.

Ice started to grow on the walls and it became too cold for me to stay in the living room by myself, so I went and got Leroy, and we sat in the kitchen and waited for the cake to defrost. We both put party hats on and had party poppers too.

When the cake was ready to eat I put ten candles on top of it and lit them with the matches from the stove. I blew them all out with one breath and then made my wish. I wished for Mommy.

I cut a slice of cake for Leroy, a slice for me and a slice for Mommy. It was carrot cake, which is my least favorite cake, and it was all clumpy, but I was happy to have a birthday cake. Last year Mommy forgot and I tried to make my own, but it didn't come out very well.

After we'd eaten and cleaned up I went and did some drawing. I drew a big picture of me, Leroy and Mommy celebrating my birthday around the table. Drawings are good because you can make them anything you want to, like having dreams on a piece of paper.

I stayed up late, right until Mommy got home. I stood at the top of the stairs and watched her come into the house. I do it a lot. I stand there and tell myself I'm going to go down and talk to her, but I don't.

Mommy sat in the kitchen for a long time, staring at the wall. I really wanted to hug her, but I was too scared the noise of the stairs would wake up winter. When Mommy finally moved I sneaked back into bed. I cuddled Leroy and listened to Mommy's footsteps in the hallway. I hoped they would stop at my room, but they didn't.

CHAPTER 2

I awoke to a splash of water on my cheek. I lay on concrete, a puddle by my side. Dampness stuck in my nostrils. Outside, the wind whistled. Through the barred window near the roof of the cell moonlight filtered in and divided the cell in half with a cone of white. It was a different cell to the one I had lost consciousness in.

My neck felt too weak to hold my head up and my body ached when I sat. A chill was in the air but my skin throbbed with heat from the beating. My right eye was swollen and covered with a patch, my ribs had been bandaged and my T-shirt was covered with splats of dried blood. I had no clue how long I'd been out for.

The man I pummelled was an undercover agent.

I was thrown into a dark cell, cuffed at the hands and ankles. First, two uniform cops beat me, and then two suits had their turn. Sometime and somewhere between there and this cell must have been a hospital stay, on my wrist a patient bracelet.

Across the cell, a pair of white sandshoes, which had begun to detach from their soles, stuck out into the light. From a corner came spluttering, and from another emerged a man, who crawled on his belly into the white cone. His eyes were dark, and his skin dirty, a long, thick scar on his cheek. In his hands he shuffled a deck of cards.

'You play cards. Blackjack?' he asked with the roll and nasal tone of a Mexican.

'A little.' This was a half-truth. I knew it well.

'So we play. Pass time. Okay?' He then spoke in Spanish, and the other two men crawled into the light. The three of them were as downtrodden as each other, indistinguishable in their desolation, the bags under their eyes uniform and exaggerated by shadows.

Through the next five days I played blackjack with imaginary currency, as if it could buy my freedom. Seldom did we talk and, mostly, the slide and shuffle of cards and the distant cry of prisoners were the only sounds to be heard.

Each night I dreamed I was back in bed with Kayla. We finished making love and she nestled into me and I wrapped my arms around her to protect her from the nightmares. The sheets were smooth against my skin, cool when I moved. I pulled her close anytime she shivered or shook. In the morning the alarm went off and the sounds of KROQ woke me. Kayla rolled over and a pair of green eyes said good morning. Her teeth massaged my neck and she bit my ear, gently and then with firmness. We showered together. I went out to get milk. As the door closed I realised and tried to turn back, but I didn't make it.

By the fifth day I was an imaginary millionaire by jailhouse currency.

The man with the deck shuffled the cards from hand to hand. 'A little is a funny way of describing your experience.'

I smirked. A little was definitely funny.

I couldn't find work as an illegal immigrant, but I needed to survive. Since shortly after I arrived in the States, blackjack was how I earned my way. It was what I did on breathers. They weren't about a break from life: they were about making the dough to keep life going as it was. I'd learned the tricks from a fortuitous incident in Mississippi after I helped a man, who I knew only as Tommy, escape some angered yokels he'd beaten out of their savings. I sneaked him onto the riverboat I was travelling on. In four days, drifting down Old Blue, I had card counting and ace sequencing to a tee. So I hit the casinos in Sin City and America's Playground for a week at a time – win, win, lose, win, lose, win, lose, I'd use as my daily pattern to not draw attention – and every time I left with thousands ...

A loud bang at the door broke the silence later that afternoon.

The door creaked open and two men in suits stood behind a guard, who had entered the cell. Both had the same slicked-to-the-side hairstyle, their faces curt with indifference. One held a clipboard while the other stood with his arms crossed. On the guard's belt there was a baton and a pistol.

They were familiar, and so were their shoes – both pairs had planted into my ribs at some point. *Agent Rogers is a friend of ours ...*

'Agent Dean Ludwitz of the INS, Gentlemen.' The taller suit flashed his ID. 'I believe we've met, but just in case it fell out of your head.' He looked down at the clipboard in his hand. 'Dane Costello, of seventeen Neptune Street, St Kilda, Australia. Stand up and turn around. Put your hands behind your head.'

'You hit the wrong undercover agent, Costello,' Ludwitz said as they dragged me from the cell. 'Now it's time to go home.'

LETTER 2

October 28 1993

Dane,

You've taken a breather, and that's fine. It's what you do sometimes and I get it: you need the money and a break from me. You don't sneak out to bars and drink away your frustrations into a glass of something-on-the-rocks, and I don't go shopping to relieve stress, and we don't take an annual vacation at the same time every year when work gives us time off, with the kids sent to Grandma Miriam's for the week to sleep on opposite sides of the same shitty little room one of our parents and their brother or sister slept in when they were the same age. I'm glad we're not normal. But you had only just come back — did you really have to go again so soon?

I left a note on the table. 'Just went to the hospital.' When you find it, you'll know where I am.

I've had the nightmares every night since I've been here. I'm back in a child's room. The walls are stone. I'm at a carnival. Something crawls on my neck. A heavy shadow towers over me from behind … and then I wake.

I expected you to be here, like I did yesterday and every day before.

People's lives revolve around expectations. No one is totally immune: we live in Western Society, which is a machine with cogs that turn with such force that it is inevitable to be taken by it at some points. Find a job, a partner, buy a house and fill it: refrigerator, oven, sofa, tables, chairs, beds, and buy a dog as a trial. Have kids, and stop doing the fun stuff. Talk about how good life used to be.

There's also the expectation for the people we're close with to be there for us. This is where I slipped up, where I fitted into a society I've never understood. The sad thing is I've grown so attached to you and so used to you being here that I'll probably expect to see you waiting when I wake up from my first chemotherapy treatment later this afternoon.

Needles are funny, aren't they? So arbitrary. They can kill, spread disease, and cure it just the same. They can cause pain, and take it away. They are human and they are inhumane; they are everything we long for and everything we despise. And they are just plastic and glass with painted markings on their canister.

The medical staff have advised me that, unless someone is at home to help care for me, I should stay in the hospital indefinitely. That's okay, though. The healthcare system sucks, but my health insurance will cover most of the costs. I'll always be financially secure. I guess I'm lucky some people pay good money for art, and that I had a big brother who looked after me … Plus, I never went on a school camp.

On my first day of Camp-chemo, the hospital was so quiet my spine jerked straight at every beep. I rolled the carry-on case with one squeaky wheel through the sterilized hallways. Patients ambled past, attached to IV drips, others wheeled along in chairs, fogging oxygen masks. I wonder if that'll be me in time.

When I entered the hospital room I felt like a kid coming in late to the classroom on their first day at a new school. I share with three other people. In the far corner is Maureen, an old lady in a coma, hooked to drips and withered to her stem. Opposite my bed is a middle-aged lady named Susan, who sits up and reads an old copy of *Vogue* with every waking hour. She glanced up, I raised a hand and her lips flirted with a smile before she returned to her magazine.

There is also the man beside me.

I set my things down at the side of my bed next to a chair. The clap of plastic against the floor sounded like thunder.

'Well how do you do, Pretty Lady?' It was a warming southern twang.

Sitting up with a tattered copy of *Moby Dick* laid on his lap was a bald, portly man, his face squashed like a pug and his skin florid: the way he was curved in bed he looked like a giant pink jellybean.

'I'm fine, thank you.' I couldn't help but smile as he beamed at me. 'And how do you do?'

'Very well indeed, thank ya Ma'am. The name's Bill Burton, but those who like me tend to call me Burty.' He stuck his hand out and then started to wobble from under his covers to meet me. The hospital gown bulged over his belly and his back curved like a snagged fishing rod.

'Stay in bed, you silly old fart.' I ushered him back under the quilt. 'Kayla Manning. Most people who like me tend to call me a bitch.'

'I'd hate to think what those who don't like you call you.' He took my hand the way a gentleman might do (I've never met one so I don't actually know).

'Probably something superficially nicer, or nothing at all.'

'Well listen, I ain't gonna call ya nothing of the sort, but it's a pleasure. I would say it's nice to see you in here, but I'd much rather see a young lady *visiting* an old man like me.'

'Pleasure's all mine, Burty.' I said it, and I meant it.

'I'll be right here beside ya if ya need anything or just wanna chat. Never ever hesitate to stop me for a good yarn. Conversations are the stories to our lives.' He held up his copy of *Moby*. It may well have been one of the first printed. 'Books are what writers write about those stories.'

The instant I met Bill Burton I liked him, and you know this is a rarity for me. He is a colorful dab on the hospital palette. Camp has only just begun but I've made a friend already.

Dr Simms and Nurse Betty are at the doorway now. I guess it's time for chemo.

∗ ∗ ∗

11:30pm, in the hallway

On the chair outside my room I'm bathed in an umbrella of moonlight. A short time ago I sneaked out of bed and left my roommates, who have sunken into silhouetted mounds for the night. I can't sleep, even though my eyes burn and my muscles feel double their natural weight. For hours I lay awake in bed and listened to the beeps, wheezes and shuffles from around the room as if all the discordant sounds blended into a melody.

Chemo this afternoon was not what I had expected. Well, I really didn't have any expectations. If anything it was less of a parade than I would've thought. I sat in a big comfy armchair and sank shallowly into the cushion while the medication was administered via an IV.

Soon after I was finished, my knees landed on the tiles in front of the toilet. The nausea buckled me in half, and I heaved from deep in my bowels. It was colorful vomit, not far from the fiery whirlpool I produced that time in Portland. Remember that? I learned Bloody Marys will be the death of me (not cancer), and although I kick your butt at most things, drinking has never been one of them. I'm still glad you held my hair back: don't underestimate how grateful a girl is for this. I kind of wish you had been here to do it again.

When I sat on the toilet to pee, my urine was a stream of fiery red-orange that coated the assorted sick in the bowl. My urethra felt as if someone held a match to it. The burning rose into my belly. When I wiped, my whole crotch felt inflamed. It entertained and intrigued me – I was delirious – how the body can make such strange colors. The contrast of red on a white tissue was not as deep as oceans of cherry-colored blood can be on white bed sheets, but it was impressive nonetheless. I marveled at this for a moment before I let it fall down and plop into the rose pool.

Until this point cancer had just been a word. Now it's real. It's hard to believe chemotherapy is meant to make me better.

Back out in the chemo lounge, I felt as if I fitted in as a cancer patient. Once my hair drops I'll be completely uniform.

'Good afternoon, Kayla. How are you feeling?' asked Dr Simms in his dopey northern tongue.

I groaned as I lifted my head. 'I've been better.'

'It's bad, but will improve.' He turned to the man beside him. 'Kayla, this is Cameron, he is going to be your primary care giver.'

'Hi Kayla,' said Nurse Cameron from the stripped, raw throat of a heavy smoker. He stepped forward and took my limp hand.

He was older. His eyes sat too far out of their sockets and his jaw stayed ajar, open as if ready to speak. He was tall and skinny with dry paper skin that looked like it could tear, and hair the same gray as his eyes. His vibe was awkward, to say the least.

'I have another appointment.' Dr Simms wrote on his clipboard and left.

Nurse Cameron sat in the chair beside me. For some time nothing was said; he just sat there and gazed at me. I've never been in hospital as a patient, but I know you have several times … is this some sort of nursing method? Like I said – awkward. He gawked at me as if I was from another world.

In the quiet he said, 'You look … you look well.'

I rolled my head over the back of the chair's headrest and sent him the stink eye. 'Thanks.' I rolled my head the other way. A colorful bird perched outside my window. It shook its feathers, raised its wings and flew away.

It reminded me of what you said at the markets in Venice when we passed the trinket stalls.

'There's something about you, Rascal.' You licked your ice-cream. 'We've been together a long time, but I get the same feeling as I did the first time we met.'

'Indigestion?'

'No.'

'Oh, sunstroke's a bitch, hey.'

'Yeah, that's it.' You tried to poke your ice-cream in my face, but I ducked back and took a mouthful of vanilla 'Nah, I mean, you're special.'

'You know that's used as an insult a lot of the time.' This time you caught me on the chin with a smudge of chocolate. I tingled when you took my jaw, lifted my head, and cleaned it with your tongue before you worked up to my lips. You've always turned me on for as long as you've pissed me off. Men.

'Yeah, you're that kind of special, too. But no, what I mean is … I'm a bird, Kayla. I need to fly. I can't be caged and stay still too long. With you, though, it feels like I'm flying all the time.'

I'm not sure whether it is this or the chemo hangover that's keeping me awake. I thought we were on an extended breather, and I remind myself of everything we've been through together: the ups, the downs, the smiles, the holidays, the 'I love yous' I never returned, the fights, the slaps to your face, you walking out the door with a vow to never return when I became too much of a bitch. We always came back, though. We didn't find each other for nothing. So now, I wonder, have you flown away for good this time? Is this more than a breather? Is it completely new air?

I don't know how many times I ever expressed myself properly. I know I've never said it back to you on the few occasions you've told me you love me, and I know I don't always reciprocate or initiate affection, but I do care, and I do want you here. You're a bird, but I am too, and some birds are not meant to fly alone.

I write these letters with hope that you will come back, and if you miss all of this then you can know what happened. And I write them so I can look back one day and know what I beat. It's something I've done before, in a past we've never talked about. It's time to let this past out of its cage.

Kayla

DIARY 2

June 8 1978

Outside it is summer, but inside our house it isn't. Mommy hasn't said much for a long time. She sits in the kitchen and stares at the wall, and sometimes she drinks the orange liquid. I make her coffee, but she doesn't drink it. I know I'm not a good coffee maker because I'm only ten, and it takes lots longer to be a good coffee maker.

I stand in the doorway, but she never knows I'm there, even when I ask 'Mommy, are you okay?'

The other day I watched her and she didn't see me. When the doorbell rang, she moved, and I realized I must have a superpower that makes me invisible. I don't always like it. It's fun to spy on people and find out things, but I don't want to always be hidden and I don't know how to control it yet.

My superhero name is Golden Girl and, from now on, instead of invisibility I'm going to have the power to make everyone smile. This way there would be no anger and hurt, because people would be happy.

Mommy opened the door. Mr Ignatius came inside. He smiled at me and then Mommy took him upstairs. The noises came from her room. When they finished playtime, Mommy came downstairs.

'Take your time, no hurry. If you want to get a drink there's some gin in the cupboard,' Mommy called after the third creak. 'Same time next week?'

Mr Ignatius called from upstairs: 'Thanks, Carol. Yes, will see you Friday.'

My invisibility turned on as Mommy passed. I tried to turn it off to say goodbye to her, but it didn't work. She gulped from a bottle and then slammed it on the table. Mommy passed me again and took her coat from the rack.

She looked to where I sat before she opened the door. I thought my power might have turned off, but she was looking at the wall behind me. She sniffed and wiped her nose and then her eyes. I jumped off my chair and ran over to her. I didn't want her to cry, but before I could turn into Golden Girl and make Mommy happy she flew out the door, using her superpower, the one to disappear.

In my room I drew a picture of Leroy. I heard the door to Mommy's room open. Footsteps came down the hallway. It sounded like an ogre was in the house. I tried turning into Golden Girl in case the ogre found me. If I could make him smile he wouldn't want to eat me up.

Creaks came from the stairs as the ogre went down. After two creaks the footsteps stopped. They groaned. The steps came closer to my room and stopped. My door opened.

Mr Ignatius stood in the doorway. 'Hello Kayla.' He smiled.

My powers worked, but I didn't feel right. 'Hello.'

'May I come in? I'd love to talk to you.'

I put away my drawing book and held onto Leroy – if someone is going to hurt me Leroy can transform into a real lion and make them go away; that is his superpower.

Mr Ignatius sat on my bed. He was tall and skinny and reminded me of a worm.

'Come here, Puppet.' He called with his hand like my teacher does when they want me to help. He patted the bed next to him. 'Come, sit.'

I held Leroy extra tight as I climbed onto my bed. Mr Ignatius smiled, but I didn't like it. It wasn't a real smile.

He ran his hand through the back of my hair, which made my spine tingle like there was a spider crawling on my skin. 'You're a pretty girl, Kayla.'

I stopped being scared, and realized he wasn't an ogre. I smiled, and hoped my Golden Girl powers would make him happy and protect me. The back of his hand felt like sandpaper on my cheek.

'Does your Mommy give you attention?'

'Sometimes. But she is busy.'

'You deserve more, don't you?' He stroked my cheek again.

I dropped my eyes.

'You're one of the prettiest girls I've ever seen. You have such green eyes and soft skin. You could be a model someday.'

His words made me feel cozy and warm, the way I do when I imagine Christmas on the way home from school in December.

Mr Ignatius reached his arm around my back. 'We are friends aren't we Kayla? I am friends with your Mommy, and you too.'

I felt as though a giant shield covered me.

'May I see your teddy, Puppet?'

He held Leroy gently and I knew he was a good man.

'What's its name?'

'Leroy. He helps keep me warm and safe and makes me happy.'

'Do you feel safe now?'

I nodded.

He passed Leroy back to me. 'How about you let Leroy rest? I have some games we can play, but lions aren't able to play.'

I cuddled Leroy. 'Why can't lions play?'

'Because these are special human games and lions can get hurt. I promise we will have fun. I want you to be happy. Do you want me to be happy?'

I nodded. I set Leroy down near my pillow. I was nervous, but really excited, too. It had been a long time since I'd played games with anyone. Ever since First Grade, when Mallory Gamble invited me to her house to play tea parties and I accidentally broke her new teapot. She hasn't asked me to play since.

'What are we going to play?' I asked.

Mr Ignatius stood and lit a cigarette. The smoke filled the room and made me cough. He kept the cigarette in his lips, and knelt down so we were the same height. His eyes were gray, like God had run out of colors.

He told me about this special game. It is a contest where I am not allowed to move my eyes from what he shows me. We are on the same team and we can win together.

Mr Ignatius undid his belt. His pants dropped to the floor. Then his underwear fell, too. I didn't want to look at his boy bits, but it was part of the game and I didn't want to lose the game for us.

His boy's area was hairy and his thing stood straight up. He brought me closer to him. I'd never seen boy parts before, except one time I saw Jamie Deangelo peeing behind the cafeteria after school. Jamie's boy parts looked much different to Mr Ignatius's.

The cigarette bounced once and then burned a hole in the rug.

Mr Ignatius moved his hand up and down and made lots of noises like when he plays with Mommy. After some really loud noises Mr Ignatius spat from his boy bits all over the floor. Some went onto Leroy and some onto my face. He huffed and did a big sigh and then pulled up his pants. I felt awful and wanted to be upset.

'Puppet, I think you should clean up.' He put another cigarette into his mouth. 'Use this.' He handed me my bath towel.

I cleaned his boy paste from my face and from the ground and from Leroy. It was yucky and smelled. Mr Ignatius put his hands on my shoulders.

'Now Kayla, remember, this is our game. You can't tell anyone, not even your friends.'

'Leroy is my only friend,' I said. 'And Mommy.'

'And me, remember.' He beamed, pulled me in and hugged me. I gripped onto him. It was the first hug I'd had for a really long time. It was nice. Mr Ignatius let go and kissed me on the forehead. His lips were like big balloons pushing softly on my skin. He stared at me, and then put the big balloons onto my lips. I had no idea what to do.

Mr Ignatius left my room. The stairs creaked three times. The front door opened and closed, and I was alone.

The house got colder with Mr Ignatius gone. I picked up the bath towel from the floor and held it in my hand. I'd made a new friend, and now I was Golden Girl. I looked in my mirror. My superpowers looked back.

I put Leroy on my lap and gripped Golden Girl's cape.

DIARY 3

October 31 1978

It is Halloween today. I am going Trick or Treating tonight as Golden Girl.

Last Saturday Mr Ignatius took me to the carnival in town. We shared a stick of cotton candy. I can never finish a big one and he has a sweet tooth. Mr Ignatius had lots of cigarettes. Every time I went on a ride, he would wait and blow smoke into the air.

We held hands when we walked and I felt safe. When I let go of his hand it felt like I was on the edge of a cliff above rocks and wobbling, but then he would take my hand and the cliff would disappear.

Mr Ignatius has a smell. Everyone has a smell. Mommy smells like pretty flowers, Susan Griffith in my class smells like cabbage and our Principal, Mr Catcher, like tang and mouth wash. Mr Ignatius smells like cigarette and cologne.

The carnival was so much fun – I rode seven rides! But there was a moment when Mr Ignatius had to go to the boy's toilet. When he left, the wind became strong and very cold. It tried to blow me over. All around me everyone moved really fast and made the wind faster until it was like a hurricane.

When we got home Mr Ignatius took me upstairs. Mommy sat at the kitchen table. She didn't see us come in.

'Sit on the bed, Puppet,' he said as he took off his pants.

We played the same game as last time.

'Stay there, Puppet.' He breathed heavily and moved it close to my face. My tummy felt sick and I wanted to cry, but I sucked in the tears because I didn't want to spoil our game. 'You want to make me happy. Make me happy.' I didn't want it to be near me, but I wanted to make him happy. That's what friends do.

His milk spurted out and got on the front of my dress. His body shook and he made lots of noise. It smelled funny.

The walls had closed in. I wanted to leave the room, but I couldn't move, they were so close. I looked for Leroy. I wanted to see him turn into a big, real life lion and protect me.

Mr Ignatius sat on the bed. 'Time to clean up, Puppet.'

I cleaned the milk from my dress and then had to get on my hands and knees to clean the mess on my floor. As I wiped up the milk from the rug, I felt the air come onto my knickers.

'My, you are a little dirty aren't you, Puppet?'

I felt embarrassed because I didn't have any clean knickers and had to wear the same ones as yesterday. Mommy hadn't done the washing. I used her spray to disguise me. If I don't, the kids at school make fun.

I prayed for the wind to come in and blow my dress back down. A tear jumped from my eye and hit the rug. I wiped it up quickly so Mr Ignatius didn't see. My face warmed and felt so swollen my eyes were pressed closed. The wind didn't come in even after all my prayers and my dress stayed up.

His finger slid onto my knickers and touched my girl parts. I was a rabbit stuck in its hole.

Then it hurt. I started to cry.

I don't want to write anymore.

Mr Ignatius said he would be here every week from now on.

The house is icy. I want Mommy to protect me from the blue and the coldness, but I don't want her to come home with any more friends. I want to run out of the house and down the road and never turn my head back, but I don't want to leave my room.

I want to have happy dreams, but I'm scared to fall asleep.

CHAPTER 3

I tried several times to break free of the cuffs until I was restrained in the airplane seat. I cursed the INS agents until they gagged me. After this I fought the restraints until I was exhausted.

I slumped my head against the windowsill and looked out over the clouds. The entire flight, all I thought about was how I'd been torn from Kayla. The possibility of not seeing her again was a blunt knife stabbing my stomach.

Upon landing, I received a yellow A4 envelope with my wallet and keys. At the foreign exchange I changed greenbacks for plastic notes, and handled them quizzically.

'Try tearing them.' The clerk winked. 'Godsend I say, no more costly affairs with the washing machine.'

The face of Queen Elizabeth II looked up at me from the mauve note, a branch of eucalypt leaves beside her. 'Life will always carry on.'

I looked at the flight screen and saw LAX. I wanted to buy a ticket and walk through the screens. But it was useless. I was red-flagged.

I inserted coins into a payphone and called the apartment. Each time the phone rang out and my coins were returned. I left the terminal with my head so low I could see dust in the carpet.

The daytime sky was as bipolar as the city itself. To one side of the horizon was a luminous blue blanket where sunlight glistened, while in the other direction a white canvas was smudged with fluffs of dark grey. Confused, unstable and without identity, it was still the Melbourne of old.

The taxi meter ticked over and white lines flashed by while we cruised down Tullamarine Freeway. It was a place so changed it was barely recognisable. Once-empty paddocks were now housing and industrial estates, and billboards soared high above sound barriers.

The driver, an Aussie warhorse with a slicked grey pony tail, rambled for most of the half-hour journey.

'Bob Hawke's no longer prime minister. Paul Keating bumped him out. Still Labor in charge, thank Christ ... West Coast won the premiership last year – interstate invasion might happen soon. Bombers got it for now, though ... Have you seen the new leg spin bowler, Shane Warne? ... Rolled the Poms!'

At the corner of Jacka Boulevard and Lower Esplanade I stepped from the cab. In front of me, the foreshore hummed with beach-goers, dog walkers and workers soaking up the sun on their lunch break. To my left in the distance the rails of the Metropolis peaked out from Luna Park. I'd spent so many nights there, fairy floss melting in my mouth, the hand of some girl in mine, flashing lights and raucous laughter with friends.

I crossed the road and entered the foreshore. Lost in a place I once called home, there was nowhere I could be except the beach. One thing that never changes is the impervious freedom of the sea. On the sand I sat and watched the baby waves curl into shore like a mother with a rolling pin on pastry.

The sea is another world. Out in the water, all the heartache and bad memories made on land can be left behind. It's like starting over, as if the salt water just washes everything away. There are no regrets, no wishing, nothing to take back.

The surf is the only time in life you can choose to catch a break.

For our thirteenth birthday my parents gave Josh and me a second-hand '76 Hansen long board to share, on the proviso that Stevie taught us how to surf. Stevie was five years older and had surfed since he could walk. He gave us wax and promised our parents he'd turn us into a couple of Mark Richardses in no time.

We learned quickly and were addicted within six months. For Christmas that year Josh and I graduated to eight-foot Slaters. Mine was purple and green with a squiggly yellow line running down the middle and a Quiksilver sticker, which I stuck near the fins.

From the summer of '79 to '80, a group of us would make the trip down to the breaks west of Port Phillip – Bells Beach, Bird Rock, Lorne and Cape Otway – whichever the radio reported had the best swell. We'd tie our boards onto the roof rack of Stevie's white EH Holden station wagon, complete with blue racing stripes. We'd squash into the booth seats in the front and back and listen to Cold Chisel, Crowded House and Midnight Oil as we tore down country highways.

Behind the break, I'd perch myself on the board and dangle my legs in the water. Every time it felt the same – as if nothing else mattered, as if nothing back on the land could hurt me. I'd sit out there for hours. At times I ignored the waves just to sit in peace. Sometimes I considered buying a boat and sailing out to sea to live. I'd catch fish, surf, bathe in the waters and forget about the world. If I never came back, so be it. It was where I was meant to be.

A sparkle of white sunlight reflected off the water and blinded me as if I'd been in a dark room for too long. I slid on my Ray Bans, and for a moment expected to see a girl wander along the sand, a white dress hugging her body, stepping as if there were cracks in the ground.

* * *

The Esplanade Hotel had changed little. Some refurbishment, a plaque to show it had been heritage listed and new artwork and posters on the walls. It had been a stalwart in past years for anyone who called St Kilda home, and anyone else who hung for the next live gig. Too many a beer had been spilled there, too many a memory to ever forget.

I had propped upon a barstool, the coaster beneath my beer saturated with a circular imprint of liquid. Of all the things I might have wanted to forget, the taste of an Australian beer was not one. The Carlton Draught was colder than I remembered any drink. It fizzed on my tongue, just bitter enough and not too dry.

The view of the beach from inside the Espy brought with it déjà vu. A birthday, an-end-of-year work break-up, a casual night on the town: maybe all at once. The shift from nostalgia to longing to regret swelled, and my throat tightened. I pushed back the bar stool and stood. I couldn't stay in St Kilda. There was too much to remember and not enough ebbing tide to make me forget.

'Another beer, Mate?' asked the bartender.

It was Gary Whitman, a middle-aged man with a pointed face and handlebar moustache draped over his mouth. As he reached for my empty glass his cologne tickled my nostrils – the same sweet musk my father wore.

'Yeah,' I replied. 'Why not.'

He tossed the empty into the wash bucket and began to pour another. The amber liquid drained into the glass. 'Seem like a man who's in dire need of more than a couple.'

'I'll just take the keg; it'll save us some time.'

He chuckled. 'Name's Gary, nice to meet ya.'

'Dane ... you too.'

We'd only encountered each other a few times, and it had been over seven years since the last, but still, how had he forgotten me? Had I fashioned a mask so indistinguishable?

He finished pouring and planted the beer onto the half-soaked coaster.

'I know it mightn't be my business, but I've been around too many years, and I've seen all types come in and leave: from the kids having fun to the musicians getting stoned. I know by now that there are normally only two reasons why folks come in with eyes like yours.

'There are those who want to forget, and there are those who wish they could remember. So if you don't mind me asking, Chief, which are you?'

I ran the tip of my forefinger through the beads of water perched on the side of the glass like morning dew on a leaf. 'Well, Gary.' I stopped and looked up. 'What if I told you I was neither?'

'Then in my experience, I'd say you're both.'

He wiped the wood grain and left to serve a pair of tradesmen waiting on the other side of the bar. By the time he returned I had finished my drink, leaving it little time to drop even a degree in temperature. He poured another and slid it in front of me.

'You seem like a man who knows a thing or two,' I said.

'Maybe I do, but only the dumbest of men ever confess to being wise.'

'Indeed. Though, there's a difference between knowing a thing or two and being wise ... What I really need is a man who knows where I might locate certain things.'

'Well I could be that man, Chief. It does depend on the things and the number. What d'ya need?'

'Three things, actually. First thing I need s a room. Secondly, I need a phone ...' I dropped my head, digging my elbows into the bar. Neither could get low enough. 'The third is difficult. I need to get to America without boarding a plane, and without a visa.'

Gary drew a long breath and then exhaled through pursed lips. 'Well, Chief, I can help ya with the first two. As for the third, I suggest you head down the Yarra and learn to row. How about I set ya up in a nice boudoir overlooking the foreshore. Phone's beside the bed.'

I tossed a fiver onto the bar and left the change.

Before he led me upstairs, he called to a waitress to mind the bar. I glanced back to see a strawberry-blonde woman with freckles on her cheeks. I vanished upstairs before she could see me. Simone would not have forgotten.

* * *

The room had a hallmark sixties feel. There were plaster cracks above the door and wardrobe, brown stains from a leaking pipe near the window and the carpet felt like sandpaper. It smelled of moth balls and sawed wood from where a new window frame, the only modern thing, had been put in – unclean paintwork and a screwdriver left on the windowsill. The bed was one of those deep-set, old-fashioned queen beds with a headboard made of pine and a mattress like a bend in space-time that would swallow you if you moved too close to the middle.

For the remainder of the afternoon I slouched on the bed and telephoned the apartment. I dialled the numbers on the keypad until they began to fade and my fingers burned. Every time it rang out.

When I woke, my head was on the pillow, the receiver buried into my cheek, the faint sound of a dead line coming from the speaker. I sat upright and gazed out the window. The sun had descended behind the line of palms on the foreshore, the purple and blue of dusk like bruises on the sky, something unhealed about the day that had been.

I pressed down the plunger, released it and the ringtone reappeared. I redialled the number, wide awake and nervous. Once again, it rang out.

In the bedside drawer there was a pen and paper. I wrote a letter to Kayla, taking five attempts to get the words right. I would send it that afternoon, but held little hope she would receive it.

At first I had thought she must be at the studio, then I had thought she might be ignoring the call, after that I had turned to worry that something had happened to her. Now, though, I realised that wherever Kayla was, she didn't want to be contacted. It occurred to me she'd left, in fact at many times I'd inferred from what little I knew of her past that she was like me: nomadic and disinclined to remain in a place.

As I pictured her, closing my eyes and reaching out for the image in front of me, Kayla moulded to my memory as if she'd never leave. Like that image was all I would ever have of her. I wanted to scream, to run, and to smash anything I could see. But I sat there on the bed; a prop, a statue, frozen as life passed me by.

* * *

Later in the evening the bar was stifled with heat and humidity trapped inside from the day just done. People were scattered everywhere, most tables and couches occupied. There was the after-work crowd finishing the day with a quiet couple, and the robust night crowd just beginning theirs with the same. The clink of glasses and chuckles sounded over the top of a record playing in the background. When I closed my eyes, the sounds reminded me of the intro to *Saturday Night*.

It was as if there was a hurricane of celebration and I was resting in the eye, some quiet distance away from the whirl of happy commotion. Each time the door opened and more patrons entered, a cool gust of night time air came with them. A man relaxed and laughed with friends on an archaic sofa, its vinyl covering cracked in many places. This microcosmic idyll of middle-class nightlife revealed a celebration of nothing greater or lesser than a Thursday night: good weather, good drinks, and above all good friends.

Propping myself in the same seat as before, I leaned my elbows on the freshly cleaned bar and pawed over the dinner menu for some time before settling for the chicken parma.

A short, dark-haired girl with brown buttons for eyes served me. On the opposite side of the crowded bar Simone laughed and poured beers for a group of businessmen with their ties loosened and shirts untucked. Like a fly on the wall, I observed her. Those light rosy cheeks reminded me of a cherry blossom, the freckles still the same S-shape they were when I'd first met her. Hypotheticals overtook my present state of mind. If I had kissed her the night we'd met then she and Kerry would never have married. Perhaps I'd have married Simone instead, and perhaps I'd never have left. Perhaps she'd have been enough to make me stay.

Some of the crowd cleared from around the bar. Simone took a plate from the bartender who had served me. I lowered my face before she approached. She placed the plate down in front of me, along with a napkin and cutlery.

I could feel her in front of me, smell her perfume. 'Can I get you a drink to go along with your parma?'

My heart sped. 'Yeah, that'd be great, thanks.'

I heard the beer drain into the glass. Her eyes felt glued to me as I hacked into my dinner and the cogs to her subconscious ticked. Did she know who I was by my posture, my voice, my smell, or somehow sense it before she had seen my eyes?

She slid the beer across the bar to me. I remained furtive, eyes fixed on the plate. I continued to cut through the chicken, cutlery squeaking against porcelain. Simone didn't move to serve other customers. She stayed and held me in her stare.

I stopped eating and peered up from my plate.

The words simply escaped her mind and slipped from her mouth. 'Oh my god. Dane, it's you ...' Her flowery cheeks turned snow white, her smile replaced with a gaping mouth.

'Thank you for dinner.' I shuffled money onto the bar. 'But I have to go now.'

I left my dinner half-eaten and beer almost untouched, and fled out into the night. The sky was clear and the Southern Cross glowed over me as if it were the watchful eyes of Big Brother and me Winston. I crossed the road to the foreshore. Moonlight flooded the surface of the water like a spotlight. At any moment it would turn and focus on me, the way it does on a fugitive in a Hollywood action movie. Out the front of the bar yellow taxi cabs waited for passengers.

CHAPTER 4

I lay on the St Kilda foreshore the entire night and thought about how I'd ended up there again. And I remembered what had brought me there in the first place …

Much of my childhood was dictated by the need to escape and run. We'd wag school to ride our push bikes into town and leave snakies in the dirt behind Old Bill Daggert's grocery store, long before it became an asphalt car park for a Woolworths.

Our house was an old weatherboard shack set on three acres of flat, open land. It was perched on stumps, with an unpolished pine veranda, chipped and with nails poking out. To the side of the house was a water tank, so often sucked to its very last drop in the long and torrid summers without rain.

We'd run through the surrounding paddocks, mowing down waist-high grass, until we reached the yellow wattle.

Every year it would flower at the same time, and wilt in accordance with the first burst of winter wind. And, like the ocean, the wind whispered the same words: 'Life always carries on.'

In a town of dried yellow monotony, a tree that flourished with yellow flowers was a paradox.

It was where my brothers and I would hide when we heard the whiskey bottle smash and Mum urged us out of the house – 'Run!'

I'd turn back to see her face masked by the flywire door, and the ominous black figure towering behind her. On a lucky night he'd pass out before he made it to her, and we'd return to find her nursing him. On most nights we'd come back when the screaming stopped and find Mum crying, with her head in her hands. Her eyes swollen, her cheeks red and her nose bloody. She'd shoo us away and try to hide the marks with makeup and long sleeves. On bad nights we'd return to find them both unconscious – him from alcohol, Mum from his fists.

This went on for most of my childhood, until Stevie was big enough, and Josh and I, too, to stay and stop him. Sometimes he'd try to beat us, but mostly we overpowered him.

No matter what, though, when I heard the glass smash, I always knew one thing: that sometime that night or the next morning I'd find myself out by the wattle.

* * *

When I woke it was quiet as if the world had decided to have a nap of its own.

I sneaked back into the hotel as dawn broke across the bay. I dialled the apartment until I fell asleep, but again all I caught was a phone ringing out. When I woke there was a note on the ground near my door.

Downstairs, the pub was empty except for a vet at the far side of the bar, his war medals and battle scars drooping from his eyes. I sat in the same seat and waited. There was no one behind the bar. I turned toward the wall clock and watched the second hand turn.

'You got my note, then?'

Simone stood in front of me, her face solemn and sunken as if a heavy hand weighed her down.

'I did.'

'Listen,' she started, 'I'm not sure what to … but … Kerry wants to see you.' She picked up a glass and dried it. 'The past is the past, you know.'

The war vet had turned his eyes downward, sinking lower into his beer with every minute. Memories are often stored in a person's choice of tipple, the courage to remember at the bottom of every glass. 'You think it's that simple?'

'Nothing is simple, Dane, but there are a lot of questions … maybe you don't have the answers quite yet, but they still need to be asked.'

I felt my legs move, ready to push out the bar stool and return to my room.

'Don't suppose a weary dog like me can get a beer, do ya?' I felt him sit down beside me, his voice still sharp like the chirp of a cockatoo. 'G'day, Old Friend.'

My heart wasn't sure how to beat. Did it skip, slow, speed up, or did it simply not change? Was it so unaffected by everything that had begun to pour back in? All those memories were meant to be a thousand miles away, but now they sat right next to me.

I turned to Kerry. He had changed little. There was an extra crease or two on his forehead, his former ginger mullet trimmed to a crew cut, and some years added behind his sky-blue eyes, but I recognised him like it was seven years ago; his sculpted cheeks, his nose bent at the bridge where it had been broken.

'When are they coming to get me?' I asked.

His face turned as stale as mine felt. 'I guess there's little need for pleasantries. They're not, to answer your question.'

Silence lingered for some time. Simone placed a beer in front of each of us.

Kerry grasped his glass and held it up. 'Cheers, Mate. I guess we'll find something to cheer in time. For now, though, just cheers. It's good to see you.'

I held up my beer. 'Cheers.' We tapped glasses and each took a pull.

Simone joined us at the bar with a vocka on the rocks. 'Not meant to while I'm on shift, but fuck it, *to old time's sake.*' She held up her glass and we rang in another cheers.

'I suppose we start at the start, hey.' It concerned me just how much Kerry was privy to, how much Josh had talked, sneered or demeaned. 'America ...'

In a matter of sentences, I relayed the last seven years of my life.

At the deportation, Simone gasped. 'Oh Dane ... that means ...'

'Yeah, it means I can't go back for at least four years.'

Again, conversation ceased.

It remained like this until Kerry said, 'Remember that New Year's Eve at Rye, the night at the carnival?'

I was taken away from the present by the bright glow of carnival lights, a hot summer night and sounds of the sea layered under celebration. 'I remember you challenged Josh to a drinking contest early in the night. It went on and on. Not sure how much you remember.'

'I remember having to carry my boyfriend to the campsite,' said Simone. 'Soaked in water without his pants, because he'd taken the clown's place at the dunk 'em game and when he got hit he'd passed out in the baby pool. Wasn't before he announced to the world, or at least a few dozen onlookers, that he was going to marry me, while his arm was wrapped around Teddy.'

'Continued the romance by trying to hold up the candy stand with a rifle from the shooting gallery,' I added.

We laughed. It continued to the point where my stomach felt the pleasant ache from joy. It was as if a dam waiting to burst had finally split its wall. Relief flowed out of me.

'Pity the bloke saw it had flowers along the side. Could've done with that fairy floss. Guess I wasn't made for the robbery game. Nearly finished like New Year's the year before with a good ole fashioned brawl.' When Kerry said it, my mind flashed to Josh's face, calm and assured. 'The boys were jawing with some locals and ...'

'Josh stopped it,' I said. 'It was the first time he ever stopped something happening. The first time he ever saw the bigger picture.' That night in Rye was the moment Josh turned a new page. No longer the angry shorter twin, he transformed into a level-headed, understated, purposeful man. Focused on something greater.

We talked until our throats ran dry, our glasses continually topped up by a still-youthful strawberry-blonde bartender. Several beers later Kerry pushed out his bar stool. 'Well, I must be off; start work in half an hour. Graveyard shift.'

'See they're still working you into an early grave.'

'An early retirement.' He winked at me.

We shook hands, his grip firm and welcoming, homely. 'It's great to have you back, Mate.' He opened the door. The bell above it jingled. Over his shoulder he called, 'I'll let Josh know.'

All joy from the reminiscence disappeared.

LETTER 3

November 6 1993

Dane,

There's something ill in my stomach that has nothing to do with chemotherapy or cancer, and more to do with you. It hurts that you're not here.

The chemo hangover has lessened. I still pee red and orange and my vagina still feels like someone has blown it up with a tire pump or slapped it. And not in the gentle way I like – would really like now – the way you used to do it before you slid your tongue to my clitoris. If I had to list the things I miss most about you, right now your fellatio would be top.

If you were to come into the hospital at this moment I'd throw away this letter, rip your shirt off and claw my nails deep into your back, hard enough for you to bleed and feel every bit of what I'd like you to feel. If you had any sense you'd throw me on the bed and make me feel, too.

I'm on edge. It is beginning to feel like I am a caged animal. The doctors are cardboard cut-outs with stethoscopes, the patients irrelevant except for Burty, and the nurses like worker bees buzzing around the place. Nurse Cameron is more of a termite.

Twice I've woken to him in the armchair by my bed, staring at me with those pale gray eyes. Yesterday, sometime in between stale-bread lunch and off-beef dinner, he was in the chair, scratching behind his ear, and staring.

I was groggy – chemo drunk. 'What time is it?' I asked. The light was weak, but my eyes struggled to open.

'It is afternoon meal time, yes.' He stood and retrieved a tray from the bedside table and placed it on my lap. 'Is something good, I think, yes.'

He returned to the chair. When I woke completely, the chemo-drunk became chemo-hung-over. You know how little tolerance I have for people when I'm hung over. But Nurse Cameron remained on the seat as I lifted the lid of the food tray. Soup spices wafted through the air – lentil soup today, yesterday it was tomato. I much preferred the tomato. Red is far more enticing.

Both Burty and Susan had their curtains drawn and Maureen was unconscious, as usual, her oxygen mask fogged with rhythmic breaths.

'I have to say, it makes me sad to see a young girl like you in here,' he said. 'It should not be this way, not at all. It's not fair, not at all.'

I stopped part-way through slurping my salty lentil soup. 'So what if it's not fair? That's life.'

'Yes, yes it is; but it should be fairer for you.'

'My tumor doesn't give a fuck about fair. Unfair is a word that cry-babies use. If you're going to be my nurse, don't have that attitude around me.'

He didn't shake, tremble or gasp in shock. He just said, 'Sorry, no more, okay, no I won't say things … No problem.'

'Good.' I slurped another mouthful before I continued. 'And why are you sad? You're a nurse for Christ's sake. It's your job to be around sick people. You chose it.'

I knew I was being a bitch, but I was right. There are few things that tick me off more than people who complain about something they chose or something unchangeable. This always made me proud of you, Babe, you never whined about anything. You dealt with it.

Nurse Cameron rubbed his hands together as if he was cold. 'Yes, yes, it is. It's just …'

I stared at him and he stopped speaking. He was trying to be nice, I guess, but it's not …

He doesn't need to be whatever he's trying to be. I'll take the needles in my arm, the vomiting, the diarrhea, the singed vagina, baldness, chemo, radiation and whatever else, but I don't want people to shower me with sympathy. Shit happens. It's life. You can stand there, smell how much it stinks and complain about it, or you can wipe your shoe and keep walking.

I know you'd tell me to go easy on him, *he is trying to help you, Kayla.*

He left shortly after: checked I was okay, and wished me well in his bumbled, coarse vocalization.

* * *

The courtyard was quiet and still this evening. A breeze swept through the line of trees at the fence and rustled the leaves before it found a way to soothe my skin. The sun was setting on the horizon, the sky a colorful sheet of stained glass. So fragile.

Burty gazed far ahead to the skyline with the expression of a man recalling fond memories. An air of discovery surrounded him.

'You know that part of the sky,' he began, his eyes fixed ahead, 'where heaven seems to start? You can't quite see it, but you know it's there somewhere.'

I sat on the bench in the middle of the grassed area and Burty hobbled to join me. 'I think so …'

'It's where I want to go when my time is up: the palace somewhere in between the horizon and a world we can never see on earth.'

'You want to go to heaven? That's not the deepest thing I've heard.'

'Not heaven, but the part before the pearly gates. You know how when you look forward to something the anticipation is almost better than the actual event? Like Friday: it's not the weekend, but you have the weekend to come, so really it's the best day of the week. That's what's up there. Friday in the sky.'

'So you want to be there and look in to see what's to come. What is to come?'

He wiped forward over his bald scalp all the way down to his bushy white eyebrows and then adjusted his glasses back up his nose. 'Well, ain't everyone's ideal but I'd have me a ranch. Like the one I had in 'Bama for most of my life. Have me some animals there to take care of the land. I'd live off the land, same as I done for years, just like them injuns do. Wide open plains and the freshest air. And I'd have my girls.' He stopped.

The sun had faded to embers and the moon was out, glowing faintly in the deepening blue dusk. It reminded me of a diorama I made in Fifth Grade art class. An exuberant colored scene, a perfect moment captured with paint and imagination, enclosed by discarded cardboard.

The first star glowed and I wondered where you were. And I wondered if you were still close enough to see the star, too. 'Do you have many visitors, Burty?'

This broke his stare; his beady eyes usually squinted from smiling wide open. It wasn't sadness in his eyes – I think he's past such a simple thing. His eyes were those of a man who had given up on something, but had disguised it with acceptance. It's difficult to tell sometimes.

He sighed, dropped his head and scuffed his slippers against the pebbles below. 'Haven't had a soul in for a while.' He paused. 'Ain't had many, ever.'

I placed my hand on top of his. This would shock you I know. 'Don't worry; I doubt whether I will either.'

'Now why in the world would a young girl, so nice and kind, have no one visiting her?' He sat upright and turned toward me.

'There's a million and one reasons – I was wondering the same thing about you.'

His head sunk lower than it seemed his neck could allow — the way a vulture stoops beyond its shoulder blades. 'Had a family once. But that's time for you. People lose contact. It's just how things go.'

You returned to my thoughts in the dull shine of the stars. The longer you're not here the more I believe you are gone completely.

Maybe time has changed us too; maybe we grew apart somewhere between getting milk and going to hospital. Has there been something missing for you, like there is for Burty? Did you just cover it up until it became too much to lie to yourself and to me? I would rather have had the truth. I wouldn't have hurt you: you're too damn big. (And this, I sigh now, is something I'm really missing. I miss your overgrown hands forming a corset around my waist, your tattoos, your shoulders, and how your thick cock stretches me: I miss everything that made me feel secure and womanly when I was with you.) You're way too big to hurt, at least while you're awake. Did I hurt you, Dane?

I stood and offered my hand to him. 'Why don't we head inside? It's getting dark.'

He took my palm and grunted as he strained to stand.

'I enjoyed this walk, Lil Lady. You done got me all thoughtful and such; nearly made a mess out of me.'

'We didn't walk much. But I enjoyed it, too. Anytime you need to be a mess, be a mess. I'd rather you be how you want than being clean.'

Burty shuffled ahead and held the door open for me.

'Thank you, Sir,' I said, stopping in the doorway to curtsy.

Real gentlemen are rare, so I think it wise to be a lady when there is one worthy of it.

You're not a gentleman, Dane, and never have been. You're hot, sexy, masculine, hell – even lovable, sweet, caring and all of that – I'd go as far as to call you beautiful – but you're not a gentleman. As I said, they are rare. Yes, I can hear you, I'm no lady either: I'm a petite little minx (your words, not mine), a seductive bitch with an androgynous, psychotic personality. That's why you love me, though. You couldn't love a lady and I don't think I could love a gentleman.

We strolled back to the room arm in arm.

I cannot comprehend how this man in his sixty or so years on earth has not accumulated friends and family. Maybe he did have them; maybe they just went out to get milk, too.

Kayla

DIARY 4

January 10 1979

Lots of nights I wake up from bad dreams and my bed is wet.

I haven't seen Mr Ignatius for three weeks. After he left I got angry and cried. Playtime isn't fun. It never has been.

It was dark outside when I left the house. My legs felt like they wanted to run so fast that I could leap into the air and fly, but my head was so full of junk it weighed me down.

I walked all the way down to the grocery store in town and passed the loud room where men laugh and drink from glass mugs. The moon was waking up when I went down the alleyway next to the bookstore. A gutter dripped and a yellow light buzzed above a door at the end of the alley.

I pictured another world behind the door. I thought that if I got through the door I would find myself in the other world, with lots of bright green grass and flowers and happy animals everywhere; beaches and sunsets and happiness.

I was playing with the door handle when someone startled me from behind. 'Hey, whatcha doing?'

I turned to the boy. He had skin like chocolate and was shabby all over; a scar under his right eye, navy blue jacket with threads loose, holes in his pants and afro hair with leaves and twigs stuck in it.

For a second I was scared, but then I saw his eyes. They were big and blue like a Husky's. I knew he wasn't going to hurt me.

'I'm just looking to get into this door,' I said as I leaned against it. 'It leads to another world.'

'Sometimes the chefs from them restaurants throw food scraps out the door.'

'It goes to a bright world with lots of colors.'

'You're probably right. I think it about a lot of doors I see. It makes them being closed okay, coz even if you're outside you know there's something special waiting for you when you finally get inside.'

'My name is Kayla, I'm ten and in Fifth Grade.'

'I'm Oscar. I'm twelve but I ain't got no grade.'

Oscar and I talked in the alleyway for ages. I told him about my school and my home – the warm parts – my favorite color and all my favorite things. Oscar liked to listen.

When it was his turn he didn't tell me much. He just said his home moves a lot and that he doesn't live with his family.

I felt safe with him and, at times, it was like my body was filled with electricity.

We strolled around the town in the quiet of night. Oscar showed me some short cuts through parks and woods to get to different places.

When a wolf howled in the woods Oscar took me by the hand and we ran like it was chasing us. We jumped over fallen trees and dodged hanging branches until we came to an opening.

'I think we're safe,' said Oscar. 'That was close.'

'What if the wolf had caught us?' I asked.

'I wouldn't let no wolf catch you.' He wrapped his arms around me. Oscar's hug was what I think all hugs should feel like.

The wolf howled again. Oscar tilted his head and howled back. I laughed and then he joined me, and we laughed so hard we had to sit down.

When it was late, Oscar walked me back to my letterbox. I didn't want to say goodbye.

He told me we could meet again in the alleyway at the same time each day, because he always goes there to wait for food.

When I got home Mommy was asleep with her head on the kitchen table. The bottle was empty. I put a blanket on her and went up to my room. The house was still cold, but inside my belly I felt a little spark of warmth. I tried to concentrate on the little spark.

This is what I do when Friday comes. After school I go straight to the alleyway and wait for Oscar. We hang out until the moon has put the sun to bed. When I get home, Mommy is passed out on the kitchen table and Mr Ignatius is nowhere to be seen. I don't have to play anymore.

DIARY 5

April 12 1979

I remember one time in English class, the teacher said: 'All good things must come to an end.'

She said it means nothing lasts forever. But I don't think she read it right or thought about it enough. It means all *good things* don't last forever. Bad things can, according to the saying. She was right, though.

It worked for months. I disappeared every Friday before he could come over, or went straight from school to find Oscar in town. But last Friday it stopped working.

Oscar and I roamed about town all afternoon. We'd gone into the woods and climbed trees, and once we even thought we'd found one of the doors to another world. We stayed out for hours until it was dark.

When I walked in the front door, Mr Ignatius was on the sofa with Mommy, who was being a statue. 'It's playtime, Puppet. I've missed you,' he said. 'I'm not happy you've avoided me.'

I did my best to be Golden Girl, but her superpowers aren't what I thought they were.

DIARY 6

August 15 1979

I haven't felt much like writing. Oscar and I hang out for as long as we can, but Mr Ignatius always finds me.

Today I didn't wear any knickers to school, because I forgot to wash my clothes.

In art class I painted a picture of a big green field with lots of flowers and happy animals, a field behind one of the doors.

Dyson Macey sneaked up behind me and pulled my skirt up. I felt the wind come onto my parts like they do in playtime and I screamed at the top of my lungs.

When I opened my eyes, the whole class was staring at me. Mrs Gaffy yelled and sent me to the principal.

In Mr Catcher's office I sat in the chair on the other side of the desk, while he tried to call Mommy. She didn't answer so I had to wait in the office for the rest of the day, and be silent and do silly arithmetic problems.

When the bell rang Mr Catcher had a big talk to me and told me I had no respect and called me an attention seeker and a disturbance to my class and said Mommy had to set me straight.

I felt blue when I left school. But when I turned the corner I noticed Oscar by the fence with all the funny painting on it.

When I stopped by home to change and pack my bag, Mommy was staring at the wall. She didn't notice me, no matter how loud the stairs creaked.

For dinner Oscar and I gathered fruit and raw vegetables and bread from George at the night market. We ate by the lake in Springfield Park. We saved some bread for the ducks and they quacked happily when I tossed it in the water.

We were having a real fun time. But then the men in suits came. Mr Black Suit, Mr Checker Suit, Mr Gray Suit and Mr Policeman. Mommy's friends.

'Hello Oscar. How's our little nigger today?' Mr Checker Suit is huge with ginger hair.

Oscar's voice was scared. 'I'm fine, Sir.'

'Aren't ya gonna ask him how he's doing, Boy?' Mr Black Suit prodded Oscar on the shoulder.

'How is you doing, Sirs?' asked Oscar.

'Well that's the thing; we could be better.'

Oscar gulped. His eyes looked like they had been polished.

'Yes indeed, Boy, we need some things.'

I wrapped my arm around Oscar and leaned my head on his shoulder. I wished away those big towers of men. I wished them away so hard that the whole world except me and Oscar disappeared.

Mr Gray Suit sniffed and played with his nose. 'I tell ya what, Sonny Boy, we'll come back and talk another time. Just remember we'll always be back.'

After they left I asked Oscar who they were. 'Just some friends,' was all he said.

'Oscar, remember when I asked you if I could stay with you and you said I couldn't because I had a nice house?'

He tossed the last piece of bread to the ducks. 'Yeah, I remember.'

'Well what if my house isn't nice?'

'But Kay-Kay, you has a good home. Why you wanna sleep where I do? It can be real cold.'

'The house can be real cold, too. It's not my home ... I just wanna stay with you.'

'Well okay, but just for tonight and you gotta get your stuff for school. I ain't having you play hooky, Girl.'

'I promise I'll go, as long as you wait for me after.'

'I'll always be there for you.'

We stood up and hugged. I don't think I've ever felt as warm as I did right then.

'You know one day we should run away together,' I said, with my head buried into his chest.

He kissed me on the forehead. 'One day, Shorty.'

$$* \quad * \quad *$$

Beyond midnight, every minute or so Oscar stirred in his sleep. Maybe he had bad dreams like me. I woke up before him, but it wasn't from a bad dream, it was because there weren't any. The mattress was dirty and smelled, but it was comfortable. The wind whistled past the opening of the cove and was chilly, but the ashes from the fire were warm. While I was awake, Oscar slept. Everything was upside-down, but perfect.

DIARY 7

December 27 1979

This year we didn't have a Christmas tree or presents. Mommy
must have forgotten. Maybe all the decorations on the streets
are invisible to her. She left on Christmas morning in the big
black car.

In the main street of town there were lots of Christmas
celebrations and a parade with elves, singers and Santa.
Snowflakes fell softly to the white ground. It was like being
inside a snow globe.

Santa came down the road on his sleigh on top of a colorful
float, with reindeer made of cardboard and sparkles and glitter
everywhere. Oscar took my hand and we squeezed to the front
between the big bodies. Santa passed and smiled. A snowflake
hit my nose and Oscar put his arm around me.

With two cups of eggnog and pudding from the Salvation
Army stall, we sat on the step of the bookstore. The pudding
was warm and crumbly, filled with fruit, and the eggnog was
sweet, steaming and thick. Oscar took a forkful of his pudding
and dropped it into my eggnog.

'Hey!' I shrieked. 'You rascal, Oscar.'

'It's good luck, Kay-Kay; it means Christmas is going to bring
everything you want this year.'

'Really? How do you know that?'

'My momma told me. She knew a lot of stuff. She also said little brown-haired girls with green eyes are devils.'

'She did not!'

'Nah, but you is as fun as one.'

I scuffed my feet in the snow. Big symphony instruments marched down the street, playing *Little Drummer Boy*. 'Where is your momma now?'

'I don't know. They tell me she's in sunshine, somewhere golden. Quick, you gotta eat the pudding before it sinks to the bottom, I forgot to tell ya.'

I gulped it down.

'Now make a wish.'

I closed my eyes and thought real hard about what I wanted to come true. I opened my eyes and then finished off the pudding.

Oscar stared at me. 'Well,' he said, 'what did you wish for?'

I burped. 'I can't tell you that, Ozzy.'

'Don't think I wanna know if it's got to do with that burp. Gutso. And Ozzy?'

'If I'm Kay-Kay, or Shorty, then you have to have at least one nickname, and yours is Ozzy. Is only fair, Afro Joe.' I ruffled his hair.

'Ozzy.' He smiled and nodded his head. 'I like it. Thanks, Shorty.'

As we hugged I looked up at the sky. I didn't see any shooting stars, but I didn't need one to make my wish come true.

The parade finished and the people cleared out until Oscar and I were the only ones left. Dusk set in while we roamed the empty streets and played with the leftover decorations. I didn't want the day to end.

We were playing soccer with a cardboard wreath when a voice startled me. 'Oscar, my little brown boy, been looking everywhere for ya.' It was Mr Checker Suit. The others were with him.

'Hey, Sweet Cheeks,' said Mr Gray Suit, a cigar dangling from his lip. 'Run along; we gotta talk to our boy. Unless you want to stay and have some fun.'

Oscar looked at me sternly. 'Head to our spot, Kay-Kay.'

I put my hand in his. I didn't want to leave him with the suit men. Oscar tilted his head. 'Go.'

I ran away, but at the corner of the barber shop I stopped to spy. They walked Oscar to the van and shoved him inside. I wanted to stop them, but I was frozen like a snowman.

The van door closed and it drove away. I was all alone. The town was still. Not even a bird flew overhead in the deep blue sky.

A black car entered the street and pulled up across the road from me. Both of the front doors opened. Mommy stepped out of the car and so did he. The world spun like the glass ball had been shaken really hard.

As Mommy began to speak, I took off as fast as my legs could take me. Down the alley behind the stores, past the door where the food came from, into the woods, and down the embankment.

In the cove I huddled. The stream at the bottom of the embankment trickled, leaves crunched and twigs broke on the ground above me. Eventually they walked away and the stream was all I could hear.

Oscar came in around midnight, lay down behind me and slid under the blanket.

'Where did you go?' I asked as he wrapped his arm around me.

'Sorry. I didn't mean to wake you. I had to go and do some stuff with those men.'

The white moonlight shone onto Oscar's cheek. His eye was puffed up with a big mouse under it.

'What did they do to you?' I softly touched his face.

Oscar took my hand off his face and held it. 'It's because I didn't do something they wanted me to do ... I ain't doing it. I'm stuck, Shorty, because if I don't, something else bad will happen.'

'Who are they, and why do you have to do things?'

'They aren't very nice men, but that's why I have to do stuff for them, because if I don't ...' He pulled me in close to him. He smelled like sweat, but he made me feel safe.

'What will happen if you don't?' I was half asleep.

Oscar petted my hair with his ginormous hands. 'Go back to sleep, Shorty. Tomorrow's a new day and the sun will be out. Somewhere.'

The light of the moon blinked. I nestled into Oscar and let my eyes close.

The next morning he woke me when the moon was still in the sky, while the sun was yawning and the birds singing their morning songs. 'Come on, Girl, we gotta get you home.'

I felt my insides drop. 'Home? I am home.'

'Nah, I mean your house, with your momma and your bedroom and some warmth.'

'But what if I don't want to go? What if I want to stay with you? It's warmer here.'

Pulling me in and hugging me, Oscar said, 'Kayla, you're my best friend. The best I've ever had, but we from different worlds.'

I wanted to tell him about playtime, but I couldn't.

We walked back to my house hand in hand. It snowed the whole way and every now and again we tried to catch snowflakes on our tongues.

When we arrived, the black car was in the driveway. Even at the mailbox I could feel them inside. They'd be talking or having playtime and I didn't want to be with them.

'All right, when you get to your room I want you to give me a signal to show me you're safe.' Oscar held his hand out and clapped his pinkie finger and his thumb together. 'Can you do a clap like that?'

I tried, but it was very tricky. 'I don't know if I can, Ozzy.'

He laughed. 'It's all good, you're allowed to use your other hand to help.'

With the help of my left hand I pinkie-clapped.

'That's going to be our hello, happy and safe signal. So promise you'll do it only when you is safe and happy.'

'I promise. But Oscar,' I said, 'you have to promise me something too. Okay?'

'Anything.'

'You have to promise me that *you* will be safe – that those men won't hurt you again.' I reached up and touched his face. His eye was purple and blue.

'I'll be fine, Shorty.

'One day you and me will run away to the sunshine. Get down to California and be free from this dull gray and all these frozen lakes. All of this. I promise we'll get out of here.'

We hugged and I trudged up the path. I glanced back to Oscar and hoped he'd call me back, but he ushered with his hands to go in.

They were in the kitchen. I sneaked up the stairs as quiet as I could, slowly so the second, fourth and ninth steps didn't creak. I could smell him from the kitchen. And Mommy too. They both have a smell that leaves a trail wherever they go. It's how I know where they have been.

When I got in my room I thought about not going to the window. But I didn't want Oscar to freeze. I wasn't happy or safe. But I went to the window and with the help of my left hand I did the pinkie-clap. Oscar pinkie-clapped back and blew me a kiss from his fingers. I caught it and put it in my pocket for later, when I needed it.

The stairs creaked and a knock came at my door. I could smell who it was.

CHAPTER 5

I approached the small metal gates at the entrance. Beyond the sea of tombstones a sky of steel blue and scattered cloud seemed to go on forever. I entered St Kilda cemetery, my blood polluted by alcohol.

Underfoot the ground was soft, as if millions of spilled tears had prevented drought reaching the earth where the departed lay, the graveyard the only place not sucked of life. It never mattered how many cars clogged the road or how many industrial chimneys poured soot into the atmosphere, the air at the cemetery always seemed clean and refreshing. I inhaled deeply. I passed the Gothic statue sitting atop an unmarked gravestone. My head felt clear.

At the end of the row I stopped. Wilted flowers sat in a vase beside the plaque, a candle on the stone was melted halfway down. The guilt I felt for not bringing a fresh bouquet surmounted any ambivalence. '*She's your mother for fuck's sake, Dane.*' Blinking, my body remembered the beer in my bloodstream. My knees became weak and I stumbled, resetting before I trampled a burial mound. I was drunk, and nervous.

On burial site DC 240, in front of her smiling picture, I fell to my knees. My heart wanted to burst, and cry oceans onto the green grass below, but my eyes wouldn't let it escape. Some things you cannot escape.

* * *

June had come and gone, along with my sixteenth birthday.

The night was so cold I had on two pairs of socks and my feet still felt like they were stuck in an Esky. I rubbed my toes and doubted they would ever regain feeling. By the fire I huddled and watched sparks fly from the logs and tried to capture the small burst of warmth that radiated from the glass.

Mum sat knitting a blanket, her glasses dipped down her nose. Josh was beside me, huddled as well. Occasionally he'd bump me in the side and try to wriggle over to get more of the heat. The house was quiet except for murmurs of the evening news from the television room, the crackle from the fire and Mum's knitting needles scraping against each other.

The door swung open and a burst of frost-bitten air slapped my face. Stevie entered, wrapped in a winter coat and muddied boots. His lips were violet and his teeth chattered. He ruffled Josh's hair – I ducked out of reach – on the way past and then kissed Mum on the cheek.

'Dinner's in the oven, Love,' she said as she crossed her needles at lightning pace. 'Tuna casserole.'

'Ripper, thanks Lynette.' Stevie had taken to calling Mum by her first name. Although she raised her eyebrows, I think she liked it. It must have been nice to hear a man in her house call her Lynette without 'you cunt bitch' after it.

Josh nudged me and tried to gain territory. I shoved him back with my hips. It was good being the bigger twin, older by four minutes. Stevie and Mum chatted in the kitchen. The usual *how was your day* stuff.

In the next moments it all changed.

A glass smashed in the television room. On all fours I peered around the edge of the fireplace and through the doorway. His arm hung limply over the arm of the chair like a withered daisy. The far brick wall was splattered with liquid, on the floor the whiskey bottle was smashed to pieces.

Dread in their eyes, Mum and Stevie fixed on the doorway. Beside me, Josh had tightened into a ball, his eyes peeping over his knees. In the television room the arm disappeared. The chair squeaked as he stood.

The glow of the television was broken by a figure crossing. His footsteps were slow and heavy, his shadow weighed a ton. He appeared by the door, his eyes bloodshot and vacant, his jaw clenched. Before me stood a monster that had been hidden away for years.

He'd been made redundant at the start of June, and had spent every day since drinking himself to sleep by noon, then he woke and repeated the same pattern into the night. It seemed only a matter of time until he drank himself to sleep forever. I wish he had, it would have been easier.

Work had dried up for Stevie, too. With only scraps of income for the household, the pantry was empty and the refrigerator dry. Each morning there was another overdue bill or threatening letter on the kitchen table.

As he opened the pantry he grunted and mumbled to himself. I jumped as he slammed the door. He glared at Mum. She kept her eyes forward as if trying to see him with the back of her head. She stopped knitting and sat up straight.

Stevie's eyes had not moved from him, while Josh's didn't want to be seen.

Then his human side returned. He snorted and wiped his nose with the inside of his wrist. 'Go to your rooms, Boys.' It was like he was a werewolf, and knew that as soon as the moon became full he would turn. 'Go!'

Stevie stood. 'No.'

'What did you say?' He stepped up to Stevie.

'I said *no.*'

The monster swayed and tilted his chin to see eye to eye with his eldest son. 'You want a thrashing, huh? Don't think you're too old for me to thump you, Boy.'

Stevie didn't budge. My arms and legs grew weak. Beside me Josh shook; his arms hugging his legs.

'Sidney!' Mum stood. 'Don't talk to him like that.'

He turned to Mum. 'Shut up, Bitch; stay out of this.' He raised the back of his hand.

Stevie grabbed his wrist. 'Don't raise a hand to my mother!' Stevie let his hand go free. 'Now go back into the other room and go to sleep.'

His attention turned back to Stevie. 'You really want a beating huh, Son.'

Stevie tilted his chin. His jaw was gripped so tight the muscles were mounds on his cheek. 'Don't threaten me. And I'm not your son.' Their eyes were locked.

My father took off his belt, snapped the leather in a horseshoe, stepped back from Stevie and prepared to strike.

'Sidney, put that down!' Mum shrieked. 'Leave him alone.'

He ignored her and lashed out. Stevie tried to avoid it but the leather whipped his back with a clap like thunder. I rushed toward them.

Mum lunged and tried to grab the hand with the belt. He turned, pulled his hand free and then smacked her square in the jaw. She fell through the air in slow motion.

'Mum!' I slid across the kitchen floor.

Her eyes were like glass. A puddle of blood formed under her head. 'Mum!' I shook her. Her eyes stayed glassed over.

Glancing up, I saw him take a knife from the woodblock. He lunged at Stevie. But Stevie stepped to the side and spun the arm with the knife around my father's back in a hammer lock. He fell forward like a sack of potatoes, the knife stuck into his spine.

Josh was by my side. 'Wake up, Mum,' he pleaded. 'Why won't she wake up?' Tears flowed from his eyes.

'Mum!' This time I shook her harder. 'Wake up *Mum*!' I patted her, frantically trying to feel for a pulse on her neck, her wrist, her neck, her foot, her wrist. 'Call the ambulance, Josh.'

He was a statue. '*Now*! Get the phone; call the ambulance.' His eyes struggled to leave Mum, lifeless at my knees, but he rose to his feet.

As Josh spoke into the phone, he knelt near our father who was as still as Mum. He touched Dad's neck, and then his wrist. I knew as soon as Josh's eyes found mine.

Stevie dropped to the ground. He quivered and beat the back of his head against the pantry door. I started CPR, pounding my palms into my mother's chest. The bone stuck out from in between her breasts; my finger grazed over the softness of her skin. Her rib snapped sometime after I'd lost count of cycles.

Her skin became cold.

I stared into her eyes, emptied of colour. I could hear voices, faint, somewhere far away, instructing me to stop. Arms took hold of me. I fought and clung onto my mother. Two policemen pulled me off and the paramedics took over.

On the far side of the kitchen, Stevie buried his head into his hands, wheezing. Josh was on all fours and wailed as another two medics covered my father under a sheet.

For a second I caught sight of his face before the sheet covered him. In that fleeting moment I saw the man he once was. The man who had taught me how to ride, who had cocked barbeques on hot summer evenings, who had taken me fishing to Bonnie Doon after my pet rabbit Nibbles died. For a moment he was my father.

I left my body, I think, and watched from two metres behind myself.

The paramedics attending to my mother called to each other, still working incessantly. They sat up straight and stopped CPR. One turned to those who stood and shook his head, while the other dropped his eyes in defeat. I returned to my body and broke through the crowd. On my hands and knees I slid through the pool of blood flowing from her head and tried to resuscitate her. The policemen pulled me away. I fought and fought and fought, right until she was covered by a body bag.

As she disappeared, a river of red the only part of her that remained visible, I collapsed at the knees. In a matter of minutes my world had been torn apart, and everything changed forever.

* * *

I wiped my cheek in search of a tear, but it had been too long since I'd cried. When I held it in that day, I closed a door that would rust shut.

Mum's picture on her plaque was beautiful. She looked so young, so happy and vibrant. She had the smile of a woman who can light up a crowded room.

It was like Kayla's. The way her eyes glowed like a warm light as she curled her lip. Smiling eyes that let you know everything is all right; you're safe and we are happy. My mother was a shield.

The squawk of a crow startled me. At the end of the row the bird was perched on a tombstone. It stared at me with beady eyes, as if to tell me something. From the corner of my eye, I saw that something.

In his hand were flowers, a fresh bouquet of pink roses turned toward the ground. He stood like a beacon of that bloody July night, still and fixated on me as if I were the monster. His head was shaved, his skinned tanned as it had always been, his body stronger than ever. He was distant and angry, and scared. It was a fear I knew – the fear of being hurt.

I stood. He didn't move. The tension rose like steam from the underground. It choked the air between us. He turned and walked away.

'Josh.' I started after him.

He burst through the cemetery gate, and swung it violently back toward me. Although I wanted him to stop, part of me dreaded to hear what he'd say. Stones flicked from the ground beneath his feet. He opened the driver's door of the black four-wheel-drive. Flowers still in hand, and with one leg inside the car, he stopped to glare at me, his face now plastered with angst.

For a moment we locked eyes. Right then Josh knew exactly what I was trying to say, and I knew exactly what he was thinking.

He sat, slammed the door and started the engine. It hummed quietly, but then the purr drifted into the wind and the old block motor took over, chugging with raw power. Last time I had heard that sound was in the middle of a convoy of cars with fogged windows.

The engine roared. The wheels spun and kicked up dust. The car disappeared down the road, leaving a dirty cloud and exhaust fumes hovering in the air. I closed my eyes and tried to picture my mother's smile telling me that everything was going to be okay. But all I saw was blood on a linoleum floor and the abandoned face of my twin brother, seared with spite, his wounds reopened with my return.

CHAPTER 6

As soon as the inquest had finished and found that Stevie acted in self-defence, we collected our parents' ashes, packed up the scarce few things we wanted to keep, and drove away in the EH, leaving behind the house still filled with furniture, and photos on the walls.

Although we left, we never escaped. What happened that night would always stay with us. At night I relaxed my guard and saw the lifeless eyes, felt the thudding skulls, and tasted blood seeping from the ground and landing on my tongue. There is a reason for nightmares.

In the summer of '82 we moved into the house on Neptune Street, St Kilda. It was a tiny two-and-a-half-bedroom, inner-suburban shack. Josh and I got the bedrooms and Stevie slept in the study – Stevie's orders. The backyard could be crossed in five steps and the front garden was infested with crab grass and bordered by a crumbling, knee-high brick fence. There was no beautiful wattle, only an old tricycle with no seat and some dirty Coke bottles.

We bought the plaque for Mum in St Kilda cemetery and hid Dad's ashes somewhere well out of sight.

Neither Josh nor I continued school. Instead, we worked with Stevie on the docks. Stevie's best friend from home, Kerry McLaughlin, had moved to St Kilda shortly after us and through a friend of his we found ourselves a part of the bustling Melbourne waterfront.

We travelled each day in Stevie's EH to the Port of Melbourne in the west of the city, where we undocked vessels for Berths B, C and D on Appleton Dock. The days were long and the work physical, but we just did what we had to do. The nights were even longer.

Some days the Union worked around the clock. Every guy wanted to make an extra buck at some point, and the city was thirsty. Someone always needs a fix of something. The higher you got, the deeper you went, the more bucks you could earn and the fewer people you had to answer to.

The crew consisted of Josh, me, Stevie, and a handful of other guys – some rough, some tired, some larrikins, and some not sure where they fitted.

Aside from my brothers, I only talked to two of the crew. One was Kerry. The other was Teddy – Bear and resident doctor-to-be – who worked the seedy hours to pay his way through medical school. He was the hardest worker and, in some ways, kept us normal.

* * *

It was an evening in mid-January '83, and the house was stuffy. All day the sun had burned like a fireball in the sky. My overalls stuck to my skin, soaked with sweat, as if I'd actually jumped off the docks into the sea, as I had wanted to. The rickety ceiling fan did little to stop the sauna. With curtains closed, the glow of the television was all that lit the living room. I was sprawled across the couch, Josh slumped on the bean bag, while we watched the third Ashes test.

The fan jingled as it spun, and the curtains whooshed with each gust from the fan. A clap sounded on the television every half a minute when the batsmen connected with the ball. It had been a long day at work in the stifling heat, and my eyes flirted with sleep.

The front door opened and Stevie bustled into the lounge room. It was difficult to see him with the curtains closed, but I could hear him panting like a Labrador. He stopped for a second and then whisked open the curtains. Evening sunshine burst through and blinded me.

'What'd you do that for?' cried Josh.

'Time to go to work,' replied Stevie.

I sat up and rubbed my eyes. 'We finished work an hour ago, Arsehole.'

'No, it's time to go to your real job, real money. And you start tonight.'

'What the hell are you talking about?'

'Captains want you there; said you've done a good job and it's time. Meet me out front in five. Don't be late on your first day.'

It took a few seconds for me to realise that he was referring to the other side of the docks. The Union ran society outside of the media's pretty little portrait: that society we all know about yet pretend not to, the darker side, the grey cloud of concern that dwells in the clear blue sky that is every parent's mind.

From the moment we arrived in St Kilda Stevie had slipped out in the middle of the night. At first I thought he was at the pub, but after some time I figured it out. My innocence had been broken with my mother's skull.

We drove while the sun set, the sky like a pastel canvas of red, orange and blue. My skin was covered in dried sweat, cooled by wind gusting through the lowered passenger window.

Stevie pulled the car into the gravel car park at the dock and wrenched back the handbrake. 'Wait here. I'll be back soon.'

Soon extended to half an hour. By now it was completely dark, the waterfront deserted and lit only by dull moonbeams and scattered lights from makeshift fixtures.

'What the hell are we doing?' Josh leaned forward through the front seats.

'Guess we're about to find out.'

As Stevie approached the car, his feet crunched the gravel. He opened my door. 'All right, let's go.'

We followed him onto the waterfront and then toward the docks we serviced during the day. The last ship that had come into Dock Seven was still moored, as was another, which hadn't been there earlier. The new ship was a shabby vessel, not half the size of the container carrier beside it.

We crossed the gangway, the quiet sound of water lapping the side of the ship coming from below. The entrance to the ship was dark. Inside it was pitch black, silent, and the smell of dust made my nostrils twitch. As we turned a corner, the cargo hold appeared, immersed in the yellow glow of handheld lanterns.

The captains sat nonchalantly on crates. Teddy and Kerry stood waiting for us in front of the rest of the crew. Teddy summoned us over to two crates on the far side. Not a word had been said. He took a crowbar and plied the crate open.

Inside, plastic bags filled with white powder were piled on top of one another. It was the first time I'd seen heroin.

LETTER 4

November 20 1993

Dane,

Although you and I aren't claustrophobic, we have never reveled in enclosed spaces. You broke the lock on the door and swore like a drunkard when I trapped you in the wardrobe that Christmas Eve. You even growled, 'I'll throw every goddamn thing I've got you out the window. Maybe the bums will bloody appreciate it!'

I laughed. 'Wouldn't quite be Christmas without the Grinch around.'

Of course, the presents remained under the tree, and once I curled up with you with a warm glass of eggnog, the Grinch disappeared. It's too early to think about Christmas, but now that I do, I know I'm going to miss you even more than I do now.

I've always looked forward to you stumbling in the front door with a live pine, insisting that, despite being on the fourth floor of an inner-city Los Angeles apartment building, we must have a real Christmas tree. It would stink the apartment out, and then we'd have stray pine needles stuck to the carpet well into January, until one of us finally cleaned it up.

I'll miss playing pranks on you, too.

I know what you must have felt in the cupboard. Did entrapment make you leave? Because I never wanted you trapped, not in our apartment – despite all those days we were holed up in the bedroom – not in this city or this country, and certainly not with me.

'You've been here for three months, right?' I asked Burty as we strolled the path around the courtyard, which has become our custom when we have the energy.

'That's right.'

'And you've never wanted to run down the street and scream and suck in every bit of fresh air you can find?'

His chuckle was like a frog's croak. 'You tickle me sometimes, Lil Lady, not because your ideas are sometimes whacky, but because most of the time I think the same.'

'I hope you put some pants on,' I said. Burty wore only his hospital gown. 'For your sake and the public's.'

'Who's for pants when crazy has your number? That's what I like about the insane: they don't have time for all this trivial nonsense like pants; much more important things to focus on.'

'Like how many body fluids you can expel, or whether the voice of Jimmy Buffet or Mama Cass is real?'

'It don't so much matter which voices are real, only matters what they're telling ya. Real folks say the dumbest of things sometimes, so maybe them unreal ones might talk sense on occasion.'

You'd see quite easily why I like Burty. Two peas in a kind of spicy, sort of sweet stew, nothing at all to do with a pod. Pods are a little too claustrophobic.

'So why don't you do it?' I asked.

'Because I see the sense in being here. I don't have to be here, even if I got cancer, but I choose to because I don't want to have it.'

On walks since, I've looked to the line of trees around the hospital grounds and realized they don't fence us in. I've stared at their branches, black and jagged in the gentle flames of a sunset, swaying and free in a peaceful blue sky, and through to the space beyond the trees – a place you can't quite see.

I don't feel as much like a caged animal, but I'm still trapped in some ways.

Under that big white vessel, beaming down its red beam onto my uncovered skin, the walls began to close in and the room continued to shrink until a microwave bell rang, and I was cooked. They've promised me it will be easier each time and I wonder, did I imply the same thing to you, Dane?

I was a baked little pig after radiation, and over the next few weeks before I begin another round of chemo, I'll be tanning for free down the hall. The good news is that the tumor has shrunk enough for this to happen.

Afterward, in the bathroom I turned on only the cold tap in the shower, and the water against my boiled skin made me feel feverish. My teeth chattered as I applied shampoo, rubbed around my scalp, and soothed over the back of my neck like you would when you applied it for me. When I washed it out, clumps of brown fell from my scalp and plopped on the white tiles of the shower floor.

I've been waiting for it. Each day I've checked my follicles to see if the time has come to join the Baldies. The day before yesterday, right after checking out of Hotel Nagasaki, was the day. What a lovely delayed side effect.

Wrapped in a towel with another turbaned on my head, I stood in front of the bathroom mirror, braced myself, then removed the towels.

In the mirror I saw what looked like a doll's scalp after a silly little three-year-old girl decides to give her a haircut, which progressively goes too far. My breasts are now golf balls, my chest as bare and skeletal as the carcass of road kill stripped of meat by vultures. And at that moment, as I clung to the last strands of my hair, my disease appeared, encasing the woman I used to be.

If you'd stuck around, you probably would have left when you saw me anyway – I couldn't even stand to look at myself. I fled from the bathroom back to my room.

Burty was out, and so Susan was the only other conscious being in the room. Rather than reading *Vogue*, she was curled in the fetal position, hands acting as a pillow, her stare fixed on the white plaster ahead of her.

I stood at the end of Maureen's bed. Her breaths were heavy, and her chest moved up and down. I wondered what her family thought. Did they want her to wake up or to go to sleep properly?

Her eyes were closed, lids wrinkled and frail, her skin tattooed with dark blue and green veins pressing to the surface. Needles connected her to a feeding tube; the oxygen mask nearly covered her whole prune face. The longer I stood and stared at her and wondered what lifetime had brought her here, the more I wanted to step to her side, touch her hand and, at the sign of no response, kiss her softly on the forehead, tell her goodnight, tell her it's going to be okay now, and then, mercifully, press down on her face with the handmade cushion from the chair at her bedside. I wanted her to feel peace, not the shit she feels now.

'What in God's sake are you doing?'

Susan had sat up in bed, the copy of *Vogue* not yet open. She glared at me.

'Nothing,' I replied. 'Just seeing Maureen.'

'Seeing what? You should mind your own business and leave the poor woman alone. She's not a circus freak to be stared at by pesky little girls like you.'

Life has taught me not to take shit from older people just because they've been here longer. So it was with a gulp and bubbles in my stomach that I brushed it aside, sat on the end of my bed and hoped for Burty to come in. You'd have been proud of my restraint.

'You know what, I'm considering changing rooms. You've been nothing but a nuisance since you showed up.'

I could no longer ignore her. 'You know what, fuck you, Susan.'

She gasped exasperatedly. 'Just the sort of response I should expect from a brat like you.'

I needed fresh air. I stood and started for the door.

'It's no wonder you never have a visitor; not even your Daddy or Mommy come to see you.'

Through the window across the hallway the trees swayed in the breeze. I don't have to be here, but I want to be to get rid of this poisonous monster infecting my tissues, and with this choice, I don't have to take crap from mother-cow bitches.

Susan's eyes grew wider the closer I got to her bed. 'What are you doing?!' She was frightened.

It had been years since I'd heard whimpers from someone realizing they've done something they shouldn't have and are about to pay for it: the genuine terror of finding out what karma really means.

I picked up the vase from her bedside table. The glass was heavy and thick – it would take some force to smash. I lifted it. Susan cowered beneath me. I forgot how big five-foot-four can be when you hold something over someone. The water soaked her and she wailed for a split second before I put the vase down and wrapped my fingers around her neck. 'Shut the hell up.'

Perhaps you thought from those times you dodged dinner plates that I was going to smash it over her head, but I wasn't. I'm actually quite a good throw and if I'd wanted to, I would've hit you when we went to Greek wedding war. It would make you laugh if I told you I don't like violence and that I don't want to hurt anyone, so I won't, but in most cases it's true.

'You're a pocket rocket with the power to fly to the moon and blow it up,' you told me after a struggle for the television remote.

The Wonder Years, really?

I released my grip from Susan's neck. 'There'll be a day when Maureen isn't here anymore, and she's not the circus freak.' I revealed my head. 'I am.

'Don't talk to me like that again, Susan. If you want to move rooms, do it. I won't miss your surliness, but if you're going to stay, remove the stick from your ass and try to be positive. There is enough god-awful shit and suffering in this place without you adding to it.'

* * *

Outside this morning, the sky appeared as if someone far above had thrown a patchwork quilt of gray and white over the earth. Stones crunched beneath my slippers as I approached the bench. Burty gazed ahead to the graceful part of life in the sky.

'Mind if I join you, Old Fart?'

I startled him, and he grunted. 'Oh … nothing would make me happier.' He tapped the seat. 'How are you, my crazy companion, making sense of Mama Cass?'

'Hardly, I'm more focused on when I'll be moved, or kicked out.'

'For what?'

'Had a run-in with Susan yesterday evening. Got a little out of hand. Think I've got a screw loose, or maybe I was never fitted with the right ones.'

'Your screws are just fine, Honey. I seen plenty of fellas and gals lose their marbles in my time, and I tell ya, I think you've got all yours. They might be colored differently and have some unusual patterns on them, but you've got all the wits you need. Earned and learned I sense.'

'I guess. I'm still worried, though. I don't want to tan and vomit without you.'

'That ain't gonna happen, Darlin'. They try and steal you away and they'll have to go through me first. You're stuck with me, I promise.'

I beamed, and rested my head on his shoulder.

'And don't you worry about Susan. She's just grumpy because her sons didn't make it in this week.' He leaned over to me as if someone was around to hear. 'She can be a downright bitch sometimes.' He giggled at his own cuss and then sat upright and relaxed to a smirk. 'Matter of fact, I might have even thrown some water on her sometime.'

'Now you're just having me on you old fool. Running down highways in hospital gowns, throwing water on a fellow patient: you're the crazy one.'

'Ain't denying that, Lil Lady. Batty as they come.'

My nose started to run. I wiped it with my sleeve, a disgusting habit you never really commented on. Did you even notice how yuck I can be? Surely, I'm downright foul.

Right then, for some stupid reason, I felt confident, so confident that I whipped off the towel from my head. As soon as I did I felt naked.

'New skin *and* a new haircut I see,' said Burty, tilting his head.

'You think I have a shot at the runway now?' I pouted and did a pathetic Marilyn impersonation: 'Now what is a girl to do.'

'I think we could do a dual show.' He chuckled, rubbing his hand over the gleam of his scalp.

I can imagine how it would feel to have Burty as a father.

Conversation dulled to nothingness. I looked at him. He looked tired. His vision was off on a porch on a ranch somewhere in his Friday in the sky.

'Can I ask you something? It's fine if you don't want to answer.'

'Shoot, Darlin', you can ask me anything.'

'Why doesn't your family visit? Who did you kill?'

He dropped his head and then sighed heavily. 'Didn't kill no one, but I sure didn't do much for their life …

'I think about them every minute of every single day. My wife Candice passed a long time ago, when my Lily was only a mite. Drunken truck driver swerved onto her side of the road.'

'I'm so sorry to hear that.'

He placed his hand on mine and patted it.

'Never been another woman to capture my eye like she did. Boy was she something. Long black hair, skin the color of just-ripe olives, eyes that made you forget about everything for a while and lips so sweet that sugar lost taste to me after our first kiss.'

If I was more inclined to cry I might have done so at that moment. I'd like to think you spoke about me sometime like this. I have no idea what you think of me now. Not enough to be here.

'And Lily?' I asked.

'I don't know.'

Our hands entwined. His fingers were thick, and his palm like a leather cushion – firm but soft. There was comfort and protection in his touch as he grasped and I squeezed back.

He explained as if he thought aloud. He told me how the land became barren after Candice was taken. Crops died and did not return: it wasn't the land, he said – he dried up long before the corn. Burty found another job and went into the usual spin – when we spend time in order to have money to spend, we lose the time to spend on the things money can't buy.

'I went down to oil rigs in Texas. I wanted to get in and get out, have enough money to retire early and spend all my time with Lily, being the father she deserved.'

Life is ironic, isn't it, Dane? It's one of the things we could never smirk enough at. Listening to Burty broke the part of my heart the silly old fool has stolen.

By the time he had made the cash he wanted, the hot Texas sun had roasted his skin enough for melanoma. That money has paid for his treatment.

He lost the time, and Lily too.

'Before I knew it she was becoming a woman. I missed her graduation, her first day of high school and when she came home and needed to talk I wasn't there. And then when she turned sixteen she requested to be placed in the custody of Candice's parents.'

Burty hasn't seen his daughter since an awkward visit to her new home in Los Angeles – the reason he came here – and eventually she relinquished contact altogether.

'Can you give up, though? She is your daughter.'

'Geoff and Margaret blame me for Candice's passing. Never going to give me Lily's details and I've tried everything. And now I can't even get out by myself, I ain't so much giving up.'

I was disappointed. I'd like to think he'd be more of a parent.

'Even if you have made mistakes … If I were her, despite what you think, I would still want to see you. It's never too late until it *is* too late. Time might leave a scar, but it still heals.'

His neck had drooped disjointedly low. We sat in silence for a long time. The clouds above darkened to a metallic gray, the skies ready to open and release the rain that still teems now as I sit here in the cafeteria and try to balance ingestion with purging.

How colorful Burty has been – a luminous flower in this dirt pile of sickness and suffering. But even the most colorful flower can be drowned in a downpour.

✳ ✳ ✳

9:00pm, in bed.

Burty's curtains have been drawn since we came inside. Entering the room, Susan glanced up at me. I was ready for her to smugly inform me I was getting kicked out, but she looked timid. From her made-up, wrinkled face with cherry-red lips, I almost pitied her.

On my bed was a paper grocery bag.

'Came by earlier and left them for you,' said Susan, as meager as she looked.

I withdrew two colored wigs from the bag, a blonde bob and a long flow of black, and rolled the hair through my fingers.

'Who?'

'That nice nurse who is looking after you.'

'Betty?'

'No, Cameron.'

I pondered for a long time and then left for the bathroom.

I presume shaving your head with a leg razor would usually be hard, but for chemo-defined follicles it wasn't. The remaining strands and clumps floated down with ease into the bathroom sink.

In the mirror I observed the alien.

When I returned to the room, Susan glanced up, this time with a smile. I returned the gesture.

I fitted the blonde mop. 'Marilyn with no acting talent?' I asked, and then changed to the black. 'Or Cher with a hell of lot more drugs in her?'

Susan laughed, and I giggled. In no time we were posing and being stupid, swapping the wigs with each other, me at one point wrapping Susan's own auburn locks around my chrome dome.

When we'd simmered to a tired after-glow, I sat on her bed and she touched my hand. It was almost motherly. 'Thank you, Kayla,' she said. 'I haven't laughed like that in a long time.'

'No need to thank me, I had just as much fun.'

My urge to beat her across the skull with a glass vase disappeared altogether.

This may sound funny to you, Babe, perhaps due to my lack of tolerance for the human race at certain times, but when I look wholly I do believe there is good in most people. Granted some people have far more bad about them, but most are capable of good. Hell, even Hitler had a wife. Susan, though, the way her eyes lit up, how her tongue poked out of her mouth as we played like sixteen-year-old schoolgirls, I believe there is much more goodness in her than the side of bitchiness that almost brought me to blows.

Cameron, too. Maybe he isn't so bad after all. It takes a while to get to know someone, doesn't it? Even then we never really do.

Kayla

DIARY 8

March 11 1980

Oscar and I hung out and did drawing for hours this afternoon. I liked my bedroom.

It was dark when lights beamed in from outside. I looked out the window to see them get out of the car.

'Are you okay, Shorty?'

I was huddled into a ball against the back of my door. He kneeled down next to me. I nodded. I tried not to make noise with my breaths. 'I don't want to see him.'

'See who?'

'Mr Ignatius. I don't like him; he hurts me; I don't want to see him.' I gripped Oscar's sweatshirt tight, stretching his sleeve.

'What …? God dammit.' He brought me in and held me close. I wrapped my arms around him and felt his shirt become wet. 'I won't let anyone come near you, Shorty. I gonna protect you forever.'

The front door opened. The second, fourth and ninth stairs creaked. The footsteps came down the hallway. They stopped near my door and the knock came.

Oscar sprang from the bed and pushed my desk behind the door. Mr Ignatius turned the handle and tried to open the door.

'Puppet,' he called and knocked again. 'It's playtime. Now move whatever you've got blocking the door and let me in.'

Panic jittered my entire body. *How is Oscar going to stop him? He's a monster, he's a monster!*

'Quick, Kayla.' Oscar was now by the window. 'We gotta get outta here.' He opened the window and put his leg through. 'We'll go down the drainpipe. I'll go first to make sure it is safe.' He held my hand. 'It's going to be okay Kay-Kay.'

Mr Ignatius yelled, 'Open the fucking door!'

Oscar put his other leg through the window, held the drainpipe with both hands and crawled down to the ground. The door shook and Mr Ignatius yelled louder.

'Come on, Shorty, you can do it,' Oscar called, signaling with his arms for me to come.

The desk started to move. I put my legs through the window and gripped the drainpipe. The desk fell on its side and the door swung open. Mr Ignatius's gray eyes glared at me and turned blood red.

He rushed across the room. I threw my body out of the window and started to climb down the drainpipe. Mr Ignatius lunged and leaned out the window, but I was out of reach. The pipe shook and, with night-time dew coating the metal, my grip slipped.

As I fell I looked up at Mr Ignatius. He snarled as I floated through the air. I seemed to float forever. Not a noise in the world.

I closed my eyes and, like in a dream, prepared to hit the ground, but just like in a dream, I woke up before the impact. 'I got you, Shorty. Lucky you little.' Oscar lowered my feet to the ground. I slid out of his arms.

Mr Ignatius was no longer in the window. Through the living-room window I saw him tramp down the stairs and toward the front door. 'Quick, we need to get out of here,' Oscar said. 'I know a shortcut away from the street.'

We ran along the street and passed three houses before we turned into the park at the end of the block. The car started up, a furious growl, while we hid under the slide. The lights drove by slowly. We stayed there and waited to see where he would go. My heart raced, and I sweated in the cool night. Beads of dew covered every part of the playground. Against the moonlight my breath fogged the air, wafting like the smoke from a cigarette.

The car drove back and forth twice before it stopped across the road. He got out and paced up and down the street. He noticed the park inlet and jogged toward it. Oscar took my hand. 'We need to go now, Shorty.'

We sneaked through a hole in the fence without breaking even a tiny twig. The woods behind were dark and might have been scary any other time. Instead they were our friend. As we started down the gravel trail, the swings in the park squeaked. Through a gap in the fence, I saw Mr Ignatius's dark shadow pushing an empty swing.

'I'm sorry I made you go back to that house … I didn't know,' Oscar said as soon as we got to safety. 'I'm not going to sleep until the sun comes up.'

In the abandoned warehouse five down in the industrial estate, I was pretty sure we were safe. I didn't know what was going to happen, but I knew I wasn't going to school, and there would be no more playtime with Mr Ignatius. I didn't want to see Mom or him ever again.

In the light coming in from outside I could see Oscar's little afro. It needed a trim. Maybe I could find some scissors and cut it for him. Yes, that's what I could do tomorrow.

DIARY 9

August 20 1980

We've been living in the abandoned warehouse since the night we escaped. It's much warmer and more out of sight than the cove near the woods.

The last few times we went back there to hide, we were interrupted by hunters across the stream, who hollered and shot at animals in the woods while their dogs barked and growled.

The other night I visited Mom's house. I didn't go in or knock. I just looked in the front window at Mom.

She sat in the same spot at the kitchen table and drank from a bottle of liquor, just like every other time I've visited since leaving. Sometimes the black car is parked in the driveway. I've seen him through the window, and I've seen them walk up the stairs.

Living away from home is different.

There are strange noises in the warehouse. I think it is haunted. I huddle under the blankets when I feel a ghost nearby, but Oscar always makes sure I am safe by wrapping his arms around me and lying in between me and the ghost.

We found a mattress and pillow. Oscar gives me the pillow, even when I try to share. When we need water there is a tap behind the warehouse. It takes a minute or so for the rust to clear. Most days Oscar gets food and any other supplies he can. It's best for me to stay hidden.

A week ago I noticed a poster in town. It had my picture and name on it and said to call the local police if I was spotted. That night Oscar and I went and pulled down all the posters. Although he doesn't want me to live with him because he says he's 'a drifter', he knows I can't go back to the house.

CHAPTER 7

'I want to run away with you – run forever and never look back. Let's go. Tomorrow before anyone rises,' I said.

She took my hand and grazed it lightly against her cheek. 'Where will we go? It'll be hard to leave here now.'

'Why does everything have to be so hard?'

'It was never meant to be easy, Dane.'

The sweetness in Rochelle's deep brown eyes took me away from the room, from the black suit and table of sympathetic flowers. My hand held her neck and drew her in … It was wrong, but everything was so wrong at the time that any happiness, even distorted, felt right.

I'd run the morning after, like I said, but not with her.

* * *

I sat at the bar and sucked down the last drops of Draught from the pot glass. Simone emerged from the kitchen with a couple of big breakfasts. She took them to the tradies seated near the pool table and then came over to me.

'You look like crap,' she said. 'Rough night's sleep?'

'Yeah, you could say that.'

She slid a photo in front of me. 'I found this last night. It's the last photo of you, Stevie and Josh all together.'

It was from Australia Day 1985, not so long before it all came to a head. Josh's arm was wrapped around Rochelle, as was mine. Hers, on the other hand, was only coiled around one brother. Stevie was disconnected from the group – with us but alone.

'Is she on your mind? I mean ... did you think about her a lot after you left?'

'I thought about everyone. Stevie, Josh, Mum, Kerry, you, Teddy, him ... But there came a time when I stopped thinking about Rochelle. I needed to forget that part pretty quickly. And once I met Kayla, well, it seemed like I could forget everything. I had something else to think about.'

There was no question I was well over Rochelle. I never forgot, though. You never forget your first love.

* * *

After I was introduced face to face to H, I became part of the biggest drug ring in the country.

In our circle Stevie, Kerry and Bear were experienced, high-ranked soldiers and answered directly to the captains, Keith Phillips and Cage Williams, who slid through the shadows and made themselves known when needed. They answered directly to the Union boss, James McCulloch, and knew their power. We broke, beat and trafficked at their command.

Alongside Josh and me, a dozen or so others made up the ground force. We worked our day shifts and earned a crust, and we worked the night shift and earned real money.

Ships came in from the Golden Triangle, loaded with crates of heroin, creeping through dark waters, guided by makeshift lights along the port. The vessels were unloaded and taken to dispersal points around the city, ready for distribution on the street before the sun had risen. We controlled the docks, so we controlled everything that entered the city by water. Sometimes it was as little as a kilogram and sometimes it was well over a hundred. Mum's House, we called them (enough cash to buy your mum a house, for some). It was ninety per cent pure, imported directly from crops between MongHong Son and Mae Sai along the Thai–Burma border.

The heroin explosion had just begun in Melbourne. After the white collars of the eighties had bled out the nose for cocaine, the seedy underbelly found something far beyond blow or anything before, and it was ten times as addictive. I was told by a junkie that the first hit of H is like an orgasm for the soul – the opiate satisfies every single orifice. A pleasure that reality cannot match. Once that orgasm comes, though, and the soul finds out what it feels like to be truly alive, life is nothing but a letdown.

Dealers pushed dope on street corners in Richmond and Footscray, every twenty-four-hour tattoo parlour and launderette a front for peddling, any train station in the greater city a hub for junkies. It was the oxygen of the streets.

Once I had earned a name, earned the cash and was entrenched in the crew – on the docks and in the nightclubs – the women fell into my lap, too easily for me to appreciate. Like every other man in this position of power I took advantage of it. If I had the balls to import kilos of heroin, risk decades behind bars, and pull the trigger when needed, talking to women and taking them to bed was a cakewalk.

Country towns aren't notorious for good-looking women, even if country music videos tell you otherwise, and growing up in the sticks meant there were just three girls that took my fancy. By fifteen two were pregnant and the other had moved north to Queensland, so when I came to the city at sixteen with hormones falling from my ears, the thing that took my eye was not the skyscrapers, smog or never-ending houses, it was the girls.

There was a little bakery in town, and although the sausage rolls were amazing, I went there for the waitress: small and olive skinned, with deep, dark-brown eyes. She was the only girl I wanted who I couldn't get. She was a peacock among pigeons. For months I asked her out, and for months she rejected me. But eventually, I got her.

Rochelle knew who I was and loved the thrill of dating someone like me, and she loved the money. Before I was legally an adult, the wage of a stock jockey was loose change to me. I could give Rochelle whatever she desired. I was young, loaded and moving up the ranks in Australia's most organised and well-disguised criminal entity.

The problem started as it always does with twins. Josh and I dressed, acted and wanted similar. We both chased Cindy Callahan around the playground in Grade Six, hoping to hit her with the stone that would get us our first kiss.

It was easy to tell when they first met that Josh loved every single thing about Rochelle. I knew because I fell for it too. The way she flicked her hair – so at ease – the way her eyebrows would raise just before she whispered something dirty, or the way she called me over with her index finger when she wanted something.

Over time Rochelle and I fell apart, and she and Josh grew closer. Sometimes it's only natural to chase what you long for, even if that is your brother's ex-girlfriend or your ex-boyfriend's twin. I didn't let it show, but I despised them being together. No more than a month after we broke it off, they started dating. It must have started long before then.

You never forget your first love, especially when they start the tear that rips you and your twin brother apart.

* * *

'Does she still work at the bakery?' I asked Simone, who was drying glasses.

'No idea.'

'What about the guys?'

'Well you spoke to Kerry. They still work down on the docks.'

'And Josh?'

Simone took some time to answer.

'He's doing fine. He stopped seeing Rochelle years ago if that's what you're wondering. I guess he's made something out of himself. Worked his way up. Lives in a big penthouse in Williamstown. Kerry's his right-hand man. Teddy lives over in America now. Got himself a job at a hospital.'

I smiled to think about Bear, and how he had got out.

'What about Gary?'

She shrugged. 'Probably best if you ask him yourself.'

From the corner of my eye I noticed a man in a balaclava stop at my side. 'Don't move.' The barrel of a gun pressed into my temple. The man stepped back and sprayed me with the black water pistol. Kerry took off the balaclava and broke into hysterics. 'Ah, Dane, you should've seen your face. Pants need changing?'

'They're fine, Dickhead.'

He kissed Simone incessantly. 'Stop it you big drunk!'

'Not drunk yet.' He let her go. 'But I'll be sorted soon, Honey.'

Simone took the hint and left us.

'Good to see you starting the day with a steady diet of hops and yeast.'

'Did you come in just to give me shit?'

'Well, partly, but that was just my lead-in.'

'To what?'

He offered me a smoke, but I waved it off. Kerry sparked a lighter and drew back a drag. 'I've got some news for you. Bad news or good news first?'

'What do you think?'

'All right. Bad news is that a bloke in our docking crew has broken his leg and will be off work for a few months. Bad break up in his femur from skydiving. Silly bastard. So that means we need someone to labour four to five shifts a week on rotation. Since your main vocation right now is to warm the barstools for Gary Whitman downstairs, which I have no doubt he is paying you handsomely for, I thought that you could do with the work.'

He was right. I had close to no money, and owed Gary for the room and my tab.

'But, what will Josh think?'

'Not his concern who I hire for day-to-day labour. Might be a chance to catch him for a conversation or two. I'm sure you gents have a few things to talk about.'

Again, he was right, though I doubted Josh would want to talk about anything.

'It's four hundred cash per week.'

'So a job that earns me peanuts is your good news?'

'Peanuts is more than you've got now, Mate, and those peanuts will help you eat, and no, that wasn't my good news. Good news is that if you start working you can start saving. Maybe get yourself a nice apartment somewhere, maybe get a car ...'

'No offence, Kerry, but settling back here is the last thing I want to do.'

'Before you interrupted, I was going to say that you can also save for something else.' He handed me a piece of torn paper with a telephone number on it. 'Guy's name is Marty Slick. Runs the pawn shop over on Acland. Industry is a little thin, but this guy will get you what you need.'

'What the hell are you talking about?'

'Don't get me wrong, Mate, I have enjoyed seeing your pretty face again, but I don't want you here – I know your heart's somewhere else. I know if I'd been ripped away from Simone I'd take the first chance to get back to her.

'Marty Slick will sort you out with a passport, Social Security card, and whatever else you need. Just remember to tell him you know me. Can be a bit funny and guarded.'

My heart went haywire. My head spun. This was my chance.

'Start work Monday, Mate, so rest up.'

CHAPTER 8

The instant Kerry left me I telephoned Marty Slick, and sank into the bed a little when the woman who answered informed me Marty was out of town on business.

'But I need to speak to him as soon as possible. Kerry McLaughlin gave me his details. Is there a number I can reach him on?'

'Sorry, Darlin'.' She paused and the click-clack of chewing gum sounded. 'You'll have to wait until he's back.'

'When will he be back?'

'Dunno. Next week, week after. Depends how much business he has to attend to.'

'Can you get him to call me as soon as he's back?'

'Marty doesn't do call-backs.'

In need of a drink, I trudged downstairs and perched in my usual seat at the bar. I waited for Gary to serve the war vet in his seat on the opposite side of the bar, his medals pinned to his jacket like a material scar.

When he served me, sleeves rolled up, I noticed for the first time his tattoo.

Gary slid a bowl of chips in front of me, along with a glass of Coca Cola. He leaned on the wood grain near me. 'I had a good talk to Simone.'

'Gather she filled in some blanks,' I said, to which he grinned and nodded. The words in ink on his forearm were visible. I read them out loud: 'From birth through life and back from the grave, we are forever.'

'That's the truth, isn't it, Chief?'

I scratched the spot on my ribs where the same words were tattooed.

* * *

Senior Detective Gary Whitman of the Drug Squad at St Kilda Police Station was a shadow that kept us out of jail, a shield from the shield itself.

Cops will never be paid enough. Gary knew the politics on both sides of the line. He had worked his way up from traffic control to beat cop to the top of his division. He knew, too, that the people he chased by day and night made his salary in a week. Most men become disgruntled crawling after their own tail for peanuts.

It took him time to crack – to walk the thin blue line straight enough and long enough that he made it all the way to the dark side. He chased the Union, understood how the docks worked, and in time realised he could never unravel the network. He crossed over and became part of the monster he had once wished to slay. A dirty detective part of our crew – it was perfect.

* * *

'I had a good chat to Simone, too,' I said.

Gary surveyed the bar, and when he noticed it was only the war vet who prevented us from privacy he replied. 'I gather she answered some questions for you as well.'

I shrugged.

'But there are probably still plenty to be answered.' He sniffed and pinched his nose. 'Like why I am hushed away in this stinking bar.'

'That'd be one.'

'Well, Chief, things changed a while back now. All fell down around the old school, Phillips and Williams. They let it slip and the operation turned to a shambles.

'It fell down for me, too. Got busted by Internal Affairs and did two years. When I came out, well, your brother had stepped up. Worked his way up fast and jumped ahead of everyone else. There wasn't much use for me around the docks. I was looked after ... owns this establishment, your brother. Made me a manager, and now I take care of things around here. It's easy, but they forgot about me a long time ago. I still get a sniff of what's going on at times, mainly from the young lads that come in at McLaughlin's hand, but really, I'm pretty much yesterday's news. Could be worse, though; least I ain't on the wrong side of the Union. You might want to think about that – I hear he hasn't forgotten, no less forgiven you. And you know what happens to people who leave …'

I knew Josh hated me. I had seen it at the cemetery, but I ignored the implication that I would soon be shot.

'Never thought I'd see Josh in charge,' said Gary. 'Don't know how he did it. But I do know that things are ten times what they were. That's why they call him King.'

I brought forth the image of Josh as I'd left him and then the one I'd returned to. 'Was shorter by two inches, younger by four minutes, dumber by a decade,' I said. 'And now he's king, huh.'

'Answers only to McCulloch.'

I thought of my twin brother's ascent to the top and smiled. I knew exactly how he'd done it. He'd used the plan we'd made while we cleaned Keith Phillips's car all those years before. It was genius, and would take things to another level. Never did I think, though, that Josh would make it a reality – the Costello name on top.

'Without you here someone had to step in. Kerry never wanted it, and well, Stevie.' He paused, and we both fell silent. The only sound I heard was the drop of beer from the tap landing with a plop in the spill tray.

∗ ∗ ∗

The living room was fogged with cigarette smoke. Pale afternoon light broke through the gap in the curtains. The lights were never on in our house. Stevie didn't like them on unless absolutely necessary. Once daytime had disappeared, the television was our only source of light.

Josh was out with Rochelle. On the sofa was a silhouetted mound.

'Dane, come sit.'

Stevie leaned forward into the beam of light, his face limp, minute rivers of red flowed through much of his half-dead eyes. He took his arm, wrapped it with a rubber hose and then patted the table searchingly. He picked up a spoon and filled it with junk. From his pocket he withdrew a lighter and heated the bottom of the spoon. The powder liquidised and bubbled. With a trembling hand Stevie took a syringe from the ashtray and filled it.

'It's like an orgasm for the soul,' he said. 'Satisfies every orifice of your being …' He drifted off as he bit down on the end of the hose, tightened it around his bicep, and then brought the needle to his skin.

My stomach rolled the way clothes co in a tumble dryer as the needle's tip punctured a protruding vein on Stevie's arm. A drop of blood rose from the wound. He pressed the syringe, his eyes rolled back into his skull and he slumped like a rag doll against the couch. The needle fell from his hand, the house so quiet that the clap seemed to echo when it hit the wooden floor. His perforated forearm hung over the chair, the fresh hole surrounded by train tracks and a minefield of red dots from old entry points. A line of blood seeped along his skin.

LETTER 5

December 1 1993

Dane,

I missed Halloween but saw plenty of ghouls: a burnt man, a bald scarecrow woman and one with a mask. This nut house deceives.

Maybe it's tricked me into missing you, or to still holding onto hope that you'll show up with some milk and a wry smile, or made me believe I'm moving on from you. I don't think you've seen my note or, if you have, it's even worse.

Perhaps I've just been judgmental.

It's hard not to. People see a tanned blonde with big boobs — she's a bimbo slut. A homeless man with a shopping cart is a deranged loser licking Hershey's wrappers. You see the blood on someone's hands and think murderer. We don't consider kindness, turns of extreme misfortune or a poorly cleaned butcher. Too often we rely on our eyes to see.

So maybe I've been too hasty to judge Nurse Cameron. Slithery as he may seem, and as charred as his voice croaks, he is here, and he is trying, that is at least something, Dane.

I laughed in between purging last week. Head on the edge of the rim, my arms hugged the big white porcelain teddy bear, and my stomach evacuated every bit of stale hospital food.

While I chuckled with vomit and saliva seeping from my mouth, a knock came at the door of the disabled bathroom.

'Are, are you okay in there, Kayla?' Nurse Cameron asked.

'Can't you hear me laughing? Physically, I'm screwed, but mentally I guess I'm doing okay – it's hilarious.' My stomach bent me in half and I expelled more. 'On second thoughts, I don't know if laughing in such a state is mentally healthy. On third thoughts I don't really care. I'm having a ball.'

'Would you like anything; is there anything I can do?'

I washed off splats of spew. 'No thank you.'

I dried, and arranged the black wig back onto my scalp. Funnily enough, it is much better being bald when you throw up. And to think I dreaded it.

Nurse Cameron was waiting at the hallway entrance. In a way it reminded me of how a monster stands in the doorway in a scary movie, and I wondered whether he'd be the type to hover above my bed or show up in the mirror.

We strolled back toward my room. 'I haven't had a chance to thank you for the wigs,' I said. 'So, thank you.'

'It's my, my pleasure. If there's anything else, just, just say.'

We turned into the hallway and at my room door as I caught sight of Burty seated in his bed, a fresh tomato from radiation, reading his copy of *The White Whale*, pages missing, for what must have been the hundredth time, something occurred to me. A crooked old back and a crooked old past.

'Actually,' I said. 'There is something.'

My request was well outside the boundaries, but I asked all the same, and he obliged.

He came back in only a few days with what I'd asked for, and then I asked him for something else. I'm a greedy bitch, I know, but screw yourself Dane: you leave chocolate-chip cookies lying around, they will get eaten. That's pure frigging logic.

He obliged to the second request as eagerly as the first, a bat of the eyelids not required. I'd like to think he helps me because he sees something good in me, but I know it comes down to the same thing. He thinks I'm pretty. Men bend over backward if they think a woman is pretty. And so what if we let them? Men have directed our lives according to their dicks since day dot, so what if we women have finally figured out how to direct those dicks, Dane?

Hospital isn't a prison, but it has it owns shackles.

Walking out of the hospital doors on that glistening white Friday morning, I felt the rush that a convict must feel when they make parole, and trade their county oranges for whatever out-of-date street clothes they entered in.

I was dressed in ripped jeans, the dirty old Nirvana tank top you bought me from Venice, and flip flops, and I had my black Cher wig on. For the time I was no longer a cancer patient, just a girl on the street.

Nurse Cameron's car was a beat-up brown Ford. The seals peeled off the door, and the ashtray overflowed with crumpled cigarette butts.

The soundtrack to the journey north to Reseda was a mix between the whir of the tires, the hum of the engine and a *swoosh swish* as we passed street poles and trees.

'Do you, do you want me, me to come in?' Nurse Cameron pulled back the handbrake, looking across at me with his blank gray eyes.

'It's okay. I'll just get in and get out. I don't know how these people will be. Could be best if you're ready at the wheel for a quick getaway – if you've got a balaclava maybe put it on now.'

The front garden was astonishing: orchids, azaleas, poppies of blue, white, red and yellow clinging to their petals in the late weeks of spring. The brickwork of the winding path was seared with cracks and tiny green weeds sprouting through.

A home. This was no house. Geoff and Margaret's was a home, lived in for years, many experiences had and memories created. This I could tell as I stood on the front doorstep, admiring the wooden sign over the knocker: **Welcome to Our Happy Home.** It filled me with optimism. I had not yet laid sight on these two old people but I was hopeful.

Moments after I'd knocked, the door opened, and a short, slender man with glasses bigger than his head, tanned skin and cloud-white hair stood there, draped in a woolen cardigan far too big for his body.

'Hello, Dear,' he said.

'Geoff, my name is Kayla, we spoke on the telephone.'

'Yes, come in, come in.'

He ushered me into a living room made cozy by the plethora of knitted blankets, rugs and adornments spread throughout. I sat and Geoff brought in a pot of hot tea. He poured me a cup and placed it down in front of me on a knitted coaster.

I was there to get in and get out, and it seemed as if I would. 'You know why I'm here, and I hope you have what I'd like. I appreciate it.'

He nodded, sipped his tea and then placed down the cup, before he stood and shuffled off to the kitchen, returning a moment later with an address book, pen and blank paper. He flicked through the book for Lily's phone number and address as I waited in anticipation. Soon, I thought, that old bum will be forced out of his slump, to the telephone and to his daughter. Soon he'll get back to being the father he once tried to be.

At almost the exact second Geoff exclaimed with relief he'd found the details, the door opened, feet wiped on the mat and an elderly but very mobile woman bustled into the living room, already huffing flustered commentary of the day to her husband. 'The grocery store clerks are terrible these days – pimple-faced teens with no concentration. I don't have a lifetime to waste, perhaps they'd like to move faster than a snail in bagging bread?'

Her rant ceased when she noticed me on the sofa, sipping from her rose-embroidered china. 'Hello, who are you?'

I stood and offered my hand to the shocked Margaret. She took it with apprehension. It was like shaking hands with the skeleton that used to stand at the back of the science classroom. Harry I think his name was.

'What are you two doing?' she asked. 'Why have you got the address book?'

Geoff was a rosy-cheeked schoolboy caught with his hand in his mother's purse. He stumbled to form an answer and so I saved him further emasculation. 'I've just come to get Lily's contact details for Bill. He's a friend of mine in hospital and he'd like to see his daughter.'

Margaret snatched the address book from Geoff. 'Please leave.' She glared. 'And do not ever come back here.'

I opened my mouth to speak but her voice grew louder with every word.

'Bill Burton or any of his friends have no business with our family. Now leave!'

If not for the fatigue, I would have stayed and fought the dragon lady. Geoff walked me to the door. Their home was a poorly cooked TV dinner: warm on the outside but frozen on the inside.

'You just let her kick you around like that?' I said to Geoff on the doorstep. 'I would've thought you'd have learned to be a man, but I guess that's why you're not allowing Burty the chance to fix his mistakes and be the man *he* can. Try to put yourself in his shoes, Geoff: he might die tomorrow, and all he wants to do is try to make up with his only living family. Just remember that, okay. For Lily, too.'

I slurred much of it, and doubt whether it had any effect. But at least I put in effort for someone, even when I was tired. At least I was there.

Kayla

DIARY 10

October 3 1980

Some hunters shot a deer in the woods. We stole it before they could reach it. We sneaked away and took it to the shed near the cabin where Mr Ignatius took me once for a weekend.

I'd never seen anything dead before. Oscar said he has seen lots of dead things.

Oscar said we didn't need the whole deer, and it would go off, so he decided to separate it. He found a long knife on the tool shelf then put his knees on either side of the deer's body and hacked into it. When the first splash of blood flew into the air I closed my eyes.

When I opened them, the shed looked the same as my Grade One art class when I spilled red paint everywhere. The deer was in pieces. It felt funny to see something that was alive like that. We found some garbage bags on a shelf and packed the meatiest parts, and then followed our secret tracks back to the warehouse.

The fire sizzled while Oscar cooked the deer. We sat and ate in warmth, safe from the rain and things outside. The meat was tender and juicy. We washed down our meal of deer and tomatoes with a drink of ginger beer. It was the best dinner I've ever had.

When the fire was embers we left the warehouse to get some fresh air. Outside, the rain had stopped. The sky was free of clouds and all the stars were out. I spotted Jupiter, and Oscar said he saw Mars, but I'm pretty sure that's not possible. I didn't tell him, though. If he wants to see Mars I'm not going to stop him. He's my best friend.

We went onto the road that connects the industrial estate with the town center. To the line of trees at the entrance to the estate and back we'd decided would be enough time for the smoke to be clear and for us to feel better in the tummy. As the trees came into sight I started to run. Oscar gave me a few seconds and then followed. He always gives me a head start to get there and slows to let me win.

Puffing, I touched the tree trunk as Oscar jogged slowly by my side. 'You'll win one day, Ozzy,' I said in between breaths.

He smiled and pinkie-clapped. 'One day Kay-Kay.' He hadn't even broken a sweat. With the help of my other hand, I pinkie-clapped in return.

'And maybe one day you'll be able to pinkie-clap without your other hand.'

A car drove by. The second it passed us its brakes screeched and it pulled to a stop. The doors opened. I held onto Oscar as tight as I could. Four men stepped out of the car. The suit men.

'Kay-Kay, run. Get out of here; go straight to the warehouse.' Oscar talked so fast it was difficult to hear.

'But –'

'*Go!*'

I ran.

I turned to see Mr Policeman chasing me. As he passed Oscar, Oscar leaped at him and punched him in the head. I disappeared around a corner, but instead of going home I climbed a tree.

They surrounded Oscar. Mr Policeman took out his baton and two of the other men held Oscar's arms. Mr Gray Suit stood in front of Oscar and pointed his finger while he growled. Oscar listened for only a second before he spat in Mr Gray Suit's face. Mr Policeman tapped his baton on his hand, *tut, tut, tut.*

I felt sick.

Snippets of words came to me in the tree. Mr Black Suit yelled. 'Where is she, you little nigger fuck!'

'I ain't never telling you where she is. You never getting to her.'

Mr Policeman stuck his baton into Oscar's stomach. Oscar hunched over, but was pulled up by the men who held his arms. Mr Checker Suit backhand-slapped Oscar across the face.

I didn't know how, but I had to help him. Another car pulled up to the curb. It was a black car.

My stomach tried to vomit, but with all my might I kept it down. I couldn't let them hear me. I couldn't let him hear me.

Mr Ignatius got out of the driver's seat and walked to the men. He signaled for them to let Oscar go. He talked to Oscar, but I was too far away to hear. It didn't matter; I knew exactly what he was asking for, and I knew Oscar wouldn't tell him.

What happened next forced the vomit into my mouth. I swallowed.

Mr Ignatius turned to Mr Policeman, who took his gun from its holster and stepped toward Oscar. He held it to Oscar's head. His lips moved, counting down from ten.

The hammer clicked on the gun. 'Let him go,' I said, standing on the road behind them.

Mr Ignatius smiled, relieved, and walked toward me. I backed up and he stopped.

'Puppet, it's time to go home. Your mom is waiting. I've missed you.'

'I'll come.' The madness rose from my feet to my stomach to my throat and my eyes. 'But you have to let him go first.'

I looked at Oscar, who stared at me with tears seeping from his puffed and blackened eyes. 'Let him go.'

The men let go of Oscar. 'Ozzy, run.'

He didn't move.

'Run, Ozzy. Go home, it's going to be okay.'

'I ain't leaving you with them.'

'You have to.'

The men walked to their car. 'Come on, grab the girl and let's go. We'll meet you back at the house. Carol is home, right? Not out working?'

'She's home,' said Mr Ignatius. 'Doesn't work these days. I'm looking after her completely. Needs it.'

Oscar stayed. The men stood at the car as Mr Ignatius walked up to me. He held out his hand. The vomit shot up my throat again. I gulped and put my hand in his and felt dirt crawl down the back of my spine. He led me to the black car. Oscar started to run toward me, but Mr Policeman stepped in front of him and held the gun up.

'You gonna pay for this!' Oscar scowled. 'I ain't letting her stay with him, or any of you. You sick fucks!'

Mr Policeman hit Oscar with the handle of the gun and he dropped to the ground. 'You're going to play ball you colored piece of shit, or little miss will find herself in the middle a five-man train.'

Mr Ignatius raised his hand. 'That's enough.'

He opened the door for me. I sat in the front passenger seat. It locked as soon it closed. The other men got into their car. Oscar lay on the ground with blood coming from his head. Mr Ignatius started the car.

As we drove off I gazed back. Oscar was still on the ground when the car turned the corner, his eyes still closed.

All of the suit men were in Mom's living room when Mr Ignatius brought me through the front door. Mom was in the kitchen. She looked at me blankly as Mr Ignatius led me past the men and up the stairs, but she didn't move from her bottle or say anything.

All the noises from below disappeared as the door to my room closed. I disappeared too.

By sunrise I hadn't slept at all. I think the men were still in the house. Mr Ignatius was snoring, fast asleep in my bed. The door was locked and so was the window. My room had no secret tracks to escape from hunters. I may never get out of here.

In the woods. On the concrete. On my bed. I saw a lot of blood today.

DIARY 11

January 12 1981

I've been locked in my room since Mr Ignatius found me. The window has been nailed shut and there is a bolt on the outside of the door.

It's been snowing for a long time and it doesn't matter how many pairs of mittens and socks I put on my fingers feel like they are going to fall off.

Mr Ignatius brings me food and water, and sometimes lets me downstairs. I've tried to run, so now he ties my wrists and ankles in rope when I leave the room.

Mom doesn't talk anymore. She just sits and stares, sometimes drinks and then goes to bed with the help of Mr Ignatius. She goes to the toilet with his help, too. The only thing she does on her own now is breathe, and drink.

She doesn't even blink.

She looks more like a grandmother.

I don't think I believe in good superpowers anymore. I'm not Golden Girl, and I'm only invisible to people who don't want to see me. Mr Ignatius and the suit men are demons and have the power to steal people while leaving their body. That's what they've done to Mom. I'm scared they are doing it to me.

It was Mr Ignatius's birthday today. The cake said he was forty-four years old. To me he's just old, scary and a monster without an age, real name or spirit. I read about demons in a book one time at school. I think one of the chapters was about Mr Ignatius.

We sat around the table, Mom in her seat, me on the side and Mr Ignatius at the other end. Mom looked asleep with her eyes open.

The whole house was quiet as Mr Ignatius pressed the knife through the cake – disgusting carrot cake – and onto the plate beneath it. I hate that sound.

I noticed drool on Mom's lip as I passed her a plate.

Mr Ignatius asked me questions from time to time as we ate the cake, but mostly the chink of cutlery was the only sound. I didn't want to eat. I hate carrot cake. But I had to. I knew what would happen if I didn't eat it and pretend to enjoy it.

'Wash up now, Puppet,' said Mr Ignatius. 'I'm putting your mother to bed.'

I cleared the dishes from the table and ran the tap with hot water, mixing it with detergent until it bubbled. Mr Ignatius took Mom by the hand and helped her from the seat at the table. In his free hand he picked up her bottle and walked her upstairs to her bedroom. The second, fourth and ninth stairs creaked.

I finished washing up and cleaned the rest of the kitchen, wiping every bench, the table and mopping the floor. Mr Ignatius is very strict on cleanliness: he needs everything spotless otherwise he gets flustered.

The stairs creaked three times again. 'Puppet, you can finish cleaning now. I want my birthday present.'

He had playtime with me.

My body hurts more each time, but inside I feel number.

Then he left to sleep in Mom's room. I wonder if Mom can feel the same thing as me in her playtime. I hope she does, but I don't think that is true.

It's going to be a long winter and I don't know how I'll get to my thirteenth birthday. If I do, I don't want shitty carrot cake.

DIARY 12

March 19 1981

Some days I wake and think there is a god and some days I wake and think there can't be.

Yesterday, the house had been silent for some hours when a car arrived. The front door opened and the stairs creaked. As usual I looked for a way to escape.

I heard the bolt being drawn back and the door opened. It wasn't Mr Ignatius.

'Shorty, I'm so sorry.' Oscar was taller than before, his afro shaved down to a thin mat. 'I'll explain when we get out of here, but we gotta move quick. They gonna be here any second. Come on.'

He took my hand. We ran down the stairs. I gazed around, and with every part of me hoped to never see the house and every horrible thing in it again. Mom was at the kitchen table. She turned and looked. I don't care if she saw me.

Outside, I gasped. The black car was in the driveway. Mr Ignatius was unconscious on the ground with blood seeping from the back of his head.

We ran from the yard. 'You did that?'

'Yeah, but he ain't dead yet.'

I hugged Oscar so tight I don't think he could breathe. 'I love you, Ozzy.' I started to cry. 'I thought you were dead ...'

'I ain't done, Shorty.'

We sprinted down the road and into the park, through the fence, up into the woods and along the secret trails. The warehouse appeared. Never had I felt more eager to enter a building full of dust, rats and rotten wood. With Oscar's hand in mine, never had I felt more at home.

A crack of thunder came from far beyond the woodlands. Oscar held the tin and I crawled through the secret hole on the back wall. Inside, we clung to each other.

'I thought you were dead, Ozzy. I'm sorry, I'm so sorry I didn't find you.'

Oscar put his finger to my lips. 'Kay-Kay, you couldn't have found me. I was locked away. Never say sorry to me. I'm sorry this happened. I should've protected you.'

'Locked away?'

'The suit men locked me in the basement of the cabin. They is evil and I mean real evil. They sell children to men who... They get them in different ways. Sometimes lure them away from their families at parks, sometimes they pick them up after school in a van. Sometimes they get other kids to help them.' Oscar paused and looked down. 'That's what they been trying to get me to do, because ...' He stopped again. Tears welled up in his eyes.

'They got my family. Years ago. That's why I ain't had no home. My momma used to sell herself and one day they came. Did bad things to me for years until I got too big. They made my momma brain dead. And they killed my half-brother. By accident, they say, but they ain't no accidents when you evil. They tried to make me get them kids. When I didn't, they started beating me and making me hurt bad. Kept trying to use me. Said they'd make me wanna die.

'And what's worse is that this whole town is evil. They got the sheriff. Who they gonna believe if we was to go to them police? I was meant to take them to you, but ...'

'They had already got to me.'

I didn't know what to feel for Mom. Was she a victim of those evil men? But she let him in the house. I didn't know if she was a prisoner to them or if she was the one who built the prison. I became confused.

Oscar kept talking. His voice drifted away and memories of the suit men came back. They came to my house from as early as I can remember, but they weren't Mom's friends.

They found her and me, for him. He'd paid them and Mom to have me.

'They do it all over the country. There's a whole goddamn network of sick people just like them ... Shorty, I'm so sorry I didn't get us out of here earlier.'

He sat and buried his head into me. I felt my sweater become wet and warm. Oscar's fifteen and six-foot-five. It was strange to see someone so big cry. After a while he sighed and wiped his eyes.

'What do we do now?' I asked. 'We can't stay here, not in this warehouse, and not in this town. They will find me again and if they find you again they will kill you, not just lock you away.'

'It don't matter where we go, they will find us anywhere eventually and yeah, they will kill me and you'll go straight back to that fucking house with that disgusting son-of-a-bitch. Nah, we ain't staying here, but first we gotta make sure they'll never find us again.'

His eyes flared and went crazy. 'We gotta make sure they can't ever do what they do again.' Oscar clenched his jaw and nodded. 'First we go away for a while and hide out, figure out how ...'

'Figure out what?'

'There is only one way we getting out of this mess alive, and that's if they don't ... they don't find us - we find them.'

My heart thudded. Oscar stared at me. 'We kill them.'

CHAPTER 9

The society of the docks had become no less surreptitious. Kerry oversaw much of the day-to-day operations and was boss to the unknowing, with Josh parked inside the site office. My days were absorbed by loading, unloading and carting containers across the waterfront. Soon November had disappeared.

There were dozens of men in our work crew, but I determined quickly who constituted the inner circle. It was an eclectic trio. Salem was a Persian migrant, his head flowing with hair as black as night, his moustache a curl of the same black, and his eyes like those of a cat. Trent was the quintessential Aussie bloke: tanned, muscles built by hard work, grit beneath his fingernails, skin wizened by the elements. Ollie was half Caucasian, half Aboriginal: brown skin with a white man's features. He was removed by child services from his family when he was young and raised in foster homes until he found a means of escaping Social Services – the docks.

During the days the conversation extended only to footy and which girl they'd like to lay. Although the workers knew who held the power, the Union blended in as it always had. If the sordid underbelly of Melbourne's dock life still gurgled with millions of dollars and a stream of kilos, it was not in the slightest detectable in this run-of-the-mill city wharf.

Days passed before I'd even come within a shout of my twin brother. He would leave the men's room and cafeteria when I was there and otherwise brood alone in his office unless absolutely necessary.

For a man as proud and pugnacious as Josh, this must have been difficult.

On my second Monday morning back at work he emerged from his office to mingle with the crew. I sat on a pallet near Kerry, who talked to the guys about something on television the night before. Every now and again Salem broke into fits at Kerry's comical imitations.

Josh sauntered toward the group inconspicuously and raised his head to Kerry, who left the crew to meet him. He was explaining something to Kerry, removing his hands from his coat pockets to speak with them and slice, chop and lift the air.

I slid off the pallets and approached.

'Come and speak to me about it later.' He started toward his office.

'Oi, hold up a second,' I said as I caught up. 'You got a second to talk.'

Josh stopped, stubbed his half-smoked cigarette onto the concrete, and then turned to face me. 'No I don't.'

This point in time I felt guilty when I looked into the pale blue eyes of my brother, and angry: at myself, at him, at everything, and longed for his forgiveness. 'Then listen.'

Josh raised an eyebrow. It would have been some time since he'd been told to do anything in his hegemonic life.

'Are you going to keep this up? I'm back. Whether or not that pleases you I don't particularly care. I've got bigger things to think about than a past that's dragging you down. So you can keep turning your back and running ...'

At this point his chortle cut me short. 'Me running? Me turning my back? You can't be serious.' He shook his head and opened the door to his office.

'You're my brother, Josh, my goddamn twin; are you going to hang onto this grudge forever, or build a bridge and get over it?'

One last time he turned. 'The only brother I had I lost a long time ago.' He stepped inside and slammed the door.

∗ ∗ ∗

Initially I swallowed much of my pride and pushed the indignation deep down inside, so that all it manifested as was a twitching eye when I saw their hands entwined.

They were better together, Josh and Rochelle, than she and I were.

By Rochelle's birthday in November '86 my inner turmoil had shifted from bitterness to a swirl of emotion. It was difficult to pinpoint what still bothered me. I had accepted what had happened, and in truth I had no deep feelings for Rochelle or hard feelings for Josh. This wasn't just the sour taste from losing. No, it was effectively my indifference that forced me to act. The fact that I didn't care scared me and I yearned to feel genuine angst, or passion, not just for a girl but for anything.

I'd stopped caring about the H trade. The money was now frivolous and the events that once aroused excitement caused further apathy. A potential life sentence at the end of each run, a loaded gun to another man's head, to my head ... Whatever.

Our still-humble abode at 17 Neptune Street, St Kilda, was decorated wall to wall with streamers, balloons and any variety of tinsel and sparkly thing. Every room was packed with friends, acquaintances, and the usual mob of nobodies that filled out house parties in those days – a friend of Jim's, a cousin of Ron's.

A girl named Sandra Ducksworth hung from my arm this night; some die-by-the-day romance that served as nothing more than fifteen to thirty minutes respite, depending on the potency of my libido.

'Suppose you could spend one day in the body of someone else,' said Kerry, who sat on an armchair, swaying his beer back and forth as he spoke. 'Who would it be?'

Josh was on the sofa with Rochelle nestled into him. 'I'd drop into Rochelle, just to see how good I actually am.'

She raised an eyebrow, slender, curvaceous.

I gulped down the suds from the bottom of my stubby. 'You spend at least two minutes in her body at least twice a day already, you need more?'

Kerry broke into raucous laughter, Josh smirked and Rochelle ignored.

'Come on, Joshy, be more imaginative than that,' Kerry goaded.

'All right, I'd enter into you just to see what it's like to feel inferior to everyone else around me.'

This time I laughed along. 'You'd have to enter that sadistic, sad little mind as well, Brother. I don't know if you'd want that.'

'Way too much man entering man for me,' Teddy said, as he rose from the sofa. 'Top-ups anyone?' A collective yes came and Teddy disappeared to the kitchen.

Kerry pointed at Josh and then me. 'I'll be seeing to it that the two of you don't wake up tomorrow morning.'

At this moment Stevie jostled through the archway into the living room, a pink streamer catching on his ear as he entered. 'Who's not waking up tomorrow and for what reason are they getting whacked?'

'The two galahs – your brothers – for talking down to their elder, and need I say superior.'

'Easy Kerry, nobody likes a bluey with little man syndrome.' If we could dish it up, Stevie could wreck us all. His wit was automatic.

'All right, Smart-arse, you answer – if you could be in the body of anyone for a day, who would it be? And give me something more than this dipshit.' He nudged Josh with his elbow.

Stevie thought. 'I'd be Gandhi.'

'Hate to break it to you, Brother,' I said, 'but the fella's been dead for a while now.'

'No one specified a time period and whether or not my day inside another would be now, future or past, so I take Gandhi's.'

To which Josh quipped, 'Coz you'd like to know what it's like to be able to grow a moustache, right?'

Stevie always struggled to break past the growth of a thirteen-year-old, while Josh and I were trimming back our three o'clock shadows from the age of sixteen.

'I'd have chosen Lincoln if that was the case. Nah,' he closed his eyes and inhaled a deep breath. The red rings under his eyes caught the light, the gauntness in his cheeks shadowed against forty watts. 'Gandhi, hell even Lincoln, because knowing what I do now, what he did, what he changed, I'd be content in knowing that I will die with purpose, that my moments here were something more than the passing of time between waking and falling asleep.'

The group fell silent. Simone entered from the kitchen, parting the crowd with a hot plate of sausage rolls.

'Geez, Stevie Boy, you'd think you've never known what it is to feel the bristles of manliness on your chin come Sunday morning ...' Kerry said before he swallowed a whole sausage roll coated in tomato sauce.

This removed the sombre air from the room. Stevie only flashed a grin, waved off a sausage roll and tousled my hair before he floated down the hallway to his bedroom, the quiet click of the door a faraway noise in the roister of the party.

Rochelle blew out the candles on her cake around ten, while Josh held her waist from behind – that sexy position women love, the one that makes them safe and wanted.

The sponge was sweet, our bellies were filled with the party mix – savouries, liquor and cake.

When the necking had taken full swing, couples retired to whatever corner of the house or yard they could find. With Sandra Ducksworth attached, I called goodnight and made haste for my bedroom. Sandra and I engrossed each other in that sweaty hard sex only inebriation and a passionate fight can bring about, all the while the same bed crashing, moans and growls from Josh and Rochelle sounded in the next room. Stevie's room across the hallway lay dead silent.

In the morning, I rolled Sandra D's naked body off my now-numb arm and trudged into the kitchen, clad only in tracksuit pants, navigating befallen beer bottles and plates and deflated party decorations. Josh sat at the kitchen table munching into jam on toast.

He tossed me a slice as I sat. 'Helluva night, ay Mate.'

'Yeah, quite the party. Rochelle enjoy herself?'

'Yeah, as she does, you know what she's like. Won't say a word then all of sudden won't shut up, and energy spurts from every olive pore on her body.'

'Yeah, sounds like her.' I bit into the toast and washed it down with a gulp of Josh's coffee. 'Bloody hell, you want some coffee with your sugar?'

'If you don't like it make your own you wanker.'

I finished the coffee and flicked the drips at him from the cup.

'Like I said – wanker.'

'We on for tonight?'

'Yeah, all's set according to Kerry.' Josh sipped his coffee and then added more sugar. 'Keith is playing absent father to the operation – haven't heard diddly squat from the old prick for nearly a week. Cage, too; he seems more concerned about romping across town, sliding around Lygon Street and King Street like a fucking celebrity.'

'You sound concerned, Little Brother. I'd be inclined to think this is a good thing, for us anyway. Figure if McCulloch gets wind of their peacocking, he'll cut them down to size. Who's next in line when they collapse on themselves?'

Josh slid the toaster over and inserted another two slices of bread. 'Logically it goes from Keith to Cage, but if Cage is indisposed, so to speak, Teddy's next in line and he can go forth and assemble the crew how he wants.'

'Yeah, exactly. Only thing being that Teddy doesn't want charge; he's in for cash, but cash for a purpose – med school, not cheap from what I hear, and he's got a lot to pay off. You know him, not a power monger, and you know that he'll bail out for the States at some point.'

'He will?' Josh was surprised. 'Thought he had inroads for a gig at Monash.'

The toast popped and I snatched a slice, oozing it with butter and Vegemite before Josh could smother both with jam. 'Does. But he knows if he stays here he doesn't escape the Union. If McCulloch's got him pegged for a captain he can't walk away; he needs a new life.'

'Shit. You're telling me Teddy's going to jump ship ...'

'Not jump ship, Man. He's throwing the anchor and running on dry land. The guy's going to be a doctor, not a bloody drug lord. The drugs he wants to work with are meant to cure people ...'

Josh stood, slinked around the bench and turned on the coffee pot. 'So what you're saying is we let him go – don't tell anyone – for our own benefit.'

'That's precisely what I'm suggesting.'

'That's a prickly little situation there.' He refilled his cup, poured mine and emptied spoon after spoon of sugar into his. 'Just one sugar, right?'

'I can't believe you still need to ask that. It's a wonder you don't forget your anniversary to Little Miss Italia.'

'Right,' he said. 'Sounds like the words of a jealous man.'

From the bathroom the violent sounds of hung-over purging echoed. Josh and I sniggered as he placed the coffees on the table and sat. The house was library-quiet. Up until the vomiting began I could have believed we were alone.

'Jealous of something I've already had, nah Mate; been there done that.'

Josh grinned. 'Whatever you need to tell yourself, and,' he pointed his head toward the hallway, 'whatever you need to screw Little Miss Chuck-Her-Guts-Up.'

'Cheers.' I raised my cup, to which Josh obliged and we clinked mugs. 'To women, love em, hate em, sometimes we even rate em.'

'Anyway,' I continued, 'what I was saying before your fine queen coated our bathroom in spew was: we let Teddy float off Stateside, become the benevolent Dr Bear: he doesn't get clipped, and we move our family stocks up toward running this façade once that saggy pile of skin loses his last tooth and pisses McCulloch off enough.'

'Keith goes, Cage goes, Teddy sets sail and then Stevie takes charge, with Bozo,' he threw his crust at me, 'and Pogo right beside him.'

'You know what they say about great minds.'

The retching grew louder from the bathroom. 'Nah, but I know what they say about heaving girls.'

We both stood. 'I've got ten that it's Rochelle,' I said as I entered the hallway, Josh behind me.

'Double says that it's your lovely lady.'

We stopped at the bathroom door and sniggered, listening to the retching. I knocked, 'You okay in there?'

'Yeah ...' Rochelle's voice droned.

I clenched a victorious fist and opened my palm. Josh slapped it four times to signal the twenty he owed me. 'Happy birthday, Rochelle,' I called, stuffing the invisible note into my pocket, patting Josh's shoulder. 'I'm going to wake the soon-to-be Pharaoh from his slumber and leave you to look after your princess.'

I peeked into my room to see Sandra still sprawled out on the bed naked, her butt poking into the air. Leaving her to rest and air out, I turned across the hall and pounded on Stevie's door. 'Wake up, Governor,' I squawked in a shrill English falsetto. 'The chillen down the abbey want to know if you got a schilling for their lollies.'

Again, I pounded. 'Hey Stevie, you dipshit, wake up. We gotta go soon.'

Still no answer. The door handle turned but the door was jammed – I thought – before I realised it was locked with that shitty hardware-store bolt he'd bought some weeks before.

'Stevie!' My hand hurt this time.

Josh poked his head out the bathroom. 'What's up?'

'Idiot's not answering,' I grumbled. 'He knows we've got stuff to do today.' I turned back to the door and shouted. 'We're part of an empire, Big Bro, not a church. We don't rest on the fucking Sabbath – we make money!'

Nothing.

I stepped back, cocked my leg and stamped open the door in one almighty kick.

The room was like night, only wire-thin slithers of daylight pierced the gaps between Venetian slats. It was a mess. Mounds of crumpled shapes, clothes thrown everywhere. From the side of the bed a foot hung, toes to the ceiling.

I flicked the light. On Stevie's bedside drawer was a mirror, a clump of H and several syringes: some discarded, caked and bloodied; some still packaged. His jumper sleeve was rolled up, a rubber hose wrapped loosely around his arm, a needle buried into his skin. His eyes were encircled with dark rings, his mouth encrusted with dried vomit.

I collapsed at him and grappled for a pulse, my elbows plunging into a pile of vomit on the mattress. I must have screamed, because all of a sudden everyone was in the room. Josh helped me roll Stevie onto his side. Blue veins were visible beneath his stony skin.

There was no pulse.

After that, I don't think I yelled. Not like when I had held Mum. I simply leaned over him and cradled his head to my shoulder. My tears soaked his forehead while Josh sandwiched a single limp hand in his.

I don't know what exactly drew Stevie to the needle – perhaps the same thing that drew me to run – but H was a monster so powerful that once entrapped there was little chance to escape its claws.

The product that freed us, also killed Stevie.

CHAPTER 10

Christmas decorations adorned every light pole on Acland Street. It had rained all morning, but stopped as I was walking along, and steam rose from the concrete with the drying heat of the sun.

Tacky red and green lights were wrapped around the front security bars of Marty Slick's Pawn Shop, like a vine. A buzzer sounded when I pushed open the door.

The shop was a jumble of second-hand goods. Musical instruments on one wall; televisions, radios and cassette players stacked on another. I stood at the glass counter under which an array of broken promises and gambling dowries lay in the form of silver and gold. I cleared my throat but the large, pink-haired lady did not look up from filing her nails.

'Where the fuck is Marty Slick?' I'd grown impatient. Every day since Kerry had given me Marty Slick's details I had called, and I'd been down on three separate occasions. And every time I tried, I received the same answer: 'He's out on business.' I'd believed it, too, until I told Kerry and he shook his head, further explaining the temperament and eccentricity of Marty Slick.

The pink-haired lady glanced. 'He's out of town on ...'

'Save it.' I slapped my palms on the counter and the glass shook.

She gasped and the click-clack of her chewing gum ceased. She leaned over and picked up her nail file from the ground.

'I spoke to Kerry. I know Marty isn't out of town. If he's here right now, bring him out. If he's not, call him and tell him he's got two minutes to get his worthless arse here before I turn this place from a garbage tip to a bombsite.'

At that moment a nasally giggle came from the back of the shop. A chunky man with straggly dyed red hair and glasses shuffled through the doorway and stood behind the counter. 'This is the finest garbage tip in all Melbourne.' He was beaming. 'Why'd you want to throw it round, ay? And I'm worth at least thirty-four dollars, not quite worthless, Partner.'

The pink-haired lady smirked. 'This is the guy.'

'Oh. So you're the guy who's been wanting to see me,' said Marty Slick, who was not at all slick. 'Couldn't find what you were looking for on the showroom floor, ay?'

'You make a habit out of being an arsehole and wasting people's time?'

He sniggered and pushed his glasses up. 'I got a lotta habits, but time wasting ain't one.'

'Well you've been wasting my time.'

'And you've been wasting my wife's time by hounding her, so if you ain't got nothing better to do, go fuck yourself or something.' The two of them giggled at this, the same way schoolkids do when they curse.

'Listen, you fat shit,' I said through clenched teeth. 'I'm stuck, and as I hear you're the only person who can help me.'

'Fat?' They both broke into laughter again. They were like oversized, real-life Tickle Me Elmo dolls. 'We're not fat – we're festive. It's nearly Christmas. Come on Mate, get in the spirit.'

'Kerry McLaughlin told me that you can do passports for people who can't get passports.'

'Kerry McLaughlin says a lot of things, and sends a lot of people down here, so what? Who the hell are you to me?'

I considered threatening him again, but couldn't stand hearing them snigger. 'I'm a guy that needs your help. Are you going to give it to me or not?

'What's your name?'

'Dane.'

'Did you get built with a last name, Dane?'

'Costello.'

The smile fled his face. 'Wait. You know McLaughlin ... and you're a Costello, as in Josh Costello?'

'I'm his twin brother.'

Now he was festive, his hair contrasted against a face as white as new paper.

'Oh, I didn't realise the King had a brother. Not except the older one who passed – God bless him. Where have you been?'

'Away … Are you going to help me or not?'

'Ah, well, ah.' Marty Slick bumbled, and wiped his palms. His humour had vanished. 'If you are who you say you are then I think I can do something for you.'

He didn't need to know that Josh hated me.

'How much is this going to cost?' I asked.

Marty Slick glanced to his pink-haired wife. 'Well, it's usually ten, but since you're royalty and such, I can do it for ya for half that.'

'Okay.' I nodded and left the pawn shop. I waited until I was outside to spit out the lump of disappointment. It was so close but, with the cash needed, so damn far.

As I walked up St Kilda Road, through the CBD and then onto Footscray Road, I became lost in memory.

* * *

'We're not home.' Kayla put her purse on the kitchen bench.

I tossed my keys beside it and took a fresh square from the Post-It note pad. 'Parallel universe? You taken some sort of hallucinogenic? Looks like our apartment.'

Nescafé, I jotted. *Oh and milk, too, Babe.*

'It is our apartment, Jerk-off,' she said. 'What I mean is there could be more of a home for us.'

'Definitely the hallucinogen.'

A banana peel slapped my forehead. Slime stuck to my skin. Kayla was on the other side of the table with another slice ready. She poked her tongue out as I started toward her and threw the peel. I chased her around the table, tackled her onto the couch and pinned her arms.

She giggled. 'Look in your pocket.'

I let go of one of her hands – big mistake – and reached into my pocket. I brought the piece of torn magazine paper in front of my eyes. 'What is it?'

'It's a house … That'll be our home one day. It's on the coastline not far from San Francisco. Remember when we stayed up on the cliffs and I pointed across the bay? This is the house I was telling you about. It has been for sale for years but no one has bought it. Ghosts and all kinds of creepy, dead shit.'

With all the nightmares she had I found this ridiculous. 'You want to live in a haunted house. Ghosts and the walking dead and things that go bump in the middle of the night?'

'Ghosts don't bother me, Dane. It's the living who piss me off.'

I took my eyes from her for no more than five seconds. Banana squelched onto my face.

'Now you've done it.' I was about to exact revenge when Kayla brought my head down and kissed me. She wiped the banana from my face with her fingertips, and somehow transformed the moment into a sensual embrace. I guess pretty girls can do that, those who are pretty enough to get away with murder.

'This is home for us, Babe.' She took the photo and looked at it. 'One day we'll buy it. We'll have our own space up on the hill – just you, me and some of San Fran's finest poltergeists.'

∗ ∗ ∗

The sound of a truck horn startled me. 'Get off the road ya wanker!' snarled the driver, leaning out of his window. 'I've got places to be.'

'Of course you do,' I thought. *The Union doesn't stop.*

The air on the wharf was cloudy: mist rising off the water, smog from the ships' chimneys and smoke from cigarettes dangling on the bottom lip of prune-faced dockers. The temperature by the bay was always degrees colder than in the rest of the city, and a southerly had just swept through, the late afternoon sun nothing more than a pretty sight setting over the distant skyline.

At Berth C I leaned on the second red container in the front row, hidden from the stream of workers on the wharf's edge. Kerry appeared with a clipboard in hand. He surveyed the waterfront and ran his finger down a sheet of paper on the clipboard.

'It's time to get rid of the mullet, Mate,' I called. 'You trying to decide on a hairdresser?'

He laughed and made his way over. 'You're keen, hanging round these parts on your day off. Sick of Gary's rambling?'

'Yeah, pretty much. What's news?'

From his pocket he took out a pack of Dunhill's. 'Same shit, different day.' He lit his cigarette. 'I heard along the grapevine you've been out and about.'

'Grapevine's a funny nickname for your wife, Mate.'

Kerry exhaled a cloud of smoke through pursed lips. 'So what can I do for you?'

'Finally got a hold of Marty Slick.'

Kerry laughed, as if Marty Slick's own giggle was so infectious it had infested Kerry from St Kilda. 'Interesting cat, isn't he?'

'You can say that. After a lot of bullshitting, I got him to agree to help me.'

Kerry raised his arms with his cigarette held in his lips. 'That's great news, Mate,' he said from the corner of his mouth.

'One problem. The cash.'

'Ah.' He butted out his smoke and scratched his chin. 'I knew the industry was tight at the moment. What's he stooging ya for?'

'Five grand. Thing is, I've got it, but it's hidden in a cookie jar in Santa Monica.'

'Shit. You're in a right pickle, Mate.'

'I need this, Kerry. I can't keep messing around here. I need to get back to my girl. You understand, right? I don't want to be here. Josh doesn't want me here. I'm just reopening old wounds ... There's only one way I'm coming up with that kind of cash any time soon.'

'Are you implying what I think you are?'

'I want back in, Kerry. I need it.'

He mulled over the idea.

'That's easier said than done, Mate. I've got no hard feelings toward ya, but I can't speak for everyone. And you know how stubborn he can be.'

'I know Josh hates me. Actually, I'm surprised he hasn't had me knocked yet.'

'You might have broken a pretty big rule by up and leaving, but things aren't what they used to be, and besides, you're family.'

It warmed me to hear him say it.

'So ask him. Maybe he'll realise that too. Besides, you both know I'm a good worker and useful. It's business after all, right? Josh might have a brick for a head, but he's smart enough to know he can use a guy like me.'

'Okay, I'll talk to him.' At the same time, we noticed Josh strolling along the wharf. In his hand were two white bakery bags, the logo on them familiar. I thought about Rochelle.

Josh saw Kerry emerge from the containers and then caught me staring. If a picture can paint a thousand words, a glare like my twin brother's threw a thousand daggers. We were matching polarities: the same end of two different magnets, which repelled one another.

* * *

Outside the local bakery on Acland Street I sat with a pie and coffee. She wasn't there when I went in, and I was unsure if I was happy, sad or indifferent.

The chair opposite me slid out. A blonde girl sat down, who was a teenager last time I saw her. Bailey was the granddaughter of Jean McLennan, who ran the bakery alone after her husband, Frank, died in autumn of '84.

'Hi, can I help you?'

'It's Dane, isn't it?'

She recognised me far too easily.

'Yes.'

'Did you come here to see Rochelle?'

'Well … No, actually I didn't. Just hungry.'

Bailey knew this was a lie. 'She doesn't work here anymore. Moved away a long time ago after your brother broke it off. Thought they really had something.'

'It's Bailey, isn't it?'

'I can't believe you remember me.' Her soft pink lips locked in a smile. 'I was only a …'

'Yes, you were only a child last time I came in.' Seven years held a lifetime of change.

'Well I was a teenager.' She paused. 'This is so weird. I was talking with my girlfriends the other day about our first crushes, and your name came up.'

'I'm flattered.'

'You were the friendly boy who came into our bakery every Saturday to order a pie and milkshake. I always wondered what happened to you.'

I pushed out my chair. Bailey was far too blonde, far too tanned, and far too fuckable for this small talk to continue. 'I best be off now. Work and all that.'

'Are you still working on the docks? Maybe we can get a drink sometime.'

'No,' I said. 'To both questions.'

Bailey smirked, one of the self-assured smirks that reflects inner confidence confined to the most pig-headed or good-looking of people.

'The second wasn't a question.'

'Goodbye Bailey.'

As I walked away, she called out. 'See you soon, Dane.'

I became frustrated with myself when a thousand would-be positions came to mind, and even more so when Kayla's emerald eyes beamed up at me.

One thing stood between me and a passport back to her. Cash. And only one thing stood between me and the cash. My brother.

LETTER 6

December 15 1993

Dane,

Christmas approaches, and I'm considering who to lock in what closet now that it's clear you're not going to be here.

The third instalment of chemo will begin soon, the 22nd if I listened correctly to Dr Simms. The date reminds me of the ritualistic lockup we'd usually undertake, a week-long bedroom coo. I'm still a woman, Dane, and for Christ's sake I need sex.

I swear that in another life I was a teenage boy or rabbit who died in their sexual prime.

I've played with the idea of asking Nurse Cameron to drive me to the adult store on Fifth so I can purchase a dildo that most resembles the endowment you took with you when you left. I think I could find one that suits, at least match the dimensions, but it's the warmth that I don't think I could find in a rubber cock.

I'll stop this train of thought, tough as it is, otherwise I won't finish this letter.

Nurse Cameron has helped me a lot lately, and not just with Margaret and Geoff.

Remember that night we stopped over just outside Minneapolis on route from Seattle to New York? I should have had the presence of mind to choose a different way, but I thought I'd be fine. It didn't matter how many layers I wore, or how many times the fire was loaded with another log, the cold in that cabin made me shiver.

You didn't see too much of a problem, most likely because my poker face was one of the first invented. I hated that night, and no matter how nice you tried to be or how many times you tried to pull me in, I felt alone, and scared, and wanted to get in the car and drive through the night. We should have.

I was petrified, Dane, and this is something you know doesn't happen often. But I was. I didn't sleep until well after your snores hit throttle. I even woke you twice to try and fall asleep with you still awake and watching me. I pushed you, even punched you in the face to make you stir and see me to sleep. It was all useless, though, and it was what happened when I fell asleep that made you wake in a pool of piss.

Nightmares like that aren't supposed to come anymore, not after everything that happened. I was meant to be safe. But that night I was reminded things were not finished.

Your immediate reaction made me feel worse. Yuk, you said, before you realized what had actually happened and perhaps connected some dots you hadn't seen before.

I felt this same embarrassment when I woke in my hospital bed, swimming in a puddle of faintly red urine.

It was just lucky Nurse Cameron was on morning shift to spare me further.

'Hell, hello, Kayla.'

I signaled him to come near. 'I have a problem.' I lifted up the sheets and showed him the artwork of my bladder. 'I'm a bit embarrassed: I don't want anyone to know.'

'Leave it, leave it with me. I will take care of it.' He left the room and a minute or so later, a cleaner came in with a bucket and mop and spread across the floor a solution I would guess was nine parts bleach, one part water. It stunk out the room immediately and Susan cringed in disgust, waving her hand in front of her nose.

Nurse Cameron appeared at the door and prompted me to the shower. Susan was distracted enough to not notice the stains on my pajamas, and by the time I returned from the shower every piece of linen had been replaced by fresh, clean whites.

* * *

I wonder about Maureen now she has finally passed on. I hope she is happier, in less pain and more alive. Death is real, Dane. When her bed was removed from the room I tried to imagine what it would be like under my final sheet. I'm not ready to go – I haven't come this far to say goodbye in my twenty-sixth year.

I didn't tell Burty I went to see his parents-in-law, and until this week no conversation had verged toward family life or even the past. The past, hey. You don't need to turn around to see it. My poor old turd of a friend sees it every time he sits on the bench and gazes to his ranch in the sky. This poor old fool may just have some hope yet.

We walked along the path. 'If you could be anything in the world, Burty, what would you be?'

He grimaced and stopped to take off his shoe.

I gave a shoulder for support.

'Darn, damn stones, always seem to find a way under my foot. Don't matter what shoes I'm wearing.'

'I like to believe most people have a stone in their shoe, Burty, regardless of which they wear. Think the more important thing is how you walk.'

He grunted, removed the stone, and we continued.

A quail flew across our path. Burty's eyes followed it. He slowed as we approached a group of pigeons pecking at the ground. He took from his pocket a handful of seed and tossed it over the pebbles in front of us. The birds cooed as they trotted to the seed and began to feed.

'I used to love bird watching,' he said, kneeling to offer seed from his hand. 'I've seen a lotta beautiful ones from the window. Saw a male painted bunting once. They're the most beautiful bird in North America ...

'You know I've been wondering something, Lil Lady. Same thing you wondered about me. Where is your family?'

I took a moment to think my answer through. I've written a lot, Dane, but I haven't verbalized any of this confusion. 'I guess I've just walked a path so unique that no one has been able to stick around long enough to be with me now.

'I had a man … I just don't get it. If he wanted to leave why didn't he just tell me? Why run away? I never told him … But I really thought he loved me. I thought he was the one person who would always be there.'

'Well, I'm here for you, Darlin'.' Burty wrapped his arms around me. I pressed my head onto his chest and held him like someone I'd known my whole life.

I've always proclaimed to be at odds with hugs; I think they are given frivolously much of the time, the same as a kiss on the cheek. Affection should be saved for those who deserve it. If you see a bitch you don't like, don't smile and say hi, walk past her. It's not rude, it's honest. I don't give away my affection like a fake bitch.

So when I hugged Burty, and wrapped my arms as far around his Humpty-Dumpty body as they could go, I was a part of every bit of warmth we shared.

He rubbed my back. 'The ones who really matter will always be there.'

As we broke I felt someone was watching us. It's an instinct evolved as a child, and it's usually right.

'Hello Kayla, hello Burty.'

Geoff Romanowski clutched at his fedora, his eyes tired and hopeful, and his hair swept across by the wind from one side of his head to the other. The brown suit he wore draped off him the way that a small boy's first suit does at a funeral.

'Geoff.' Burty was flabbergasted.

Apprehensively, they shook hands. I took seed from Burty's hand, and while the two men sat on a bench, I slid into the background to feed the birds.

The two old bats sat on the bench for a long time and I believe they could have sat there for days. Old people can talk, so when you get two of them together it is a recipe for time consumption.

When they finally finished, Burty had to rouse me after I fell asleep somewhere in the twentieth hour of their marathon. In his hand was a piece of paper. I didn't need to ask what it was, and he bore a wide smile, showing teeth I didn't know he had.

Burty called his daughter and from her answering machine discovered she was out of town on business. He left a message.

Later in the evening he told me about Lily. He said I reminded him of her in many ways. How she looked. Her determination.

'I didn't answer you earlier when you asked me what I'd be if I could be anything,' he said.

'So what would you be?'

'A father.'

He has not stopped grinning. Even now, in his bed, the hopeful look of a man who has so much to look forward to covers his face.

Outside in the halls the Christmas decorations are up. It is a different feel this year, but as with any, there is hope this Christmas. I'd like to say I still hold out hope that you'll return to the apartment, find my note, and be here. But I know this is naïve.

I hope you're thinking of me, Dane, wherever you are. And I hope you're happy, looking forward to the 22nd, whoever you'll be doing. When she comes and sighs heavily under the fluid roll of your body, when she tingles at being stretched by your cock, know that she'll never feel you like I did, and know that you'll never feel her like you did me. I just hope for her sake that you don't abandon her. I don't wish this confusion upon anyone. In advance, Merry Christmas, Babe. I hope it's white.

Kayla

DIARY 13

May 15 1981

I don't know what I should believe: my heart, my head or my tummy. I love Mom. I hate Mom. I don't feel anything for Mom.

Most kids my age are going to school, playing outside with bicycles or having sleepovers. I'm thirteen years old and searching for something I can't understand. I don't think I ever could.

Outside the window the sky is speckled with stars. I imagine somewhere up there someone is looking down on me and guiding me. In the distance I can see the lights of San Francisco, the arch of the Golden Gate Bridge and what I hope will be a new start.

Gray Suit is in San Francisco. Oscar found out, but wouldn't tell me how.

For the last few months we have laid low in different towns across the northwest, only going out at night to gather food and water. Oscar knows how to do it and I am slowly getting better. You do what you have to do to survive: in a house, or on the street.

This afternoon while I sat in a Greyhound bus, I gazed out the window to the changing land. Oscar slept beside me. He was exhausted like most days because he stays up all night to guard me.

We boarded the bus at Saint Paul Airport, having traveled to the big city by foot, car, train and truck. The hustle and bustle of Minneapolis and murky lakes became crystal-blue waters and gray-green misty woods of pine as we left the city. We traveled west to Seattle, where we changed buses some hours ago. I walked in front of Oscar and he held my shoulders between his huge hands, looking at each person we passed in the aisle.

Down the west coast through Oregon and now into northern California, white lines on melted tar flashed by.

People got on and off. There were old people, some alone, some with another old person. There were families with kids just like me and Oscar. There were people with bright eyes, some with tired eyes. I wondered which people were running away and which were going home. I didn't know which type we were.

The afternoon turned into dusk and dusk into night. Outside the window I can see the shorelines and stretching out into the moonlight the water of the ocean. I've never been to a beach, but I've imagined so many times what the sand would feel like between my toes. I think it would feel like a massage every step. I can imagine the refreshing feel of the water; the feel of hope, like the first day of spring.

Oscar just snorted and started to sleep-talk. 'Shorty, I got five horses waiting for us. They gonna get us a win on the tracks and then we be rich. Blueberry pancakes, too.'

I'm excited. One time on the TV someone said, 'Tomorrow is going to be the first day of your new life.' I think tomorrow will be that day for me. We made it out, and when we return to La Mont it will only be for one reason.

DIARY 14

September 20 1981

I think if I had to live in any century or place on earth I could do it, as long as I had Oscar with me.

San Francisco is the prettiest city I have ever seen. The houses are like colorful shoeboxes cut with window holes, the streets are clean and the weather is always warm. Every morning I walk to the beach from Sunset District where we live. The feeling of sand between my toes excites me.

I don't remember being born, but I think I will always remember when I was reborn. It was when we got here.

With a lot of shoving, I woke Oscar. I ran, like my legs had jetpacks attached, from the Greyhound bus. I ran all the way across the lawn, through the playground, over the rock wall and with wings I flew onto the sand. The moment my feet touched the soft yellow grains it felt like life started over.

'Come on, Kay-Kay, time ta go,' Oscar called from over the rock wall.

Even if I'd wanted to, I couldn't have gone back to him. He hollered some more, and then dropped our bags and jumped the rock wall.

Oscar caught me, and around the beach, through the waves and all over the universe he piggy-backed me, whinnying and grunting like a wild animal. We laughed until our stomachs hurt and we were covered in sand from rolling around so much.

'Look at that house, Ozzy,' I said from his back. 'There, up on the cliff.'

It was a beautiful, old-fashioned house far in the distance, overlooking the sea.

'One day, Shorty ...'

The first three weeks here we stayed on the streets – mostly behind Rushes bakery in Western Addition – until we were able to find our way into a share house for people like us in Tenderloin.

It was smelly and sometimes I got really scared at night, because of the strange people. Some of the residents would bring in drugs, and inject them into their veins. They would do it over and over again and when they no longer had a sleepy smile, they would wake and want more, and when they couldn't get it, they would cause trouble.

I saw my first dead body in the shelter. He threw up and choked on his vomit. We left because Oscar said it wasn't safe.

We slept behind Rushes for another week before we won on the horses, like Oscar said we would.

'Kay-Kay, wake up.' Oscar was shaking my shoulder. 'Shorty, we gotta get outta here.'

From the prickly concrete, I stood. I don't even come up to Oscar's shoulder anymore.

'Where are we going?' I asked, rubbing my eyes.

'Well it's nearly daytime, so we gotta move, but I got something.'

We packed our blankets and bags. Oscar led me by the hand all the way across town. We passed shopping malls not open yet, schools that were hours away from their first bell, bakeries still baking, homeless men still asleep under newspapers, and crossed to the west of the Golden Gate.

The first cable cars were not yet running when we trudged up the hilly road that curls over the horizon.

Oscar darted his eyes around. 'We're here.' He pushed open a small white picket gate and led me to the front door of the pastel-blue house.

'**We come**' read the doormat. Oscar jumped from the doorstep into the long grass under the front window. He slid the dusty window up and then dived head first into the house.

The front door opened. 'Welcome to our mansion, Lady Kayla,' he said in his best posh accent. He can't do very good impersonations anymore because his voice has become deep as a tuba.

The house was filled with cobwebs. It was as if dust was growing out of the walls and furniture.

'Whose house is this, Ozzy?' I stopped by a piano and hit one of the only non-cobwebbed keys. 'Or does it belong to the millions of spiders?'

'It's our house. Them spiders just guests for the spring; they get gone once we get them gone. I tells them the holiday is over.'

'You're a damn mean landlord.'

'I'm harsh but fair. They had their stay ... It ain't been anyone's for a long time. I been doing some homework since we got here. Ain't nobody come here for years.'

After the dust had been sent to sail with the ships in the bay, we had a home.

The water works, but there is no electricity or gas. If it wasn't for the streetlights that watch over us, I would forget about electricity altogether. It is best to shower when the day is hot, and for meals we eat fresh food we gather, or we cook using a small barrel I found in the byway. Sometimes we have steak. Those days are the ones when Oscar's horses win. Those nights we usually have blueberry pancakes, too.

We've been spying on houses all across the city, sometimes we stalk and sometimes we hide. They all have the same last name as Gray Suit – his real name Oscar knows, but I never remember (Ginder, Ginnersberg, Ginner?).

The city is so pretty, the water so fresh and the sunshine so warm that often I forget why we are here.

We haven't found him yet, but soon we will. The phone book is running out of names staring with Gin ...

Ginger.

That was the name of the cat.

We spent a day waiting in bushes near the front of a house. The man had finally come home, and at first as he climbed out of his car in a gray suit, I thought we had him. Then he turned, and his young, happy face wasn't the Gin we were looking for. It was another day, like a lot of others.

The sunset was near its end when we walked into our front yard, the sky was red over the sound, the way it looks when it is trying to say that tomorrow will be hot.

Our street is usually so quiet that at night I can hear the wind whistle through the trees and blow fallen leaves along the concrete. So quiet that the whooshing of the tide rises up the embankment, all the way through the roads and right into my bedroom. Sometimes the quiet is scary.

When we came into our street, it wasn't as quiet as usual. There were strained meows.

We found it under the front steps.

Ginger belonged to Polly Albertson, the old lady who lives at the end of the street. I've heard Mrs Albertson call Ginger in for supper. I'd petted it once, before anyone else in the world was up.

I've never had a pet. Leroy the Lion was the closest.

Ginger was so pretty, with big blue eyes that reflected the light from the darkness under the step. I crawled under and brought her out, while Oscar jogged down the road to Mrs Albertson's house.

'She ain't home, Shorty,' he said as he came through the gate.

Ginger lay on my lap and cried in pain. 'It's dark, we need to get inside and take care of her.'

Oscar lit the candles in the living room and I stayed with Ginger. He brought a saucer and candle over to me and held it to the cat. On her belly was a big, swollen lump, red and purple, seeping blood and puss.

Oscar checked Mrs Albertson's house twice more. Why did she have to be away that night? If she was there it wouldn't have had to happen like it did.

On the grandfather clock it was one o'clock, which meant it was ten minutes after midnight, when we decided to do something.

Ginger's meows worsened by the minute, and her wound throbbed.

'Shorty, what we gonna do? We can't just leave her like this?'

'Is there a vet? What about the other people in the street, or the other street, or the other one after that?'

He looked down glumly. I knew what he was going to say.

'You know we can't let other people take too much notice of us. If we tell them ... If they come in here and find us they gonna tell someone and we'd have to leave.'

'What are you saying, Ozzy?'

'We have to put her down.'

At first it angered me, and I looked at Oscar to tell him *fuck you* with my eyes, but then I looked at Ginger in pain and knew it was the only way.

'We have to make it quick, you promise.'

I don't know if Oscar had ever killed anything, but he knew how to make her pain go away. He went to the kitchen and returned with a knife.

Oscar took Ginger off my lap and put her on the floor. I covered my eyes.

The mews stopped. 'It's done.' Oscar sounded flat.

When I peeped through my hands I saw Ginger. She was like a stuffed toy. I ran into my room, huddled into a ball and cried. Oscar buried Ginger in the backyard. He came in after to talk to me, but I just wanted to go to sleep.

Mrs Albertson has walked along the street every night for weeks now, in search of Ginger. She has put up posters with its pretty blue eyes reflecting out: Find me, they plead. She has knocked on every door of every house in every street in every town for as far as I can imagine. Every door except ours.

DIARY 15

December 25 1981

The house is speckled with tinsel and all sorts of Christmas decorations from the box I found in the attic. Oscar brought home a tree – not a pine like a normal Christmas tree, it's actually closer to a cactus – and we have decorated it so barely any green shows.

In bed I always wake when Oscar goes to the toilet. He is so tall that he collects hanging tinsel on his way and becomes tangled.

When I gazed out the front window this morning I felt what Christmas is really about.

Winter sun glowed off street signs. Mrs Albertson's grandchildren played in the street. (She has stopped looking for her cat.) One of her grandchildren built things with left-over wrapping paper and boxes, one rode a bike with training wheels and another one bounced a basketball. They screamed and laughed.

We are resting until the New Year. Oscar says we need it.

We have made a list of things to get, and will finish shopping soon. I am nervous. I look at our list and I feel a shudder from my spine all the way out to the prickled hairs on my arms. But I will check it twice, check to make sure we have everything we need. And we have a plan, too. Gray Suit, whose last name is Gin-something, is no more than a fifteen-minute bus ride away.

Right now the sun is setting in a purple-blue swirl over the bay. I imagine what Gray Suit is doing for Christmas. I can see his house, now that I know what it looks like: two stories, red tiled roof, and small, cracked brick fence with a black metal gate that creaks when the breeze moves it. I can see his gray suit through the window, his lonely table with one serve of meat and vegetables. I see his face and I see his eyes. He can't see me, though.

CHAPTER 11

For a Friday afternoon the bar was quiet, only a handful of people inside: a pair of mullet-sporting teens played pool, a group of suits seated around a table sipped early-knock-off brews, and by the bar a familiar ginger crew cut.

Kerry was laughing with Simone when I sat down, both were wearing Santa hats.

'Look what Rudolf dragged in,' said Simone.

Kerry turned to me. 'Speak of the devil, hey Grapevine.'

'Didn't think that one would take off,' I said.

'Many didn't think Apollo 11 would take off,' Kerry joked.

He ordered another round and Simone slapped down two beers on the bar mat. An unusual ringing sounded as Kerry took his first pull. He reached into his coat pocket and withdrew a hand-held telephone the size of a brick. I'd seen mobile phones in Los Angeles here and there, but this was the first time in Melbourne.

He pulled out the aerial. 'Hello,' he said and then played with the aerial. 'Stupid thing. Hello? Oh, yep, I can hear you now.' He pushed a finger into his free ear to block out the noise. 'Slow down … Okay, I got it. I'm onto it.'

'You right, Mate?' I asked.

'Shit,' he hissed. 'Up the creek. A package was meant to go to a buyer but the bloody truckie has flipped and never showed up. The amount is nothing, but this is a new product and the buyer is a major player … This is not good. We've known Remy's got connections to bikies for a while. Josh has had suspicions about him slipping them bits and bobs to undercut in the north and west. Dumb bastard has no idea what this package is worth.'

He pushed the aerial back in, leaned his hands on the bar and simmered for a few moments, then exploded. 'Fuck! No good son of a ...'

The back of the phone broke off and hit the floor. Kerry threw the other part out the front of the bar onto the footpath.

'Isn't that valuable?' asked Simone.

'Not compared to what we've lost. Besides, those stupid hunks of junk will never take off.' Kerry began pacing, and muttered to himself. 'I don't know how I'm going to get this shit back. The boys are all on the road. I gotta move ... But I can't go alone ...'

I gulped down the rest of my beer. 'Well then let's go.'

Kerry had stopped. I pulled his coat as I passed him and marched out of the pub as if I was as tall as the Rialto.

Outside, Kerry caught up to me. 'Dane. We could run into some trouble. You don't have to ... You know how dangerous this is.'

'I know. I've done this before. Remember how Josh and I retrieved ten keys from an Outlaws' warehouse when Keith Phillips was off with some whores?'

'Yeah. It was one of the things McCulloch noted when he handed over the reins to Josh.'

'So trust me, we can do this.'

Kerry picked up his phone, and put it back together as we jogged along the Esplanade toward the car.

The phone rang. 'Okay, yep,' he said and then hung up. 'Josh has word that Remy is meeting a bikie near Kirby's Kiosk. We're loaded in case we need it.'

✳ ✳ ✳

We crept along Pier Road until we caught sight of the truck. We parked opposite, some thirty metres behind it.

I slid down the seat. Kerry laughed. 'Mate, there's no way they can see through these windows.' I sat upright, and Kerry nodded to the truck. 'That's definitely it, but I can't see Remy. Little prick.'

'I'm guessing that's his connection.' I pointed to the young bikie, patched and with sleeves of ink, crossing the street toward the truck.

'He's a Prince,' said Kerry. 'Princes of Hades. New crew in town. Making a name for themselves. Not as organised as some of the bigger outfits but they're volatile bastards.'

The truck door opened and a small man with a handlebar moustache stepped down. Kerry reached into the backseat and brought out two balaclavas and handed me one. As I put it on I felt something plonk on my lap.

I picked up the sawn-off shotgun. It'd been a long time since I had handled one.

'Sorry about that.' Kerry pointed his head, now covered in black, at my gun. 'Just what I had lying around.' The magazine clicked into place in his sleek handgun. 'You still know how to aim?'

'Guess we'll find out.'

'Hopefully we won't.'

Remy and the bikie walked to the back of the truck. Remy opened the back doors and they climbed in.

Kerry undid his seatbelt. 'All right, let's go.'

We got out of the car and skulked to either side of the truck. We peered around and into the back. The men were exchanging the parcel for cash. Kerry nodded, and then leapt into the truck. I followed.

'Hands up and don't move a fucking muscle.' Kerry pointed to the bikie, and both men obliged, Remy holding the package. I held the shottie to Remy's head.

'Who the fuck are you?' the bikie snarled.

'We are the owners of what you were about to purchase, and we're here for our property.' Kerry then spoke directly to Remy. 'You've got on the wrong side of the wrong people. Give it up now and don't make it any worse. Go on, drop it.'

Remy laughed. 'What, the Union? A bunch of has-beens. It's a sinking ship, Mate. Get off while you can and take what you can get. That's all I'm doing.'

Kerry took his time to respond. 'Drop it, or I shoot.'

Leaning down, Remy put the package on the truck floor. The bikie swung his arm out and knocked Kerry's gun from his hand. I pointed the shottie at the bikie for an instant and then buckled over with the gut-churning pain from a kick to the balls. Remy jumped over me and out of the truck with the package. Kerry and the bikie broke into a wrestle. I got up and chased Remy into Catani Gardens.

He had twenty metres on me, but I got closer with each stride. He was near the drinking fountain when I caught up and tackled him to the ground. The package spilled free from his hand onto the grass. We wrestled momentarily before I punched him twice in the nose. Blood splashed like water from a burst balloon. He moaned and grabbed his nose.

I got off him and rushed to the package. I p cked it up and left Remy huddled in a ball.

To my relief, Kerry stepped down from the back of the truck with both guns in hand. 'Shit, Mate, what happened?'

I followed his eyes. The right shoulder of my T-shirt was soaked in blood. I felt around and found the knife wound. 'I got the package,' I said. 'That's all.'

'We better get you back and cleaned up.'

* * *

The staff bathroom at the Espy was closed off.

Simone held a sewing needle in her lips. 'You'll feel this.'

She cleaned the wound.

'Ouch!'

'Told you. You're lucky this didn't go in a few centimetres to the left. Just muscle damage. Could've been a lot worse.'

'I know, good thing this T-shirt was cheap.'

She shook her head. 'Okay, don't move. I'm going to start.'

I winced and gripped my fists while she stitched me up.

Kerry popped his head in the door. 'In the tcilets with my missus. I'm onto you, you sly dog.' He chuckled. 'In all seriousness, great work today, Dane. Package got delivered fine and everything's cool. Saved a very important deal for us. Come speak backstage after you're done here.'

'I'll finish with her soon. Ouch!'

'Oops,' said Simone. 'Must've slipped.'

Backstage, Kerry and Josh were seated on crates, smoking cigarettes. Kerry slid a milk crate for me to sit. 'Like I said, you did good today, Mate.'

I waved off a cigarette at Kerry's offer.

'And, since I've been bugging the boss here for a while, we'd like to offer you a chance to do some work for us again. Real work. We need more soldiers like you. Dying breed.'

'I'm in.' I looked at Josh.

He was preoccupied by the lighting cables in the rafters. He finished his cigarette and crushed it on the wooden floor.

'You'll start with some tasks next week,' he said to me, without looking. 'Kerry will oversee what you do.' He stood and started away from the stage.

I stood. 'So, King. When are we going to do this?'

Josh turned. 'Do what?'

'Don't be stupid. You can wear that mask all you like, but I'm here and I'm sticking around – we can't just keep avoiding each other. I don't give a shit if you're the King of bloody Scotland, I know you better ...'

He stepped toward me and raised a finger. 'You don't know shit. And you can't just come around telling me how it goes – not how it works. You didn't die today. Congratulations, but all that means is you've got a chance to work for me. That's it. So keep your happy-family bullshit to yourself.'

He remained in front of me. I stared him down. 'Happy? No. But we're still *a family*, whether you like it or not.'

CHAPTER 12

The passenger window was wound down as far as Kerry's VP Commodore wagon would permit. Fresh sea breeze gusted in and ran through my hair as I gazed outside to the sand and water.

The sun had risen while we passed through Werribee, illuminating a deep-blue dawn with the glisten of yellow and white, a sparkle that shone from far away over the straw paddocks right into the car mirrors.

At the moment we veered onto the stretch of road in Torquay, the famous track that leads to the Apostles, those paddocks turned to swell. With surfboards strapped to the roof rack we trailed the winding Great Ocean Road behind the others.

For the first time in seven years, Josh and I were together on a route we'd travelled too many times to recall. A Christmas Eve tradition in years gone by, it was a day of relaxation out in waves before the rush of the season.

The sets of Kennett River Beach appeared as we rounded a winding corner. A dollop of nerves shot from my gut up my trachea all the way to the back of my throat. We turned down the gravel road, kicking up dust, and there in the car park was a black four-wheel-drive I knew.

Kerry pulled the handbrake and cut the ignition. 'Look a tad shaky, Mate.'

'Has been a while,' I replied.

We dressed in wetsuits and loped toward a loose wire fence. On the dune I surveyed the shoreline: jagged brown rocks to the left. By their near side an inconspicuous rip flowed out behind the breakers, which crashed onto the rocks. To the right were more rips but fewer hazards. As he reached the group on the dune Kerry continued and planted his board in the sand like a pitchfork.

I became a fly on the wall. The Josh in front of me, with broad shoulders, ripped muscles, shaved head and skin covered with tattoos morphed into a skinny teenage boy with curly hair and clean skin, who would patiently survey the shoreline for an easy rip to ride out to behind the back set.

He would tell me how this morning we could ride the sea and a grin would form before he goaded me into the first contest. *Last one to catch a break does the other's chores for the next week.* Off we'd run toward the water. Stevie would still be dressing, and call out, 'Oi, take care you two,' as we bounded through the shallows and leaped prone onto the boards. When I entered the water, salt rising high into my sinuses as my head submerged, it was as if nothing else mattered, not even the extra chores at stake.

'The one and only great mystery of Bass Strait!' Ollie's hands were raised in the air, coffee still in hand.

The rest of the group turned, Josh included. Every man except my twin brother greeted me jovially.

Josh slid his arms into the sleeves of his wetsuit, tied the leash to his ankle, picked up his stick and strolled toward the water.

Salem shook his head. 'Flying solo this morning, hey Boss.'

'Eh. Let him be,' said Ollie. 'Too early for grumpy folks.'

We grouped together around Kerry and waxed the boards. While the others talked I watched Josh. He waded into the shallows, ankle breakers lapping against his lower leg. As the water became deeper he broke into a stride. He lowered the board beneath his body, leaped onto it and paddled out. *Last one to catch a break ...*

I slid on the top half of my wetsuit, and then jogged toward the water.

Against my ankles the water was refreshing. Only adrenalin and impulse propelled me past anxiety. My strides lengthened. The water splashed onto my knees, and then my thighs, and then, just after the inevitable crotch splash, I felt myself soar into the air. I landed on the board, and the bond formed when the wetsuit gripped against the wax.

Josh had swerved into the rip on the left of the breaker, some ten metres ahead. I paddled with long, powerful strokes and followed him. As I caught the undertow the pressure of the incoming waves disappeared and the rip dragged me out. To the right, the back set of waves formed a tube, curling perfectly into a tunnel.

I clawed at the water and steered right to pursue Josh to the back of the breaker. Another five surfers bobbed up and down while they waited for a wave. Josh settled, and as he sat up I paddled to his side.

He raised an eyebrow, his lip twitching. 'The fuck you doing?'

'About to surf, Dickhead. Pity I can't say the same for you, presuming you still throw your weight around on the board like an overweight yoyo.'

'Clever, aren't ya.' He scowled.

I beamed a smart-arse smile. 'Always been smarter than you.'

A wave began to form and swept under us. Two surfers paddled like madmen to catch it, and as it curled over and formed a tube, one dropped in, while the other left to regroup. Neither of us feigned interest.

'What do you want?' he asked.

'You know what I want, but seeing as though that's not going to happen, I might as well come out here and kick your arse for old time's sake and at least put you part-way back into your place, Little Brother.'

Josh sneered. 'Twins, Moron, and I know my place well enough to not have some strange outsider come in and try to tell me otherwise.'

'We'll see just where you wind up.'

'We both know once a wave comes along that's too big for you to surf easily, you'll bail out and paddle back to shore. Curls over a little too late and what? You stay under water. Or better yet, you paddle all the way to another country, not before you steal a break off someone first. Quitter.'

'With the cash you've made using the structure we created I'm surprised you couldn't get some therapy. If you've got something to say, say it Josh.'

'I've said all I need to say, so if you're done with the shit talk get the hell out of my way and let a real surfer do what I came down here to do. Go on, paddle in and let me be … *Brother.*'

Presently, another wave began to build beneath the surface of the water. Josh turned to see it rise. Before he could move, I flopped down on the board and splashed him. I caught drift and it continued to rise: building, building and then curling. Over the crest I dropped in and caught it. With slippery hands and a fluttering heart beating purely on adrenalin, I stood up on rubbery legs. For just one second, I was a candle in the wind. I was delicate. Before I remembered something – something remembered me.

The tube formed, and the edge of the board sliced through the water, breaking the face of the wave with a beautiful tear. I dropped lower and moved with the flow of the water. Reaching my foot to the tail of the board, I brought the nose up. A rush came as I emerged from the end of the tube and began to carve. I cut out and then cut back.

And then a missile appeared from over the crest, and before I could be hammered by the board, I bailed out.

I surfaced and clung to my board. Josh cut in and out of the wave before he wiped out. In surf law, he'd committed the grossest offence by dropping in on me. Even worse, he'd come dangerously close to taking me out. I had every right to chase him, rip him under water and flog him.

Behind the breaker, Josh sat up on his board and I sat beside him. For the first time since I'd been back Josh broke a smile, albeit a nasty smirk. The temperature of my blood rose high above boiling point.

'I'd rather be a quitter than a dog.' I cocked my foot and kicked Josh in the chest. He fell from his board, and as he surfaced and tried to collect himself, I paddled with the wave, caught it and sliced through the tube, carving, climbing and cutting in and out like a pro before I let myself wipe out this time.

Josh waited for me with fists ready. From behind him another surfer approached. We reached Josh at the same time.

'We're fine, Dude,' Josh said over his shoulder and turned back to me.

I was ready to throw down, but the spiky-haired surfer interrupted before we could start. 'Nah you're not, Mate. Far from it actually.'

'What's the problem?' I asked.

'There's no problem.' Josh turned fully to the local. 'Now fuck off and keep out of our business.'

Four other surfers who'd been out the back minding their own business paddled toward us and formed a half circle. 'This is our spot and you snaked in on us just before. You're treating this place like it's a bloody garbage tip. If you're even half-schooled on etiquette, you know what happens now.'

Another of the surfers, who wore a Pendleton, laughed. 'I doubt it. They're posers.'

Josh floated beside me. 'We didn't do a thing wrong, Dickhead. You were positioned wrong and you lost your wave – deal with it, we're just better surfers.'

They moved toward us. As stubborn and pugnacious as he was, Josh knew what it meant when I tapped his foot below the water. We back-pedalled a metre as a wave began to form behind the locals.

'Example A,' I said and we both turned and paddled. 'Amateur hour in the west,' I called as I sliced down the face of the wave. Glancing back, I saw Josh drop in and carve in the opposite direction. He didn't cut back toward me. We glided into shore and joined the group sitting on their boards.

'How was the therapy session, Ladies? Kerry grinned.

Josh thumbed over his shoulder. 'Came out with some trouble.'

From the water, the locals stood and paced toward our group. 'Shit,' hissed Ollie. 'Trust you two morons to get us into the crap. You know what these boys are like at Kennett? Rep bigger than a bloody Yowie. They don't take shit.'

'Keep it in your pants, Ol.' Josh was humoured, and coolly sat on his board as the locals dropped theirs short and continued toward us. 'Just a bunch of wannabe bunnies. Remember who we are. The fucking Union.'

Salem and Kerry stood. Salem cracked his neck side to side. Josh leaned back on his elbows. Nonchalantly, he whistled a merry tune, not a worry in the world.

Ollie stepped up to the men as they reached us. 'Problem, Lads? Ya look a tad frazzled.'

The spiky-haired leader pointed at Josh and then me. 'Your boys snaked us; cut in on our waves. You know what happens now.'

I felt myself smile. Why, I'm not completely sure. I guess in the middle of all of this I was happy that for the moment I was closer to Josh. On the same side at least.

The locals surrounded us. Some bounced up and down and some shook their shoulders in preparation. We were a man down at best. But we knew who we were, even if the poor locals didn't.

It all happened too quickly, as most fights do, to really gauge just how we conquered them in spite of numbers. I struck one, two, maybe three of them in some capacity, and to their credit they even landed a few blows of their own. The fervour was such that the only memory I kept was one of my brother when he sprang from his board, and with two punches felled two men before he returned to his seat on the board.

When the locals limped off, one of their unconscious comrades carried, we stood like guard dogs around the boards and the boss. Josh smiled the same self-assured smile he'd worn when they'd approached. Like everything involving my brother, there was a reason for it.

'Well, after all the excitement, thanks to the two of you.' Kerry pointed at me and Josh. 'I think maybe it's about time we actually did some surfing. How'd we all fare anyway?'

The group was a little bruised and scratched, but nothing more. If Josh had been in a fight it was undetectable.

Kerry, Salem and Ollie left Josh and me and headed for the water. 'You going back in?'

He ignored me; so like before, I trailed him and this time caught him before he got to the water. 'Hey.' I took hold of his arm.

Josh spun and struck my ribs with a body rip. I hunched over, gasping for air. 'That's for kicking me off the board, and snaking my wave. Kook.'

It took me some time to regain my breath. My rib wasn't broken, I knew that feeling and this wasn't it. Most comforting of all, though, was that if Josh had intended to break it he would have. The pain was the most uplifting I'd felt.

For the rest of the morning I surfed, rode waves and chased Josh as he avoided me. At no point did I catch him.

When the heat had risen so high that the water trapped inside wetsuits began to warm, we turned it in for the day. Bruised and battered by fists and the sea, we cleaned our boards among idle chatter under the taps outside the toilet block.

After I'd finished, I walked up the small grass mound toward the car park and rested my board on the ground while I stripped from my wetsuit. Part way through pulling my right leg from the rubber, a set of feet trampled across the bow of the board.

Josh took one more step. I hooked my legs around the back of his knees, push-pulled, and he planted flat on his face on the slope.

I stood. 'That's for trampling Kerry's board, Dickhead.'

I awaited the spear tackle. But it didn't come. Josh found his feet, dusted himself off and picked up his board. He scowled at me.

'If it were worth the energy,' he said. 'I'd put you on your arse.'

'If you could you would, but you can't and you know it.'

Josh stepped up, but as he did he dropped his head and sniggered to himself. 'Nah, you don't get it like this, Mate. Nah.' His constraint alarmed me as much as it relieved. He'd changed, and as much as I knew him, I could not know everything I'd missed. He raised his eyes and met mine. 'You're a coward. You run. Cowards don't get to fight. Men fight.'

He climbed the mound.

'Only a coward would say that to shy away from confronting their family,' I called. 'Only a coward would hold a grudge like this. Maybe I am a coward for leaving but you are just as much for shying away. Talk big, walk tall, but you're still the boy who'd run second to any scuffle behind me.'

Josh whirled around, his eyes red as blood, teeth clenched, a vein popping from his forehead. 'You fucked my girlfriend the night of our older brother's wake!

'And then you left before you were forced to face the music, so don't talk to me about facing things, because I was left to deal with everything that Stevie lumped us with – everything – and all the shit you put on me as well.'

He pointed at me as if to poke holes in the air. 'No mum, no dad, no older brother, no twin brother and no girlfriend. You weren't here to go through it. The day you left you died.'

He was close to tears, frustrated and enraged like the boy I once knew. It was as though he stood on a mountain top. I felt a profound urge to crumble at the knees, though my eyes were dust dry.

'You think I didn't go through anything?' I pointed back. 'Just because I ran away doesn't mean their goddamn ghosts didn't chase me. Not a day went by that I didn't think about everyone. Most of all, you. I don't know why I did what I did, but I'm here now, Josh. I'm trying to make something up to you. We're not even thirty and we've lost everything. There's not one other person in the world who understands what we've been through.'

'That's the thing, *Brother*. You don't know what I went through. You might have thought about me, but all I've done is try to forget. You betrayed me and you ran.'

My voice dropped in time with my hand, 'I know what I did, but think about when you first screwed her. You betrayed me a long time before I did it to you, but I let it go because she made you happy.'

All rage vanished from Josh's face. He opened his mouth to talk, but stopped short and said nothing. Lowering his arm, he looked away, turned and trudged over the hill.

LETTER 7

January 3 1994

Dane,

It's been some weeks since I've written. I'd like to say it's because Christmas was so full of fun and festivity that I haven't had the time, but I can't.

The calendar has rolled over the last picture of birds on the wall in my hospital room, replaced by twelve shots of London town: black and white, parks of green, red telephone boxes, cobblestone streets. Jolly Old. You once told me you'd like to go. So I wonder, as I've done so often over this holiday season, is the universe talking back? Are those voices that aren't there telling me something, like Burty suggested they might?

While I sat across from Nurse Cameron and gazed out the café window at the glistening sidewalk outside, I recalled Christmases past in white surrounds with only paper-thin rain boots to conceal my frostbitten toes, and I thought about my big brother. About the times in the cold north, huddled against each other. Oscar's selflessness the only thing keeping me warm. As the years flew by in my head, I inevitably turned to you, Dane, and how I was sitting in the very same café you first managed to break me.

It was the first time in the weeks we'd known each other that I got you.

'You're born, you live, and you die,' you said as you stared out the window. The waitress brought our food: sloppy French toast for you, which I hadn't yet taken to, and scrambled eggs for me. 'Everyone's life is scripted the same, isn't it? We're just floating in the breeze like leaves.'

'Or caught in a drain like a wet plastic bag.'

'Or that … Can I tell you something?' you asked, to which I nodded, and realized that when you speak deeply, or attempt philosophy, you are just delaying expressing yourself or what something really means to you. I think you do it to build the courage to get hurt.

'I'm not sure what I believe in, or if I believe in anything, but the more I get to know you, the more I'm starting to think that something pretty amazing must exist.'

I don't know if you could tell, because I was quite tanned at the time, but I blushed. Later that afternoon we screwed for the first time.

Those days seem a lifetime ago. You seem a lifetime ago.

The café is only a few blocks away, but it's far enough for the towering hospital to be hidden. The walk there had been nothing short of amazing, for no reason other than I was walking down the street in casual clothes to meet a friend, I guess, for breakfast. Nothing about cancer got in my way, just morning sunbeams and streets decorated in holly, wreaths, tinsel and all things Rudolf and Santa. So I breathed in as if it was my first time doing so.

Nurse Cameron ordered a slice of carrot cake and a coffee and I selected French toast with bacon and waffles. Cancer has taken some things, but not my appetite – I still eat like a pig.

I gulped down a glass of water before I refilled and repeated. It's become a pattern to be dehydrated leading up to another bout of chemo, for reasons Dr Simms doesn't know. I piss like a horny tomcat – and so I left for the toilet, wiping my hands on my dress when I returned.

'You, you are looking well.' Nurse Cameron refilled the glass.

'The wig makes a hell of a difference. You wouldn't be saying so if I was wandering around bald. Thank you again.'

'It's no, no trouble.'

The food arrived, and I tore through the toast like a wild dog before the waiter had even put the plate down. Between mouthfuls of ketchup-coated French toast I asked: 'Then can you do something else as well?' I burped. 'I just need something little, I'll give you the money, but if you could get it that'd be amazing. I haven't been able to find it in the hospital stores.'

In his bumbling, barely coherent stammer, Nurse Cameron agreed.

'So I was thinking, that maybe, maybe you'd like to g–g–go home soon,' he said as we exited the café.

'A sleepover or to stay?'

'It, it would be your, your choice.'

'What does Dr Simms think?'

He nodded. 'If the tests come back, show improvement, yes, then I think, I think it will be fine.'

'But I thought I needed someone there?'

'I would be there.'

'You don't have to. I'm fine in the hospital. Actually to be honest,' and I was being honest as I thought of Burty, 'I think I'd rather stay in the hospital for the time being.'

He made a noise with his tongue, a click–clock and slither.

The day following he came back to me with what I'd asked for. I wrapped it in Frosty the Snowman paper and tied it with the best demented bow I could before Susan called me over and helped me tie a pretty one. The old cow is pretty nice these days, and I'll miss her when she goes home.

Christmas morning I awoke like most mornings after day one of a new chemo cycle, hung-over, punched in the pussy and cotton mouthed. The dreams I had on Christmas Eve involved nothing of a Grinch, just a big muscular dick wrapped in Santa pants. I think I climaxed in my sleep at least once, and if not for the I-don't-give-a-fucks that come with chemo-induced moodiness, I'd probably have blushed on waking. You looked ridiculous but sexy in a Santa costume the year we had Christmas in Maine. I still enjoy some of the memories we made together, despite how you ended this. It's a strange feeling to appreciate someone and at the same time feel a jagged spike from them, and be angered for it.

I mumbled 'Merry Christmas' to Susan as she sneaked out the room with her sons. She returned the sentiment merrily, looking special in her red velvet jacket. 'I will be back tomorrow,' she whispered.

From my bedside drawer I took out the present. Burty slept quietly, for him – no snores, snuffs, groans, sleep talk or farts. His florid cheeks drooped as he lay on his side, the glasses usually covering his beady brown eyes placed over the old copy of *Moby Dick*.

'Wake up, Burty, you old fart!' I yelled with all the energy I could muster, now excited by the day.

He didn't stir, so I tried again. 'Burty, time to see Santa!' I shook his shoulder. 'Wake up.'

Lightly I slapped his face. 'Come on, Burty, wake up.' His skin was cold. I lowered my ear to his mouth. The silence was sickening.

I felt my face scrunch. I threw the book at him. It bounced off his cheek and fell to the floor with its wrapping torn.

I shook him harder, like a rag doll, and I hit him, over and over and over again. My screams brought nurses into the room.

I fled once they'd removed me from slapping Burty back to life. There's only so long you can beat a dead friend.

Passing the hospital's reception, I caught wind of the tail end of a conversation.

Receptionist: 'Yes, of course, he is in room four-zero-two.'

The woman she spoke to was dressed in a pencil skirt and small black suit jacket, the uniform of a business woman. Her hair was long and flowing, waves upon waves of silky brown, her tanned Reseda skin smooth, her figure tiny; her eyes the brown of rich chocolate. I'd never seen her, but I knew her.

If I die in here, I hope you walk in the hospital doors and discover the same thing as Lily did. Sometimes the universe talks back to us, Dane, and when it does sometimes it just says fuck you.

Kayla

DIARY 16

January 21 1982

It doesn't matter how much I try and warm my feet near the drum, they stay cold. Oscar's too. He doesn't try to warm them, but he paces and curses himself and sometimes hits the wall in frustration. He smashed every plate last time we failed. They were stained and smelled, but they were all we had. Now we need to buy new ones.

We've tried three times to do it, but each time we've been too chicken. We haven't gotten further than Gray Suit's front garden. It's been a relief to run away from the yard each time, I admit. It scares me to face Gray Suit. So I don't know: Do I really want to do this?

'Do you want more kids to get hurt like us, huh, Shorty?'

'No, of course I don't!'

'Don't forget what they done to us – they fucked us, bruised us and they tried to crush us. But we still here and we ain't going to let em get away.'

Oscar keeps me on track. I don't want any more kids to feel the way they made me feel. I don't want their nightmares to be like mine, their beds to be wet when they wake, the dark to scare. None of it. We have to do this.

Oscar's cousin Dee showed up in town from Sacramento a few weeks ago. He helped us get all the things on our list. His head is bald, shaved, and he has a thick black beard. He wears baggy jeans, a white tee and colorful red rags, sometimes. He says they are his colors, but sometimes he can't wear them.

There were street gangs in Minneapolis. I remember the news reports. La Mont didn't have street gangs, only monsters.

'You right to do this, Cuz?' Dee asked Oscar as I lay on my mattress. 'Big move, yo.'

'I'm good, Man. I need the dough.'

Oscar did whatever he had to do for Dee. Dee stayed at home and guarded me – that's how Oscar put it. 'Pfft,' I said back. 'I don't need anyone to guard me.'

When Oscar came home later, his clothes didn't go in the washing pile. He didn't know I was awake.

Dee has money to give Oscar. We need the money. Cough it up, Dee, and then go back to Sacramento.

DIARY 17

March 14 1982

I've been having the same nightmare. I'm walking with Oscar, or someone who I think is Oscar – I never see him and I never remember his voice. We walk through a long tunnel. If I look back there is daylight where we came from and if I look ahead I can see the other side of daylight. Ahead of us is something. At first I only feel it. At first I don't know what it is. As we move further through the tunnel I become more anxious. Eventually something appears in the shadows. We stop and it stares at us. It looks like a rat, but it's not. It twitches its nose and dust flies through the tunnel, and I sneeze. When I open my eyes the rat is gone, and so is Oscar. I'm not alone, though, something is behind me. It bears down on me, and is about to swallow me. Just before I turn to see it, I wake up.

One night I woke to breeze blowing the torn white lace curtains in my room. I'd had the nightmare. I got up and sneaked into Oscar's room. 'Ozzy, are you awake?'

He didn't answer, so I crawled under the sheet with him. He grunted and woke. 'Wha what ya doing, Shorty?'

'I had a nightmare. Do you mind if I sleep in here tonight?'

'That's cool.' He rolled over to the wall, and shook himself comfortable. I was wide awake. I nestled into as much of his ginormous body as I could. He was warm. His muscles grow bigger by the day. With all the push-ups and pull-ups and sit-ups and whatever-ups he does, he is growing into a man.

I wrapped my arms around his tummy and felt his muscles. He had fallen back asleep. I felt his arms, his back and his hair, which I had trimmed the other day to a smaller afro. Then I slid my hand down to his dick. I wrapped my hand around it and started to play.

'Holy shit!' He woke, flipped around and sat up. 'What the hell you doing, Kay-Kay?!'

'I was just ... I wanted to make you happy, for looking after me.'

He got off the bed and lit a candle. His face looked as if he had seen a ghost. He sat on the end of the bed.

'Shorty, we gotta talk. What you was going to do - that's something you do with a boyfriend or girlfriend. You is like my little sister.'

'But I thought you'd like me to? I thought men want that and need that to be happy?'

'Look, you is growing into a pretty woman, but that is something I don't want you doing to anyone, for a long time. That sick fuck might have said that's what friends do, but it's not. Friends hug, friends look after each other, but they never makes the other do something they don't wants.'

'But ...'

'No, you don't want that with me. Never feel like you have to do that for me, or for anyone. One day you'll find a man that loves you, not like a sister or a friend, but something more, and only then do you do anything like that. You got it?'

I felt embarrassed. But then we lay down and he turned to cuddle me. His dick wasn't hard or pressed into me and his hips were well away. I felt safe, I felt at home, and I think I started to understand what he meant.

* * *

Dee went home some weeks ago. He gave Oscar the money he owed him, which was a lot, and he left Oscar with a bag of something that he said will help him 'make that cash.'

I wasn't meant to hear this, or see this, but I've grown sneaky and I need to know what is going on with Oscar. As much as he thinks he is the protector, I want to protect him, too.

I'm not stupid. I know Oscar sells drugs. We need money, so I understand. Still, I don't like it. I don't like to worry about my big brother.

DIARY 18

May 22 1982

I can't sleep for more than an hour. When I wake it is like there has been pounds of soreness added to my head. I can stay in bed for ten hours and still feel tired. It's been a week. I still feel sick and when I look in the mirror I can't figure out whether I am proud or ashamed, happy or sad, or nothing.

It was a scorching hot day. I'd never felt the sun so hot. Night fell and the temperature was still high. Crickets chirped as we crept along the hedges in the street in Westwood Highlands.

At Number 12 we crossed the road and checked for onlookers. It was a nice street where people have a lot of money: away from the city with lots of trees and two-story houses.

I felt the same freeze-on-the-spot fear of each failed attempt, but Oscar marched on into the yard and around the side gate before he stopped and summoned me.

With shaky legs I slid my feet up the front path, backpack attached, under the rusted archway and up the front step. I waited ten seconds and then knocked.

My jaw was trembling when he opened the door and I stuttered: 'I'm sorry ... to bother you ... but I'm lost.'

'Well,' he said, 'where you tryna go?'

'My aunt's. She lives somewhere around here.'

Oscar slid through the window and crept up behind Gray Suit.

'Maybe you'd like to come inside.' He smiled, the way Mr Ignatius used to smile at me before he made me suck his dick or spread my legs. 'You can use my telephone.'

He turned and Oscar smothered his mouth with a chloroform-soaked rag. Gray Suit struggled for a moment, but Oscar is so damn big now, he easily overpowered the bald creep. I closed the door and handed the bag to Oscar. Gray Suit's knees buckled and we carried his unconscious body to a kitchen chair. We gagged him and bound his arms, legs and body so much that he looked like a mummy, so tight his hands turned purple.

His curtains were already drawn. From the backpack I withdrew the long knife and handed it to Oscar. At first he did nothing.

'What are you waiting for?' I asked.

'He's bound so fucking tight he gonna lose his hands and feet. I wanna wait until he is awake, so he can feel every single second of pain. He killed ...' Oscar stopped and gulped.

Gray Suit was the one who killed Oscar's brother.

We waited, and didn't say a word the whole time.

Eventually, Gray Suit woke, groggy and disoriented. His eyes flared with shock, and then fear, and he started to mumble 'Please'. Oscar held the knife in front of Gray Suit's eyes and allowed the yellow light of the dining room to shimmy off the blade.

'You gonna die, you sick fuck; this is your last night on earth.'

Oscar ripped open Gray Suit's shirt and ran the blade along his skin. I shivered, and felt myself smirk. Last time I saw Gray Suit he struck Oscar over the head and made sure Mr Ignatius got me back.

I followed the blade with my eyes until, 'Stop, please, I'll give you anything. Take it all – my money, everything.'

The gag had come loose from Gray Suit's mouth.

Oscar stopped. 'You don't even recognize us, do you?'

He shook his head.

'Look harder.'

Gray Suit's jaw dropped to catch flies. 'It's you ...'

I moved in front of him and stood by Oscar. I felt fifty feet tall. 'Nice to meet you,' I said, thinking, *My name's Karma, Bitch.*

'You ain't got nothing to bargain with.' Oscar started to replace the gag. 'We're gonna track down the rest of you and do the same. It's only a matter of time. This is life biting back.'

'Wait, wait! I can tell you where they are and where she is. Just have mercy on me.'

Oscar paused.

'Top drawer. Bedroom at the end of the hall upstairs. There's a black address book. It has all their names, addresses and phone numbers. They are in a special section.'

I hurried from the room and retrieved the address book. On the way back I noticed how his stairs creaked. The third, fourth and eighth.

'Turn to the back under P, and look for professionals.' His voice quaked. 'The home where she lives is in there, too.'

Oscar flipped through the book. 'He ain't lying.' He turned to Gray Suit. 'Okay, we gonna spare you; it's your lucky day. But let me check something first.'

I heard Oscar on the phone. His voice started out full of hope, but then it dropped. When the receiver clicked, I knew what had happened.

He didn't say a word when he approached Gray Suit, but the fire reignited in his eyes said it all. He replaced the gag, and Gray Suit tried to scream.

Together we ripped off his pants. Oscar cut away his underwear. We've both seen pervert's dicks too many times to be scared of them.

Oscar pulled up Gray Suit's cock, and laid out his balls on the wooden chair as if it was a chopping board.

Oscar sawed through the skin that attached his scrotum to his body.

Gray Suit screamed.

As the blood splattered, I broke from a trance and wrapped my hands around Gray Suit's throat. We hadn't thought this part through. Just chloroform, tie up, gag, chop off their nuts and let them bleed to death. Who'd figured they'd scream?

Oscar shoved the knife into his stomach. His eyes became lifeless as I choked him with every last ounce of anger. When I let go, his head flopped limply onto his shoulder. On the floor his detached testicles lay in a massive, spreading pile of blood.

'Come on, Shorty, let's get the hell outta here.'

On the way out the side door I looked back at Gray Suit, sitting dead on his kitchen chair, surrounded by a red pond. I never knew humans had so much blood.

He was there, and then he was gone. We had made something go away. He is never going to hurt another kid again.

On the way through the back streets toward home, Oscar said only one thing. 'She's dead.'

* * *

In the days that have passed since we became murderers, I've scrubbed my hands and clothes, but blood is by the far the hardest thing to wash away, even after all the color has gone.

I've felt like crap. But yesterday morning things started to look up.

'Hey, Kay-Kay.' Oscar stood at my bedroom door.

'I got you something.' He came and sat beside me. 'Got it cheap down at the thrift shop.'

He handed me the paintbrush set and I clutched it to my chest. 'Thank you, Ozzy.' He started to get up, but I pulled him back down. 'I'm sorry about your mom.'

'It doesn't matter. She was already gone a long time ago. Now I'm just sure we gotta do this.'

I could hear the tears he sucked back behind his words. I wrapped my arms around him and he leaned his head on mine. He's right: there's no turning back now.

Oscar stood and walked to the door. 'Hey, Shorty.' He smiled and held up his hand and pinkie-clapped. I pinkie-clapped three times in return.

It was the first time I didn't need the help of my other hand.

CHAPTER 13

The festive season was as I needed it to be: quiet and inconspicuous. Not at all festive. On Christmas morning I left presents for Kerry and Simone without a note and broke a rare smile when Simone brought me up a pudding in the afternoon. New Year's was seen out in the pub. I was surrounded by happy people, and women falling everywhere, but I felt alone. There was only one girl who crossed my mind.

I wondered if Kayla was still in Los Angeles, and if she was where she'd gone for Christmas dinner, which parades she'd watched and which cove she'd seen the fireworks from. I wondered if she was still alone, or if she'd found someone else, or if she had buried herself in her art, and what these paintings would look like. I wondered what she'd look like, too: had she dyed her hair, had she cut it? I wondered if she thought of me each day like I did her, and more than anything I wondered what she thought about me.

My tasks in the Union increased and night shift became part of my routine, but by mid-January I was still well short of the cash I needed.

'You're keen, Mate.' Kerry appeared in the ring of light. 'I offered you the nights off.'

I hugged the crate and moved it onto a pallet. 'Need the cash.'

'I know, but you've worked nearly every graveyard since New Year's. Have a rest tonight.'

The sun was peeping up between where the water meets the skyline. I looked at my watch. 'Well, it's the morning now.'

'Shit. Six. Time flies, hey. Go on, knock off now. I'll finish moving this stuff.'

'Mate, you should be knocking off. You've got your girl to go home to. I'm just trying to get back to mine.'

'Well, maybe that's what I'm saying. Knock off, and go back to America.'

I moved and dropped another crate onto the pallet. 'Kerry I don't have the bloody ...' I stopped as I turned to him.

'Cash?' he said with a smirk, holding out an envelope.

'What are you doing?'

'You need money and I've got it. Consider it a belated Christmas bonus.'

He handed me the envelope. I opened it and flicked through the bundle of notes. 'It's five grand.'

'I'm aware.' Kerry chuckled. 'I believe that's how much it costs.'

'Kerry, I don't know how to ...'

'Save the lovey-dovey shit, Mate. Now knock off and get some sleep. Marty is expecting you when he opens at nine.'

* * *

I'd worked sixteen hours straight every day for the last week but I couldn't sleep when I got back to my room. By eight o'clock I couldn't lie around any longer and went to the bakery for a coffee and pie. Bailey smirked and winked at me when I took the baked goods. I left in a hurry.

On the step to Marty Slick's Pawn Shop, I sat, ate my pie, sipped my coffee and waited for Marty. Each time I checked my watch, I had to wait to see the minute hand move. Time dragged.

A high-pitched laugh made me jump. 'First time anyone's been waiting for me,' said Marty Slick. 'Come on you poor transient.'

He opened the door and let me in.

Once inside he turned on the lights and locked the front door. 'So you've got the money?'

I withdrew the envelope from my pocket. Marty took it, counted the cash and then smiled. 'Excellent. Follow me.'

We went into the back of the shop, past an office filled with mounds of paper and scrunched chocolate-bar wrappers, and entered a dark room. It looked almost like a workshop. In the corner were two large money-printing machines, and on a wooden bench in the middle of the room was a row of printers and computers. Marty put his keys down on the bench, waddled over to the front wall and pulled down a white screen.

'Stand on the feet marks.' He moved behind the tripod. 'Big smile for me, Cutie.'

I stood in position and he adjusted the camera height. 'Nice face, but no smile.' He snapped three photos and then peered at them with one eye. 'Excellent; all done. It'll be about a week. A pleasure doing business with you.' Marty held out his hand and I was about to shake it when he pulled it back and turned to the door. He waddled over and placed his ear on the door. 'I'll be back in a moment,' he said. 'Someone doesn't realise I ain't open.' He laughed. 'Silly dicks can't read a sign. Hold on.'

Through a thin gap in the doorway I saw him in the shop. 'Not open yet,' he yelled. 'Come back in half an hour.'

A loud bang sounded and the front door flew open. 'Go, go, go!'

Cops flooded the shop and threw Marty to the ground.

The back door was locked. I shoved and shoved against it but it was too solid. I glanced around the room in search of something to break a window.

'Where's the gear?' a cop yelled.

Marty squeaked. 'I don't know.'

'Don't bullshit us. You're going down for fraud.'

The police were tearing through the shop and moving closer to the back room. On the bench I noticed a cricket bat. Perfect. When I picked it up something fell to the floor. Marty's keys.

The second key I tried opened the back door. I slinked out into the alley and began to power walk away.

'Don't move!'

At the other end of the alley was a cop with his weapon drawn. My mother's voice echoed: 'Run!'

The policeman yelled for me to stop as I sprinted out of the alley. I crossed Shakespeare Grove, sucking in air.

In O'Donnell Gardens I hid behind a tree. The policeman appeared from the alley and stopped. He surveyed the street and stopped passers-by to ask if they'd seen me. One shook his head and the other shrugged. The policeman nodded, and spoke into his radio.

I sneaked between trees and onto the Esplanade, and then remained inconspicuous all the way back to the Espy.

As I climbed the stairs and unlocked my room door I realised what had happened. Sitting on the side of my bed, I looked out the window to the beach and put my head in my hands. Tears welled below my eye. But before they could break free the toilet in my bathroom flushed. I looked up and the door opened.

Gary Whitman appeared in the doorway. 'Quite a morning, hey Chief.'

'What are you doing in here, Gary?'

He wiped his hands together, walked to the door and locked it. 'You've got a problem, Dane. I'm here to help you.' He stood at the end of my bed. From his coat he removed a bundle of papers and tossed them onto the bed next to me.

They were photos. Josh and Kerry exchanging packages. Ollie, Salem, Trent loading a crate of guns. There were old photos, too. Josh and Stevie, and me, when I still sported a glam rock mullet. We were handling bags of H and cash stacks, all of us smiling from ear to ear.

My heartbeat sped and rose into my throat.

'You're ...'

'Still Senior Detective Gary Whitman of the AFP.'

CHAPTER 14

'The rooms are all empty and upstairs is closed for maintenance.' Gary Whitman perched on the windowsill, his favourite spot.

The telephone in my room was unhooked. An hour or so had passed since I'd found out.

The Union, Melbourne's most clandestine and organised crime syndicate, had been under surveillance for a decade. Some had sold out already. Some would soon. Gary had been undercover from the start, and had built a monumental case against everyone. He'd been onto me as soon as I got back, and knew almost everything: my deportation, my re-joining the Union, and trying to attain a false passport.

He shuffled through documents and photos. 'As you can see, you have some pretty serious problems, Chief, with serious consequences. The good news is I can help make those problems disappear.'

'What do you want?'

'We've got you all — trafficking, money laundering, small-time distribution — but you know better than most that they're good at keeping themselves hidden. There is something I need that will make this concrete. We need the Asian link — your brother and McCulloch. We get them and we can get the suppliers.

'The Yanks have been after the Golden Triangle for years. Khun Sa supplies over sixty per cent of the world's heroin and he's offered his empire in exchange for hundreds of millions. Exportation would be stopped overnight. But that's not happening, and it's just enraged the Yanks even more.

'We need to know how it comes in, and how it goes out. We need to catch them in the act.'

'This is Melbourne, Gary, not LA, New York or Paris.' I was desperate. 'How can we possibly provide them with a link if they can't get one themselves? We were making bucks but we were small time compared to the States and Europe.'

'*Were*, Chief, *were*. Your brother.' He shook his head. 'Your brother has turned Melbourne into one of the most profitable markets for H in the world.

'It goes for triple in our streets what it does in Harlem or Compton, and the mullet junkies around our back streets have the shit on a drip. Add in poorly guarded waters and a shorter distance from the Triangle and there's a hell of a lot less risk with much more profit ...

'I have intel' that there is a shipment coming in early to mid-February that is the largest in Australian history. High-level Asian associates will be present and we need to catch Josh with them. What we need from you is the specifics of the deal – how, when and where. We need to bury the Union, and we need your help.'

'What if I don't want to help?'

'That's your choice. You can honour men who would kill you in a second and you'll spend the next decade in Pentridge dodging bikies' cocks in the shower for it.'

'Shit.' I rubbed my eyes. 'And what happens if I help you?'

'Firstly, I make sure you don't end up in a cell like your brother.'

'Can't you spare Josh and just take down McCulloch?'

'Sorry, Chief, Josh is one of the biggest players. He's going away for a long time.'

'I can't rat him out,' I stuttered, my mouth desert-dry. 'He's the only family I have left.'

'He isn't the same person he was when you left. He's something far more dangerous. How's he treated you since you've been back?'

'You don't know what happened. He's treating me how I'd expect.'

Gary stood. 'How you'd expect? He's acting like a bloody five-year-old. I know what happened, and I know you've tried, and still he's not moving on. You don't owe him anything, Dane, but you owe Kayla something.'

My head throbbed with confusion. 'What do you mean?'

'The other problem you have is that you are here, and potentially in danger after you help us. I will make sure you are safe and you can go back to your girl. You get the info I want and you get an authentic American passport and flights to LA.'

I closed my eyes. Kayla's face appeared, lying next to me in bed, her skin softer than the silk sheets.

'But I can't ...' I said to myself as much as to Gary.

'It's funny when you think about it ... I'm sure you feel bad for leaving, but isn't it the best decision you've made? If you'd never left you would never have met Kayla.

'It's simple, Dane: a brother who hates you or the girl who loves you.'

I brought my head from my hands. 'An authentic passport?'

'Clinton himself will have grazed his eyes over your ugly mug. Do we have a deal?'

He held out his hand.

I reached out and shook it.

LETTER 8

January 18 1994

Dane,

Before 1993 ended, another man had disappeared from my life. The morning of the 28th was the first time since admission I'd returned to the apartment. Nurse Cameron collected my mail from the PO Box for me. Just bills. He waited at the kitchen table with a black undrunk coffee under his chin, evaporating via silky steam. I managed to pull together a half-suitable black dress and cardigan for the funeral, and I stole your Wayfarers to hide behind. Thanks for leaving them.

The grass was lush and speckled with beads of morning dew. In the corner of the sea of tombstones a small crowd of black suits and dresses clustered around the grave. It was a pine casket from Ibis with a white floral arrangement on top. I pictured Burty inside: his eyes closed, hands clasped respectfully and cheeks still florid. 'That's his body,' I told myself, 'and who gives a fuck about a body when it comes to death? If there is anything more, then something far deeper than flesh and bone will float freely in their open-plain ranch.'

Across from me, Geoff and Margaret Romanowski stood, and sandwiched in between them was Lily, her face concealed in a black-netted veil.

The reverend read aloud in a strained monotone from Revelation 7:15–17 and finished with Matthew 5:4 – *Blessed are those who mourn, for they shall be comforted.*

I was unmoved, and hated myself for it, as like dominoes the small congregation shed tears from beneath their choice of mask. Even Margaret Romanowski let a solemn, lonely tear fall into a waiting tissue by her cheek. Crying at funerals is contagious, so why at this moment, when the sobbing crowd was invited to shovel dirt and place any last goodbyes onto the lowering Bill Burton, did I not break? Your Wayfarers hid me well, but I was dry as a nun.

I approached the casket at the same time as Geoff, Margaret on his arm. He caught me glance as he offered Burty something final, a bottle of old scotch they'd probably shared years before all of this shit.

When they backed away I tossed the unread copy of *Moby Dick* onto the casket. I scooped a handful of dirt and sprinkled it down over the shiny book.

I hadn't seen Lily cry, but then she came forward and lifted her veil. Her makeup ran black rivers down to her chin. She threw to her departed father a collection of pictures, and letters. I saw what real regret looks like.

It wasn't until I was away from the grave with Nurse Cameron at my heel that I let anything out. Under an oak tree tiny cracks began to open. Nurse Cameron must have seen the tears not even your oversized Wayfarers could hide, because he came forward and reached out his arms. It's not his fault that I don't like hugs. I fended him away with a push.

He stumbled back and fell to the grass then scampered to his feet and mumbled 'Sorry.' I slid down the trunk until my butt hit the dewy grass.

At first I wanted to disappear. And then I wanted the world around me to disappear. Everything except that oak tree and the grass. Every last person: the Lilys, the Geoffs, the Margarets, the Nurse Camerons, the Dr Simms, the Susans, the receptionists, the building supers, the shopkeepers, the friendly lady from Apartment 16 who tried to talk to me when I saw her. Everyone. And when the world had disappeared I wanted all of you assholes who have gone to come back.

I bawled until my eyes hurt from rubbing. I don't think there is any water left in my body. I've held back grieving you, but Burty brought on the monsoon. He was the last good thing I had.

You ran away. You broke my fucking heart, Dane, and now that old fool has taken the deformed bit that was left. I should have learned a long time ago that you all leave.

DIARY 19

August 1 1982

It was sad to leave behind our house and San Francisco. From our street I took one last stroll down to the beach that morning. We'll always find our way back to the shore, but I hope the sand and the water make me feel as fresh on other beaches.

At the pier I stopped, looked to the distant house on the cliff and wished we could fast-forward to when we've finished, and all the monsters have gone.

I wish we could be in that house right now and live in peace with no anger or sadness ...

'Is something, isn't it?'

I was startled by a short old lady walking her cat. Its brown and white swirls were like the foam of hot cocoa. It was Mrs Albertson.

'What is?' I asked.

'The house.' She pointed to the cliff in the distance. 'I heard a lot of things about it. Would you believe no one lives there? A beautiful house like that, towering over the most perfect ocean views.'

'What have you heard about it?'

She picked up the cat and cradled her. I petted its head and it purred.

'I'm not sure it's right for you to hear; you're so young and sweet. Not the type of thing for a child's ear. How old are you?'

'I'm fourteen. It's fine. You'd be surprised what kids see these days.'

She nodded. 'Yes, this generation ...

'Well, there's been more death and pain in that house than most of San Francisco. Let's just say people don't want to live there anymore.'

'So no one lives there?'

'Been on sale for as long as I know. Only things there are a whole lot of ghosts.' She squinted at me. 'Where do you live, Child?'

'I'm from out of town, just here for the day. I better go, actually. Nice talking.' I petted the cat, and left Mrs Albertson, the shoreline, the house and San Francisco behind.

* * *

Mountains were the first thing I noticed about Utah. Mountains and lakes. That's Salt Lake City.

Dee came and went in the first week. He left another big bag of crack. Oscar has sneaked out every night to sell on street corners downtown.

I followed him once. I figure if I can follow him and catch him selling drugs, how easy is it for anyone else? I told him this after I crept up and surprised him on the corner. He was mad at me for following him, and from his cocoa skin I could see a red flush of embarrassment.

'I hate you doing it,' I said as he came in that night.

He ignored me, and locked himself in his room and cried. His sobs were muffled – the ones you want no one to hear. But when you really listen for tears, you can hear them.

When he came out some time in the hours normal people sleep, I rose and caught him in the kitchen and hugged him so tight I thought I could actually hurt him.

'I know why you're doing it, and I love you for it. Thank you.'

'I love you too, Shorty.'

Oscar started to his room. I picked up a broken piece of crockery and tossed it at him. He turned and I pinkie-clapped. He grinned and clapped back.

The bag gets smaller each day he goes out, and soon there'll be none left. I suppose Dee will be back.

The crack money pays rent and feeds us. Our apartment is on the eighth floor of a never-ending stairwell. The elevator smells like urine, the carpet in the hallways looks like urine and the stickiness of the door handle feels like urine. It's pissy and shitty, crammed and boring, and everything else beautiful about public housing. Our neighbors are clients of Oscar's. There's always yelling, swearing, fights from all around us: above, below and both sides. Oscar fixed two extra locks soon after we moved in. Funnily enough, I feel safe here. Not much outside a small circle of beasts in my mind scares me after what we did, and what we are soon to do.

Checker Suit lives at 32 Mountainside Drive.

It's Rob-something. Robinson. Roberts. Robolo.

One by one we'll work through the names, city by city, and we'll finish them all. Mr Ignatius is back in La Mont. The only time I'll go back to that hell hole is to carve him up.

DIARY 20

November 22 1982

We're on another bus. Our next stop is Portland.

I used to think I had superpowers. First I was dumb enough to think I could go unseen by people while I slinked around a giant igloo. Now I think that invisibility is more about the person who is looking. I also thought I was Golden Girl, the girl who could stop all the bad things happening. But I know that's just crap, because bad things make evil people happy.

After Oscar finished selling the bag, Dee arrived with another.

I tried to earn money for us, so Oscar wouldn't have to. Art. Not the shit we were made to do in school. I drew pictures and made sculptures with whatever I could find. They were images I'd kept in my mind for a long time.

'Dark,' said Oscar, looking at the charcoal drawing on paper, which I stole from the craft store. 'Real dark, Shorty.'

I tried selling in the street. There were occasions when people enjoyed the works, but mostly they sneered. There was a Monet exhibition in town during our stay. Monet doesn't paint like me. It wasn't very good timing. I made fifty bucks from fifteen different pictures in Salt Lake City.

Oscar hides his crack money in a jar labeled **'Sweetness inside'**. It makes me laugh.

Checker Suit's house was perched on a mountainside. From his back porch I could see the snow-capped tops of Wasatch all the way down to the city and the enormous Great Salt Lake.

Inside, the house was beautiful: marble floors, polished-oak bench tops, high ceilings, hand-crafted furniture, huge windows hung with turn-of-the-century English blinds and Persian rugs.

We waited for him inside.

I was behind the sofa, and Oscar was ready to attack from behind the front door.

Checker Suit lumbered in and stretched out his huge arms. His brick head nearly hit the door frame. When he placed his car keys on the kitchen bench, Oscar was only a few feet behind him with the chloroform rag. He lunged and tried to smother the creep's mouth, but he must have caught Oscar from the corner of his eye.

Checker Suit grabbed Oscar's arm and it began.

'You fucking dirty nigger!' Checker Suit growled as he shoved Oscar back. 'What do you want? My money? You ain't getting a sniff of it ya dirty coon!'

'I want your fucking nuts,' Oscar said, and back-pedaled near the sofa where I hid.

Checker Suit stopped. 'Wait. I know you ...'

'Yeah, you do.' Oscar took from his belt the long knife. 'Judgment day, Bitch, God's talking.' He swung the knife, but Checker Suit slid back and avoided the slashes.

He chuckled. It made me think of the devil. 'God don't have a voice here, you sniffling bastard.'

Gray Suit had been easy. I'd felt so big. But I was scared in Checker Suit's house. He came back at Oscar and they crashed through the coffee table and knocked over a bookcase. They punched and kicked and head-butted each other. There was biting and gouging, and blood spilled across the room.

Checker Suit got on top of Oscar and cocked his fist. He clobbered Oscar in the face. He hit him again, and again, and again, until Oscar no longer fought back.

I don't remember picking up the wooden horse.

I swung it down on the back of Checker Suit's head with every bit of strength I had.

He howled and then rolled off Oscar. He wasn't knocked out. Instead, he stood, and glared at me. He lurched at me. I backed away and dropped the horse.

'Well. Hello.' He licked his lips. 'What's this tasty little slut? This could turn out all right. The nigger's dead and I've got something to play with. I'm gonna tear your asshole, Cutie Pie.'

I was up against the curtains. A little girl gasped for air. I believed she'd gone after we killed Gray Suit. I thought I no longer feared these monsters. I was wrong.

Checker Suit grabbed me by the neck. I trembled. He smelled like sweat and bourbon.

'This is going to feel good.'

It was the last thing he said before his eyes turned to glass.

He dropped. Oscar rushed on top of Checker Suit and beat him over the head again and again.

'Go into the kitchen, Shorty. Don't look,' he told me, but I couldn't help peeping. Oscar took the long knife and sliced his throat. With the smaller blade he carved out the words 'Kid Fucker' on Checker Suit's torso. Blood streamed out of him. The letters were sharp and jagged as if carved in wood.

Oscar sighed and dropped his head when he'd finished. I scampered back to the pantry and rummaged for food.

'He's done,' said Oscar.

'Ozzy, come here.'

'What?'

I handed him the cookie jar labeled '**So Sweet**' and his face lit up. We were thousands of dollars richer.

Bleach worked well for the blood stains this time, though after drying on the concrete in fading sun my clothes turned to cardboard. At least it's clean cardboard.

There was a headline in the newspaper.

Man Found Mutilated in Home

'The scene was a mess — one of the worst I've ever seen.'

This was how Senior Detective Royce Johnson described the discovery of a body in the city's outskirts early Monday morning.

Paul Martin Roberton was found dead in his home when a friend stopped by to check on him. Mr Roberton had not been into work or answered phone calls for three days. The friend, who wishes to remain anonymous, described Mr Roberton as honorable, caring and reliable.

'He was an upstanding member of the community. It just doesn't make sense for someone to do this,' they said.

Detectives believe the perpetrator may have been known to Mr Roberton …

It went on about how good a person he was, but left out the truth, which was carved on his body.

CHAPTER 15

Rather than partying with the crew, I stayed in my room on Australia Day Eve. In the morning I rose early.

For twenty bucks I rented a '74 Ford Falcon convertible. The gears were rigid, the clutch sticky and it smelled of damp clothes, but it was perfect. It was ruby red with white-rimmed tyres and an engine that hummed.

I drove out of the city, west onto open roads that were surrounded by a dried yellow expanse. There was not a cloud in the sky. Rich sunshine heated the leather seats like it was a passenger right beside me.

A cloud of dust followed me as the car kicked up stones on the dirt road. An old white ute passed. In the tray sat two boys, who laughed and tossed rocks at moving trees.

I counted one after another the rusted tin letterboxes every few hundred metres. Another car passed, an EH Holden station wagon complete with blue racing stripes and surfboards on the roof rack. Teenage boys were crammed inside – some older, some younger. The sound of *Khe Sanh* shot out the window as it passed.

This time I didn't look back. I knew the car was long gone.

At the Kaman's maroon letterbox my heart started to beat like a scared animal's.

The next letterbox was a rusted shell with barely a lick of its former green. It clung to the post by a loose nail. No letters were inside.

Trees still lined the driveway, but instead of thousands of tiny lush green leaves there were only frail dead branches, which diverged like the capillaries of a bloodshot eye. As the driveway curved right, the house appeared.

I parked and stood on dry dusty ground in front of the house I'd grown up in.

Broken windows, and paint crusted and peeled off the parched weatherboards like a dead fish drying in the sun. It was a carcass, gutted and decayed. The yellow grass sprawled as far I could see, blades raised no less than a metre high. A bright bob of yellow peeked out from the straw desert.

The second step to the veranda collapsed under my weight. Much of the veranda had rotted. I followed the line of nails fixing beams to joists. The front door was open, the screen door hung by one hinge, oblique to the doorframe, the flywire screen curled over and no longer joined.

Behind me the screen door clapped against the doorframe. In the kitchen the linoleum's white tile pattern was barely visible beneath the dirt, dust and broken glass. The table and chairs were in the same position we'd left them.

Outlines of pooled blood seemed to rise from below the grit, one to the right where Mum had been lying with a twisted neck and lacerated skull, the other where Dad had fallen to a knife wound and been human for a moment.

The floorboards in the hallway creaked. I pushed open the bathroom door, which had been hollowed by termites. On the inside, I felt the key still shoved in the lock. It wasn't there for privacy. Mum had kept it there for when she'd try to hide from him.

In the living room, tiny speckles of dull glass remained on the ground near the crumbled and faded bricks. The shadow was still there where the television had been, and I could see the glow of light from night-time sitcoms flood the room. Laughter spilled out as *Hey Hey It's Saturday* played on the screen.

The room Josh and I had shared for fifteen years was covered with cobwebs. Our beds lay there, the sheets mouldy and coated in dust.

* * *

Two childish ghosts remained awake long after their bedtime, while the rest of the house kept still to the whistle of wind across the plains outside.

'Shut up and tell me,' hissed Josh as he turned in bed. 'I told you.'

'So? I don't have to do everything you co.'

'Don't be stupid, Dane. Now you're going to tell Cindy I like her; I know you are. You have to tell me who you like.'

'All right, but you can't say a word.'
'I won't tell anyone.'
'It's Kelly Brown.'
Josh giggled. 'Smelly Kelly?!'
'She doesn't smell, you butthead.'

* * *

Suddenly the air became thick. I fled down the hallway and out through the screen door and sucked in oxygen like a fat man forced to run. On the edge of the veranda I sat, legs hanging off as I'd done when I was a child waiting for Dad to come home with groceries.

Dust clouded the driveway. A jet-black four-wheel-drive with dark windows parked at an angle to mine, so that even if I'd wanted to run, I couldn't have. It was pleasing to be trapped there. Josh climbed from the driver's seat, eyes covered by shades.

He shut the door and sauntered over. Some moments passed without speaking. Josh did not meet my eyes.

Eventually, he removed his sunglasses and looked at me. 'It's been a while.'

'What is it, eleven years now?' I asked. 'Time goes fast.'

He forced air out of his nostrils. 'Yeah, flies.'

'They were so happy on their anniversary. Like we were a true family. I could've sworn he loved her at some point.'

'He did,' said Josh. 'But people change. It's true – leopards can't change their spots. But we're humans, not leopards.'

Josh stepped over the dirt as if the azaleas still sprouted from it, lifted himself onto the veranda and sat beside me. 'You know, it's funny. I followed you here.'

I pointed to a patch of dirt near the blue gum. 'You remember playing cricket on the mowed pitch out there? Anything hit past the wattle tree was six on the full, four on the ground, and if you hit the house without getting scolded you got an extra wicket.'

Josh smiled. 'I remember you couldn't play my off cutters to save yourself.'

'Pull the other one. You threw the ball down the pitch like a rainbow, Mate, bloody toffees. You remember the games when everyone played?'

'Yeah. All of us, ay.'

'Stevie couldn't bowl a ball on the pitch, but goddamn that prick was impossible to get out, and Kerry was the left-handed master, swear he could've played for Australia with his goofy stance and swing. And Mum, she gave it a good crack didn't she?'

We both laughed. Nerves that had built now poured from our throats. 'Too right she did. Old girl had a mean bouncer!'

I thought of Mum in her gardening clothes, as she took a break to throw down some swinging, high-bouncing balls, warning *'Don't underestimate your mum, Boys.'*

'And bloody Dad; remember the shit he'd toss up?' Josh imitated Dad's crappy bowling action. 'He told it like a legend but that was as far as it went. Old prick went for six most balls. Think Mum got sick of playing just because she had to field when he bowled.'

Dad. My stomach dropped. Our laughter flattened.

It was Josh who broke the deadlock. 'Do you hate him?'

I'd thought about it occasionally, if at any time he had found his way to the forefront of my mind when my guard was down. 'No.'

Josh turned to me.

'I don't think so. I mean, if I think about him, yeah I wish he was alive just so I could beat him to death myself. Maybe I do hate him. But something I've come to realise is that hate is something that affects those who harbour it more than those it's directed at.

'If I hated him then I'd be hanging onto anger that he created inside me. If I let go of the anger, I can let go of him and he can no longer hurt me. Just like if I still love Mum, and I still love Stevie, they are still a part of me, and I can be happy with what we shared, not so sad at what I lost.'

'I've never really thought about it like that. For most parts I've just blocked it out until late at night.'

We slid off the veranda and walked toward the ocean of overgrown yellow grass. 'It always survived even in the most drought-riddled summers,' I said. The bright bob of yellow shone from the paddock. We parted dry elbow-high blades with our arms and legs.

'It was a resilient bush,' said Josh.

'Tree, actually.'

'Shut up, Dickhead.'

We ploughed through the straw and made a path the way a mower does. The internal compass led the way.

'You know you look about ten years older than me with your head shaved,' I said. 'I know you've got a tough-guy reputation to live up to, but surely it doesn't fare too well with the ladies.

'Listen, Kurt Cobain, I go just fine with the women. You, on the other hand, you're old news. Unless you can play guitar your look is passé. You might as well start sporting a mullet again.'

'Mullet?' I fended off a rogue blade of grass. 'You were the only mullet bearer in this family.'

'I had a curly afro, not a mullet. That pathetic style belonged to you and Stevie on the odd occasion he had a girlfriend and found no need to look at all decent.'

'Better than Kerry – *he* still has one.'

'Doesn't matter how he trims it: crew, shaved, ponytail, undercut, he'll always have that goddamn ginger mullet.'

Like children, we broke into a guffaw that scared the cockatoos from a neighbouring blue gum. Josh stepped ahead and up over a rock. I knew it well. It was the point to which the safety net extended.

We emerged in the small circular opening. The wattle stood in full bloom.

Josh picked a yellow ball from a branch. 'Can't believe this is still here.'

'Seems like most of what we left is still here.'

'Yeah, you can say that.' He knew I wasn't talking about possessions.

We walked around the tree. I was caught up in the big old wattle, running my hands over the flowers. Josh stopped in front of me. 'Looks like there's something new, too.'

A small wattle had sprouted, only as high as my hips.

Josh looked back over the paddocks. 'Wait here.'

He ran through the path we'd created and then returned with a shovel. 'Was still in the tool shed.'

I grinned and nodded. I knew exactly what he was thinking.

In the shade of the large wattle – the hope of our childhood – with sweat on our foreheads, we dug up the new tree. Its roots extended some metres out. We swapped the shovel every minute or so and relived fond memories. There was no pain from the world outside: no fallout, no betrayal, no hatred, and no tear in the fabric of our brotherhood.

Together we picked up the tree by the roots, and trekked back through the makeshift path. We left the ocean of straw with the only beautiful possession on the property. We bundled the wattle into the back of Josh's four-wheel-drive, its branches reaching over the flattened back seats all the way to the centre console.

I leaned against the side of Josh's car. He joined me, took out a smoke from his pocket and sparked a lighter into his cupped hands. He inhaled a deep drag and blew smoke upward like a chimney.

'I've thought about coming here for as long as I can remember.'

'This is the first time you've been back here, too, isn't it?'

Josh nodded and then pointed to the top of the old wattle peeking out from the straw. 'I always wanted to jump on it and fly away into the sunset, you know, because the wattle was also a magic broomstick.'

'I thought about using it as a jetpack most nights when I couldn't sleep. I'd look out the window and then consider which outfit would be best to fly through the night sky in, and maybe enter space on the wattle rocket.'

'Kids, huh … Hey, I'm sorry that Marty Slick got pinched. I know he was getting you a passport. Good bloke – weird, but good. Did a lot for us. We're going to bail him out, but they've set it at a hundred grand, so it might take a couple of weeks to get the funds. I spoke to him and he's promised the first thing he'll do when he's free is your passport.'

'Thanks.' I dropped my head. 'I really appreciate it.'

'You really love her don't you? It's why you stayed. Why you've done everything since you've been back … Kerry filled me in.'

'Yeah.' I was lost for words. I didn't want to think about everything that lay before me.

We remained silent for some time.

Josh stood straight and opened the passenger door. 'There's something else I came to do. I'm glad I'm not here doing it by myself.'

He brought out a grey plastic case. With Mum, we'd found a beautiful plaque at St Kilda cemetery, and with Stevie …

I didn't know what had been done with Stevie's ashes.

But I knew what was in this case, or rather, who was. Much more Hyde than Jekyll.

'We never knew what to do with him,' Josh said. 'We never really talked about it, did we? I only ever came to one conclusion.'

And then, without hesitation, I did something I would always do when my younger-by-four-minutes brother became anxious or worried as a child.

Josh didn't move when I put my arm around his shoulder. For a moment I was a brother worthy of the name.

From his boot he passed me a can. Josh held the case like a stack of fine china plates, and I cradled the fuel can as we approached the house. He led me up the steps, and through the frail screen door.

In the living room, Josh placed the case of our father's ashes on his chair.

I poured the petrol around the house. The screen door clapped three times before coming to rest. On the bottom of the steps I shook the last drop of petrol from the canister. Josh bent down to the trickle of heady, transparent purple and sparked the lighter. Flames shot along the wooden beams, through the front doorway and into the house.

On the dusty ground we settled ourselves and watched the inferno build.

There are few things I've seen as beautiful and depressing as that fire. Screams screeched from the crumbling wood as shackled ghosts burned, feeling every lick of orange.

Josh finally spoke. 'Burn in hell, Monster.'

'Burn painfully,' I said. 'And rest in heaven, Dad.'

'Rest peacefully,' Josh said.

Fire crackled and beam by beam the house fell to the ground. We stayed there until there was just a chimney. A slither of smoke rose high into the blue sky, and closed off that ugly chapter of our lives.

CHAPTER 16

I rose in the afternoon and dressed for my last graveyard shift, which came with January's close. An agitated knock sounded at the door. I opened it and Gary Whitman burst past me.

'We need to talk, Chief.' He paced, his hands corseting his slender waist. 'More accurately, you need to talk.'

'Gary, relax. Sit down.'

He turned and pointed at me as if his finger was a dagger. 'You need to cough up something, right now, Sonny. I'm hearing things from everywhere except you, the man who is central to it all.'

'For chrissake, Gary, sit down and then we'll talk.'

After he paced back and forth twice more, grinding his teeth all the while, he finally leaned on the windowsill. From his pocket he withdrew a half-crushed cigarette and gripped it between his shaky lips. He held the smoke and relit, and then sucked on it like an asthmatic on a puffer.

'What can I tell you?' I said. 'I haven't got anything major yet. I've told you everything I've got wind of.'

'I got whispers things are moving, and I know you're back in with Josh. I'm not stupid, Chief.'

'I'm on better terms with Josh, yes, but I haven't got anything yet.'

Gary butted out his cigarette on the windowsill and resumed pacing. The floorboards groaned. 'So say I believe you and you know nothing, you better get moving in on your brother like he's a skirt, if you want what I can give you.'

He stopped pacing.

'The documents are signed off. Passport is ready, but you don't get squat unless you get me what we agreed on. You want to see

Bright Eyes again don't you? Better get back there or else she'll go find another dick ...'

In an instant I had Senior Detective Gary Whitman of the AFP pinned against the cracked plaster wall. 'You say another word about Kayla and I'll rip your fucking throat out, you dirty pig.' The words escaped through the gaps between my teeth.

He laughed like a madman. I pushed his collar to his throat and forced him to wheeze between fits of laughter. And then I realised and released him; if Gary's cracks had become visible, so had mine.

'You've been in this undercover business too damn long. You're starting to lose your bloody mind. Seems like you've got too much at stake.'

'Maybe, but you've got more to lose, Chief. Don't forget what's on the line. It's my career, but it's your life. Think about that.'

* * *

That night I crossed the boardwalk toward Berth C and then knocked at the office door. Josh called from inside to enter.

'You wanted to see me?' I asked as I closed the door.

It was the first time I had been inside the site office since the days Keith Phillips used it as an occasional brothel. It was cleaner now. A water cooler sat in the corner, a kettle by the sink and in the middle of the room Josh's desk, neat and organised. He sat behind his computer and I sat opposite.

'You're not dumb, Brother, even if you try your best sometimes,' he started. 'I think you know why. You've worked well, and reminded me how damn good you are. This haul. It's big – maybe the biggest. I want you to help run it.'

I nodded and tried to hide it when I gulped a rather large, and growing, ball in my throat. 'I'm in.'

'Good, well, listen carefully.' He handed me an A4 envelope. I reached inside and removed the documents. Josh explained as I read. It was encoded, but every last detail of what was going to happen was there. I had the information I needed.

* * *

In the week that followed I worked during the day and, when I wasn't in the bar considering things over a beer, I lay on my bed and clutched the documents, every so often glancing to the phone. One call to Gary Whitman and my passport was stamped, but I held onto hope for a resolution that didn't involve selling out my brother. Marty Slick might still get me what I needed.

It was a Friday night when the phone rang.

I rolled over and picked up the receiver. 'Hello?'

'It's Kerry. Have you got a moment?'

'Yeah, sure.'

'I've got some bad news. Marty Slick got taken out today. Fucking pigs put him out in the yard with those animals in Pentridge. The Princes of Hades knew he was associated with us and took revenge. I'm sorry.'

I didn't answer.

'I can ask around for other sources, but it might be hard – industry is thin.'

'Ta.'

'I'll leave you be. Don't give up, Mate.'

Soon after I hung up the phone, I trudged downstairs to the bar. I needed to drink away the knowledge of the hope I'd just lost.

The crowd clustered, drinks flowed and the band played rock hits from the previous decade, along with classics and new anthems. Six drinks later, the alcohol in my system caught me unaware when I stood. 'I'm fine,' I thought. '*Oh wow, I feel ... good, I think ... Since when did the floor slope to the left in here?*'

Out the front, scantily clad women and clusters of hopeful men climbed the steps and entered the bar. I drew in a deep breath of fresh air. With the taste of hops on my tongue, I'd dumbed myself down enough to no longer think. I followed the pretty girls back inside.

I felt jovial as I wandered through the sardined bar, smiling, and bopping to the music. It was all so good; I was open, free.

∗ ∗ ∗

When I awoke my head felt as if it were pressed between a vice. The room was stuffy but I felt too shit to reach the window. I groaned and discovered that the sheets moved without me.

The smell of flowery perfume seeped into my nostrils. Beside me, with her back turned, lay a woman with blonde locks covering half of her spine, her back arched and buttocks just visible under the thin white cotton sheet.

She turned and opened her eyes. 'Good morning,' she said.

As I looked at Bailey, bare breasted, the night before returned to me in as much entirety as it needed to. A chance meeting at the bar – fate as Bailey, out for her nineteenth birthday, would tell me – a drink, another drink, stupid dancing, stupid flirtation, stupidity at its finest. Her lips, how they pressed on mine, sweetened by the taste of liquor, the feel of her smooth skin beneath my hands, her body and sweat against mine, how she felt inside, how she tasted. Everything came back to me ...

Still naked, I sprang from the bed and ran to the bathroom. Until now I'd only vomited the morning after once in my life, and that time was as much to do with a suspect chicken kebab.

'You did yourself proud,' she said when I emerged from the bathroom.

I hmmed. 'Something like that.'

Bailey stuck around for I don't know how long.

When I was younger and still stupid, which seemed the present, any amount of time a girl stayed for after sex was too long. Kayla's eyes were the first and only pair I wanted to fall asleep and wake up to. She made me hate the cool feel of empty sheets, and treasure company in bed, not just sex.

'Life's a funny old thing,' Bailey said as she dressed. 'I thought I'd see you again.'

'You find what you need,' I said, unenthused. 'When you need it.'

'So, there's every chance I'll see you again.' She winked. 'When I need it.'

I couldn't look at her anymore. 'There's every chance you won't, too. That's life.'

She giggled to herself, kissed me on the forehead and left the room.

It took me a long time to move from the bed.

I once heard that guilt is the toothache of the soul. In that stuffy hotel room, naked in every way, I had the worst toothache of my life. For every careless, idiotic thing I had done, this was the worst. I'd dealt drugs since I was sixteen. At eighteen I'd broken a man's shins with a baseball bat because he tried to undercut Keith Phillips. I'd run from my problems and abandoned my brother. That all paled in comparison while I sat on that stinky, poorly sprung mattress.

I'd followed my dick like a common slob who'd never stared into the eyes of something greater than any part of this confusing, fucked-up life.

Kayla would have killed me if she had been there in the moment. I don't think I'd have resisted, either, if not for the urge to make things right.

I put my head in my hands and left it there. I'd spat on the one truly beautiful thing I had in this ugly word. I was weak and worthless.

Broken.

I picked up the telephone and dialled his number.

'Gary speaking.'

'You want Asia; you want the Union; you want Josh? I've got your information.'

'I knew you'd come through, Chief.'

'Just organise my passport, and get me the hell out of here.'

LETTER 9

February 3 1994

Dane,

I lasted only another few days in hospital. Despite Dr Simms's advice, I couldn't be there.

'Kayla,' he started. 'I know you were close with Bill, and that you are hurting right now, but I can't recommend that you go home.'

'Why not? Cameron will help care for me.'

'Yes, I know. But the tests came back. Things haven't improved. In fact, the tumor on your thigh has grown.'

Maybe I'm scared, or maybe I just don't care, but I know if I'm going to go, I want to go in comfort, not in that sterilized hell-hole.

I still miss you — that I can't lie about — but I'm okay. I used to consider how doleful life would be without you, and thought I needed you here for me to be happy, but I don't. Aside from needing to self-gratify, there's not much else I need you here for. I climbed the kitchen bench to bring down the candy jar, I had Nurse Cameron refill it, and with the aches that quite often permeate my joints, there is no issue bending my arm enough to scrub my back in the shower. Life just carries on.

Susan was not in bed the morning I visited. Burty's bed was empty. Maureen's replacement, a lady named Caroline Clements, was in her bed. She was unconscious and fogged an oxygen mask.

Sickness and suffering are horses on a carousel. It doesn't stop when someone dies. Standing in my former room, I wished I could've torn apart that carousel, or at least gotten off. I fell into the trap of asking why – why do we have to suffer?

It's ironic, Dane, that the older I grow and the more I know, the less I really understand.

I left the hospital with a reminder from Dr Simms that I was making the wrong decision for my health. He urged me to reconsider my treatment plan to the point he uttered the word reckless. I'd love to see the old Wisconsin clod try to force me back into a gown.

That was over a week ago, and since then I haven't ventured outside the apartment. One thing I thought I wanted to do when I got back was surf. Use the board I bought you, remember it? But I haven't. It's something for the future when I've got my hair back, or at least a wave-proof wig.

I follow Nurse Cameron's instructions, and for once am not running around of my own free accord. This is painfully difficult. Almost as much as the cancer.

'Just sit, sit and rest, rest please, please Kayla,' he stutters as I pace the living room, my thigh and insides aching, sometimes with the dusty board under my arm and a bikini hanging from my body. Dammit I miss my boobs, nearly as much as your dick.

'It's a hundred degrees out there, how am I meant to stay and rest?' I say, still pacing. 'I'll go crazy before I die, but this way I'll take any comers with me – be warned, Cameron.'

He gets anxious when I talk like this – I don't think he gets my sense of humor yet. It took you more than a few threats and shin kicks to get it.

Chemo at home's just like chemo at hospital. I get injected with the poisonous crap, sit like a brain-dead slob for an hour or so, vomit and repeat. Day 8 always comes quickly after the first of a new cycle. Nearly as soon as my genitalia is no longer a pink balloon I'm back at it and ready to inflate all over again.

There's something different, though, and I can't pinpoint it.

If I let the worried part of my mind take over, I begin to think that my body is writing its letter of resignation. I'm glad I'm home, Dane, but I've been tired, very tired, and even if Old Strep Throat let me out into the waves, I doubt whether I'd go, and if I did, I think the first half foot of swell would take me under and keep me there.

It's the pain. He gives me more meds to combat it. They're prescribed, he says, and will help me get through it.

'Okay, okay, relax now Kayla. Just be still,' he says after the pain makes me groan.

'I'm a fucking statue, Cameron, now just inject!'

After this it's kind of like a snake slithering through my veins, dripping venom as it goes that turns into sugar.

He adjusts something and I feel less pain. I don't feel better, just different. It's the different feeling that makes me worry. It is soothing, but scary. I expect pain, but not to float. I feel free, but I know I'm still chained to a chair.

Last time after I'd come back to the living room with coffee-stained carpet – another reminder of you – the shelves had been cleared of the pictures of you and me.

'Where has everything gone?' I asked in a chemo-drunk slur.

'I cleared the apartment. Re-remember you said you, you wanted a fresh start.' Nurse Cameron sat at the kitchen table, no steam coming from the coffee under his chin. He was right, I did say that, but I didn't expect to feel so empty … How is he the only person I have left?

'You're still here.'

He gazed across. 'Yes, I was waiting, waiting until you were, were awake. I didn't want to leave you here, when you weren't.'

I stood and passed him. I thought to reheat the coffee and make him drink it, or pour it on his head. You might have been a whiny bitch and needed milk like a newborn baby, Dane, but at least you drank your coffee.

'You like having a decorative drink with you, don't you?'

He didn't get it and just fiddled with his hand without response.

It was dark outside and regardless of the many traits that might make me a horrible person, I actually have some tolerance for very small sections of the human race, stupid as it is.

'It's late, dark, and there are probably wolves outside, so if you're okay sleeping on a sofa bed out here then you're welcome to stay.'

It was like watching a retard froth at the mouth when Mr Whippy jingles down the street. He stuttered and stumbled and his hands trembled with excitement.

I locked the bedroom door, the first time it's been used as anything other than to keep you in there. I don't believe he's stupid enough to think anything could ever happen, but he is a man.

That was the first night Nurse Cameron stayed. I don't need him here, but it's nice to have someone to look out for me. And when I become tired with every injection, I float off into another world, weakened, it's good to know there's someone on earth to make sure I land safe.

'G–g–goodnight, Kayla,' he said, tucking into the blankets on the sofa.

'Goodnight.'

'It is, your birthday next week, yes, isn't it?'

It is, and to think I'd forgotten Valentine's Day.

Kayla

DIARY 21

February 24 1983

Portland is a wonderful city, so far. This apartment is quiet, like the house in San Francisco. Wind gusts through the trees in the front courtyard, and each night I lie here and let it sing me to sleep.

In the morning I wake to see the paper boy toss rolled-up missiles from his basket to the doorstep targets, and to wave hello to the milkman when he brings fresh bottles just after seven.

Our building in Goose Hollow backs onto Washington City Park. When I climb the stairwell up to the roof, I can see the rolling heights of West Hills on one side and the banks of the Willamette to the other.

I might forget about why we are here for a while.

The headlines we left in Salt Lake City have crept north. On a stopover in Boise, I found another:

Salt Lake Murder Link

Investigators believe the murder of a man last month in Salt Lake City, Utah, may be linked to his involvement in a child pornography ring.

The search for a killer began after Paul Martin Roberton was found murdered in his Salt Lake residence in late November. Detectives from the Homicide Squad called in the FBI when video tapes containing child pornography, both homemade and purchased, were discovered by police while searching his home.

No witnesses or suspects have emerged in the murder case.

It was only a matter of time before our work drew some attention. Murders happen every day in this country, as do rapes, bashings, fraud, molestation, lottery winners and cats stuck in trees. It's not as common for wealthy, well-to-do pedophiles to have their balls chopped off, and their dirty secret carved into their chest.

I like to think we're faceless, but I worry about the attention. A tall Negro with a little white girl, who if I imagine hard enough in the mirror, could pass as cheer captain. I hope we don't stand out.

Sometimes I think about what my life could be like if I hadn't been born into the family I was, if I was just a regular fifteen-year-old girl. I see the school kids from the local high school in the street. Sometimes it makes me sad to think about what I'm missing, and sometimes I get sad to think about how much I wouldn't fit in.

People are a dime a dozen.

If there is a hell I might go there for what I've done, and what I'm going to do, but I try to think that I'm special because I'm trying to make the world a better place.

DIARY 22

April 30 1983

Dee collected money and left more crack for Oscar to sell.

We don't need the money, not with the cash we got from Checker Suit's cookie jar, and everything Oscar's already made from dealing. But Oscar still hovers on the street most nights and sells. I found him unconscious in the stairwell Sunday morning.

He wouldn't tell me exactly what happened. 'Rival dealers. They got me, all four of them whooped me. That's it, Shorty, now drop it!'

'Drop it! Your eyes are blacked, one's fully closed and I found you unconscious ... and you want me to drop it?! We've got enough money already, Oscar; just stop before you get in too deep. Before you *really* get hurt.'

Oscar stayed silent for a moment. 'It ain't that simple.'

'You're my big brother. Without you, I have nothing. It is that simple.'

He hugged me. 'I'll be fine. I just gotta be more alert, right.'

I couldn't say anything. He didn't yell. I think he thinks he has to do this, like eating, but he doesn't.

He rested all week, and I loved having him here when the sun went down. I loved playing Snakes and Ladders, Celebrity Heads and all sorts of games. I loved his company on walks at dusk. I loved how we were just Shorty and Ozzy. For some crazier moments, I even thought he might stop it altogether.

Then the next night, I had the marker and sticky notes ready, and had written Cher on his, when he skulked from his room dressed in black, and slid on his puffy coat and beanie.

'Where are you going, Ozzy?'

He looked at me as if still trying to be invisible and sneak out. He's six-foot-six.

'Out.'

'Yeah, I got that. You're going to sell.'

'I gotta.'

I turned away from him and scrunched up the notes. 'If you don't come home, I'll kill you myself.'

He snickered. 'You're much scarier than gangbangers, Shorty. Trust me, I'd never do you wrong.'

I turned back, and his smile caught me.

'I'll be home later,' he said.

'You better be.'

At sunrise he still wasn't home. I didn't care about money. I just wanted my big brother.

DIARY 23

August 2 1983

Serial Killer Asks Questions

The FBI has recently confirmed a link between three killings. The most recent occurred here in Portland a week ago when a father of two was found in his basement. Circumstances have led detectives to declare a serial killer is at work.

Markings on the Portland victim are consistent with the other two murders. The Bureau confirmed on Friday that the victims are linked to child pornography and what they believe to be a nationwide ring.

The killer, dubbed the Castrator, has escalated in violence and method of execution. Detective Dom Victors described the scene at the most recent homicide: 'After fifteen years in this position it still shocked me.'

The public response to the murders has been varied, with some people claiming these killings are not a simple case of murder, but rather a justified act of revenge, while others insist that taking a life is never right.

These murders have raised moral questions for many. Child molesters being murdered. Is there a time when the light shines differently?

I'm confused. I'm a serial killer, but I tell myself I'm the good guy. We've got a reason, don't we? But doesn't every killer? I think we're right. But it's becoming harder to tell.

∗ ∗ ∗

Black Suit was hard.

We did it last Tuesday, when Mrs Black Suit had gone to have her nails painted, when the kids were at school and the neighborhood was as quiet as distant traffic of the highway.

We crept into the backyard while it was still dark, and hid. Shortly after sunrise Black Suit and his wife sat on the porch and ate breakfast together. We lay on our backs and gazed up through the gaps in the wooden deck.

'Yes, I think I'll go with the pink you like today,' said Mrs Black Suit as her cutlery clinked against the plate.

'You treat me well,' replied Black Suit. 'I can't wait to see them.'

They kissed. 'I treat you as you deserve.'

Little James and Julie rumbled down the staircase. The children jumped on their father, one on each leg, and he bounced them up and down and sang songs. He listened to their stories about animals that weren't real and the adventures they had in their imaginations.

'You're okay to pick them up this afternoon, right?' asked Mrs Black Suit from somewhere.

'Of course. Wouldn't miss it for the world.'

He lied. He had no choice.

'Okay, Kids,' their mother called, 'time to go to school.'

I heard the pucker of kisses and began to feel sick as I thought of what approached.

We waited beneath the porch. Black Suit went inside. Some muffled conversation, the front door opened and closed, a car started and pulled away and then silence. It was time.

Oscar started to shuffle out first, and I followed. Crouching beside one another we waited ... the front door opened and closed.

Swiftly, Oscar climbed onto the porch and skulked to the kitchen window. He stood up to peer over the sill and then relaxed and stood up fully. 'He's gone out. That was him leaving.'

I relaxed. 'So what do we do; can we risk waiting around here?'

'We go inside. He'll be back soon, we know he's home every second Tuesday.'

My skin crawled, and the gurgle in my stomach rose as we sneaked into Black Suit's house. I followed like I was still a stupid little girl doing whatever she's told.

Oscar inspected the house while I stood like a statue near the back door. A car parked in the driveway and its ignition cut.

'Come on, Shorty.' Oscar summoned me from the hallway entrance. 'We gotta hide.'

I didn't move.

He turned back and hissed, 'Kayla!'

I didn't move.

As Black Suit turned the front-door key, Oscar took me by the wrist and pulled me into the den, stuffed me behind the door, and stood in front of me, waiting like a cat about to pounce.

In the crack between the door and frame, Black Suit flashed past. Oscar signaled for me to follow. This time I did. Peering around the corner, I saw Black Suit disappear into a bedroom and return with a set of keys. He walked to the end of the hall, opened a door and pulled the cord to a light, which lit up the top of a basement staircase. Oscar withdrew chloroform from the backpack and went to follow. I took hold of his arm as Black Suit disappeared down the stairs.

'Ozzy,' I said, glancing to the family photographs on the wall. 'I don't know if I can do this.'

A loud sliding noise came from the basement.

'Kay-Kay, we have to.'

'But he has a family. Imagine how scared his wife will be when she comes home and finds her husband ... And his kids, what will their lives be like, knowing their father was cut up and left to bleed dry?'

Oscar clenched his jaws and dropped his eyes momentarily before he looked at me. 'He was the one.'

I was still holding his wrist. 'What do you mean?'

'He was the one that used to tie me down ... he has a taste for little black boys. Says he loves the niggers.'

This punched the wind right out of my stomach.

Footsteps came from the basement and up the stairs. We swept back behind the den doors. Black Suit moseyed down the hall, into the kitchen and emerged in the hallway a minute later with a plate of food. He strode down the stairs into the basement.

'I'm sorry for them kids, and his wife, but I gotta do this. It ain't always gonna be easy but it's always right.'

I followed Oscar down into the basement. It was lit by a low-watt yellow bulb. We didn't make a noise – we've gotten good at being silent.

The basement was normal – stacked boxes and old furniture - aside from two things.

Black Suit was not in the basement. And, at the far end of the room where a bookshelf had been partially pulled out, a door was visible in the shadows. Side by side we slinked toward it.

Oscar leaned over me. I could see through the slither of the open door into the room.

Light flickered from a video player. Black Suit crossed the beam of vision with the tray of food. He crouched and held out the tray.

'It's time to eat, Eric,' he said. A small African-American boy, no older than five, crawled toward him, took the tray, and disappeared, as did Black Suit.

I glanced up at Oscar. He looked insane. I ducked out from under him and stepped back.

'Are you enjoying the food, Eric? You look very pretty today.'

It was the last thing Black Suit ever said.

Oscar burst in the room the way I imagine a hurricane would burst through the doors of a house. A video of Eric and Black Suit played on the television. Black Suit turned and noticed Oscar. The pervert looked like a deer just before a car hits it.

Oscar punched Black Suit three times, and before he could drop to the floor, had him by the scruff of the collar. He slammed him head first into the television and cracked the glass. Blood ran down Black Suit's forehead like sweat.

Oscar turned to me. 'Take the kid and close the door!'

Little Eric was against the wall, hugging his knees tight to his body, on his dirty, cum-stained, single bed with an inch-thin mattress and cuffs and ropes on each corner of the metal four-post frame.

I held out my hand. 'Come on, Eric. It's okay. I'm not going to hurt you. We are here to save you. I promise.' I said it in what I hoped was a motherly voice.

He held my hand. I picked him up, took him outside and closed the door. We walked slowly up the stairs.

'Who are you?' Eric asked in a squeak.

Crunches, slashes and whimpers sounded. I closed the basement door quickly. I thought back to when it was me trapped in a shitty room. 'I'm just someone who is here to save you.'

I put him down. He was tiny. The top of his head was in line with my boobs. 'Are you going to take me back to my mommy?'

'I hope so. No matter what, Eric, it is going to be okay ...'

We waited in the living room. My eyes switched between the abused child next to me and the loved ones in the photo frame.

When Oscar emerged from the basement he was dressed in fresh clothes from the backpack.

'Let's go.' He hurried past us.

'What are we going to do about Eric?' I asked, standing up from the sofa, Eric's tiny hand in mine.

Oscar stopped at the front door. He looked back at Eric, and then came into the living room. He kneeled in front of Eric and put his hands on his shoulders.

'You've met the devil. But you haven't met God yet. I promise you, though, He does exist, and He will find you.'

Eric reached for Oscar. 'Will you take me back to my mommy?'

Oscar's eyes welled. He opened his mouth to speak, but then gulped and picked up the tiny boy. He walked to the door with Eric in his arms. 'We'll take him with us. Figure it out later.'

We returned to our apartment in Goose Hollow. I cleaned Eric up and gave him a pair of my shorts and a tee to dress in.

When we were done, Eric sat with Oscar on the sofa. I stood in the archway and watched them, feeling warm inside. Proud. Eric ate SpaghettiOs and smiled at Oscar's animal impersonations. After Eric finished, Oscar took away his bowl and wiped his mouth. They talked and laughed and played games.

Oscar came over. 'He told me where he lives. Not the address, but I know the neighborhood. We take him there, and he'll know his house ... we just gotta be careful.'

I felt sad for a moment. I enjoyed playing family. 'Okay. We just need to make sure he's safe.'

Oscar put his hands on my shoulders. 'Won't leave 'til we see his momma. You stay here. I'm going to get something.'

Eric and I watched *Looney Tunes* while Oscar was out. He came back about an hour later with plastic bags and a set of keys.

'Here ya go, Lil Homie.' Oscar emptied the bags onto the sofa.

He'd bought Eric a hoodie, new tiny jeans and sneakers. Oscar dressed him and then tossed me the keys. 'It's a white Ford pickup. Parked across the street. We'll be down in a moment.'

'You got a car?'

'Bout time. We need it.'

I waited in the car for Oscar and Eric. When they came out of the building hand in hand, they looked like brothers.

I slid across the bench seats and Oscar helped Eric into the middle. He glanced up. I wondered if I ever looked like he did.

Oscar closed the door and started up the car.

For the entire journey Eric was still, until we turned into a street in Alameda. At a double-story brick house, Eric kneeled up on the seat, his eyes glued to the house. Oscar braked. 'Is that your home?'

Eric nodded.

Reversing, Oscar parked two houses back. 'You home, Eric. Go on.'

I opened the door. Eric crawled across me and I held his hand as he climbed down from the car.

As he ran up the sidewalk and through his front garden, we began to drive away. Eric reached high for the doorbell.

Moments later a large African-American woman answered the door.

She picked him up and clutched him to her shoulder as tears streamed down her face. Eric hung on.

'That's her,' I said.

Oscar planted his foot and we burned away.

CHAPTER 17

There was only one other car in the lot when I ripped the handbrake of the beaten-up wagon. Too early. It always was, at the docks. Too early for the coffee to kick in. Too early for good conversation.

Before Peter Harvey had shuffled his papers that evening I would be in a cell *or* on my way back to America.

It really was too early to look my twin brother in the eye, while I still hung for his forgiveness, and betray him all over again. *Too fucking early.*

I slammed the car door shut at the same time Josh stepped down from his four-wheel-drive, shades masking his eyes. He removed the sunglasses and wore a smile. 'Too early, isn't it? Least it ain't so cold today. Proper summer morning.'

'Yeah, least it's warm.'

'How you doing?'

'As good as I've been,' I said. 'I guess.'

He bounced on the spot, more spritely than I'd seen him since he sported a dirty glam-rock mullet.

'Yep, too damn early.' Josh laughed and truthfully I almost did too. 'Only about one thing in the world that it's not too early for.' He turned and motioned for me to follow. He opened the boot of his car. 'Come on, Man. Let's ditch work. We don't need to be here. Besides, I am the boss.'

Laid out in his boot through to the backseat were two boards. One was pink and blue with a peace sign near its tail fin, the other pearl-white with candy stripes at its bow. One was Josh's board and the other was mine – the board I'd left behind. These two boards, simple fibreglass and plastic, were us: two brothers, two animals of the sea.

A wave of new beginnings crashed over me. For a time everything disappeared. 'Since you're the boss.'

'Come on, Brother, we've got surfing to do.'

* * *

It could have been a decade before. The car was newer, not so charismatic, and some soldiers were missing, but our old mix of eighties Aussie rock – Cold Chisel, Hunters and Collectors, The Angels, Crowded House – was enough to make me believe that everything was going to work out okay. We were teenage boys again, cruising freeways, hope in our hearts for the surf to be ripe, because this was all there was to think about.

Josh turned the volume down on *Cool World*. 'Hey, you remember the speeches at Stevie's twenty-first?'

'Wasn't a dry eye in the house,' I said. 'Everyone choked themselves with laughter. Geez, Kerry really put it on him. Told the world about Stevie's little drag indiscretion, the run in with a bouncer after he stole a bar mat when he was pissed on his first night out as legal. The one about him and Gina.'

Josh grinned. 'Kerry really did do him over.'

'Stevie got him back, though. I don't think you remember that one as well.'

'One of the few nights I drank more than I could handle.'

I patted his thigh teasingly. 'Don't worry about it, Mate – not everyone can handle the piss. Doesn't matter how big and heavy your head is, you're still a lightweight.'

'Shut up, ya moron. I've seen you in the same state about a hundred times. Least I didn't make it a weekly thing.'

'Touché. The bottle did the best of me more than a few times.'

Joy dropped from his expression. He took his eyes from the road. 'Least you never let the bottle change who you were, never led you to hurt anyone.'

It gripped like barbed wire around my throat. But I wouldn't let a defunct ghost we'd set to rest in flames affect this time. 'Maybe a bin here or there.'

Sniggering, the gleam returned to Josh's face. 'Had a thing for knocking bins over didn't you? Why was that?'

'I dunno. Just a jerk I guess.'

'That's true.'

The indicator ticked and Josh steered into the car park at Bells Beach, the slice of heaven where I'd learned to carve, shred and cut through waves and discovered the freedom of the surf. Upgrades to the asphalt, a new sign warning not to do something or other, and a new toilet block. Otherwise, everything else was exactly the same.

The waves rolled into the shore, separated in wonderful time, curling crisply to become barrels that an architect could not replicate with the finest tools. The water appeared brighter than sea water should. The often cloggy sand was like fine, soft powder that could run without hassle through a sifter. Sunbeams shone so light and pure they could have been mistaken for false.

We took the boards from the back and Josh handed me the towels and wetsuits. In his free hand he lifted an Esky from the boot. 'Beers and snacks. Going to be a decent session I reckon; could get hungry and no doubt thirsty.'

The water wasn't cold but fresh enough to wake me. We paddled out, and positioned ourselves behind the back set of waves. With not another surfer in sight, I perched on the board opposite Josh. My legs dangled freely on either side of the board, soft sea breeze caressed my hair as if it were a woman's hand, my mind as clear as the blue summer sky. Up until this point, I didn't realise he had something with him.

'I always wondered what you did, or didn't do with him,' I said.

Josh massaged the box. 'Never felt right. Never felt whole, I guess.'

'This is how he'd have wanted it.'

'Do you want to do the honours or should I?'

The water lapped against our boards as building waves passed beneath, *click-clack, click-clack.*

'How about we both do it?'

He nodded.

I paddled beside him and placed a hand under the container. Josh unscrewed the lid. Although I looked down at the grey gritty ash Stevie had been for over seven years, mostly I saw the wonderful man he always was.

As I peered up at Josh, I knew he thought the same thing. *'It was never your fault, Brother. I love you. Thank you.'*

'On the count of three.'

'Three, two, one ...' And together we heaved the container. It happened slowly: for a moment the ashes remained clustered before the ocean breeze picked up Stevie and blew him far and wide across the water in a beautiful cloud of grey.

'He's free now,' Josh said. 'It was never right to keep him cooped up in this container. Fresh air.'

'The freshest I've ever breathed.'

If in passing Stevie had relinquished the weight that had pushed him down, in this moment Josh let go of something that pressed him down. From the horizon he turned to me. 'I forgive you, Brother.'

I reached out, our hands slapped together and we gripped. Then suddenly Josh pulled me in. I held him close, and he buried his head into my shoulder. I wanted to cry as his warm skin pressed against mine.

Nothing else in the world mattered right then. Any problems were left back on dry land.

* * *

Until the morning sets became dull ankle breakers, we surfed, often catching waves together like we did as teenagers. Just as often we perched on our boards and reminisced.

At the point our stomachs groaned loud enough to be heard over the sounds of the sea we paddled back in and set our towels down on the sand. We stuffed our faces with potato chips and sandwiches before all that remained was two bottles of beer.

'So how about it?' Josh held out a stubby. 'Not for old time's sake, for now, the present.'

'Cheers.'

Raw summer sun bathed my skin, leathered by sea salt, as we sipped on suds. The beer was chilled, refreshing and relaxing. Few finer moments come than sharing a beer with your best mate, the first for Josh and me in this lifetime.

'So how are things looking for tomorrow?' I sipped a tiny mouthful, savouring the lone stubby.

Josh burped loudly. 'Yeah, all set. There's only one thing that might change, but it's nothing to worry about. I think everyone's going to come out happy on the other side. They might take it a bit funny when I tell them, but they'll understand and they can make their own decisions from there.'

'Tell them what?'

He wrapped his arms around his legs, dangling the beer bottle between fingers. 'I'm stepping away.'

'You're leaving the Union ...?' My heart paused for a moment. 'You're a captain now; how can you ...'

'They'll take it fine, Man, doesn't affect them. The Union is a sinking ship, and I'm going to get out before I drown.

'We took over this, and built it into something beyond any dropkick-bikie, wannabe Mafia or try-hard Triad could imagine. Built an empire. But I've been feeling what it's like to be on top of the mountain – every man and his dog wants to take you down.'

I didn't know what to say.

'This has been my life for a decade, and you know what I've learned?'

I wanted to say something deep. But I kept my mouth shut, and then Josh said something I'll never forget.

'I learned that if you work hard enough without joy, you'll work yourself out of life … You can spend time and you can spend money. Money you can always get back. Time you never will. So which is more valuable? Cars? A bigger fucking house? More worthless cash to buy more meaningless possessions? Screw that. I've become a number, Man, and I'm bloody tired of it.'

'I suppose it doesn't matter how pretty the v ew is,' I said. 'If there's no one there to share it with, it's just a lonely view of others having fun on the ground.'

'Amen, Brother.'

I thought for a moment. 'I need to tell you something.'

His eyes were tired. They showed the heaviness of his crown.

'Gary Whitman …' I said.

'Yeah. What about him?'

'He is still a cop, an AFP agent.' I sighed and took time to gather the words that were about to come. 'He's been undercover since day one in an investigation to bring down the Union, and most importantly you and McCulloch. After that shit went down at Marty Slick's he came to me and put me in a corner.

'If I give him information on you and the haul, I have a passport back to America. If I don't, he has set me up on trafficking and possession charges.' I stopped and braced for Josh to pummel me into a corpse.

Contrariwise, he gazed out to the embers of the skyline, a peaceful look in his eyes, and smiled. This scared me more.

'I guess you've got a choice to make then.'

'But …' I wanted him to be angry, to scream at me, to punch me in the face.

'But nothing. This doesn't change anything. It took a lot of thought to forgive you, and I'm glad I did. I've done a lot of shitty things in my life. If I go away for something I've done then so be it. I can live with that. But I can't live with creating any more regret. I can ignore any part of me that is peeved you've talked to a fed, but I can't ignore the part of me that is glad to have you back. If me getting done in as the Union disbands means you get to make it back to your girl, I guess that's my way of trying to make up for all the shit. Chalk down one thing in the positive column.'

'But, if I give Gary what he wants you will go away for a long time: not a year, not two or three, but decades.'

He shrugged. 'I hear it's not too bad inside these days, and getting better. I'd sit in my cell knowing I helped you get back to your girl. As long as one day you bring her Down Under to meet me.'

My heart pounded like a techno bass drum. My hand holding the beer tremored.

'Just do what you need to do, and remember this choice isn't about me, you, or even Kayla, it's about life, and righting it as much as possible.'

* * *

Stevie's picture hung above the pine casket, the white of his eyes clean as porcelain, irises the deep blue of fresh hydrangeas come springtime in a dry yellow yard. He smiled from the other side of the glass, the sweet, saddening smile he always wore, like a beautiful necklace that weighed too much and caused his head to dip.

'We are gathered here today …'

Black suits and dresses, veils and sunglasses hiding the sallow faces of grief. So many people cared for Stevie, so many more than would come to my funeral even if people knew I'd departed.

For every word, gentle sob, painful moan and air of silence, tears pressed at my eyes like prisoners pushing walls of confinement. I had clenched my jaw too tight, strengthened the prison bars so nothing could escape. The day before, while I wrote the eulogy the tears had come, but not now at my brother's funeral, and not since.

* * *

Josh leaned over and took me in his arms. Sand lightly grazed my skin and sunlight forced my eyes closed. With my head pressed into his shoulder I doubted I could ever give him up again. And then, in my brother's embrace, I cried.

CHAPTER 18

Gary Whitman's car was parked in the vacant lot. Over the back boundary stood power lines from Richmond station. The brick wall of a neighbouring warehouse was covered in sporadic graffiti. Thinning grass sprouting from the ground resembled the balding scalp of a man; scraps of garbage were strewn throughout.

I parked.

He stepped from the car, leaned against it and sparked a cigarette. In the fading afternoon light the creases n his weathered skin cast dark shadows, a tired, relieved look on his face.

I stuffed the envelope in my coat pocket anc approached. Gary shot out his hand and grinned. 'It's good to see you, Chief. You've made the right choice.'

'Yeah, much of me finds that hard to believe.'

'You're doing the right thing, Dane. Not only for yourself or for me, but for society. You're brother has filled this city with junk. He needs to go away.'

'Have you got the passport and all the other documents?'

Gary became aloof. 'They're at the station, Chief. Right after you give me what I want, we'll head down there and get them.'

I pictured the passport and the Social Security card, and the shock and joy of Kayla's expression as I entered the apartment. And then my twin brother's smile on the beach. Was this the right decision? Could there be such a thing?

I reached into my coat pocket and removed the A4 yellow envelope. 'This is everything you need.'

Gary took the envelope and peeled it open, reached inside and removed the paper. He stared at it, wide-eyed. 'What the hell is this?'

'It's everything you need,' I repeated.

'No, really, what the hell is this?' He held the almost blank paper, marked with only a single sentence.

'Like I said, it's all you need to know. It says, "Fuck you, Pig," in case you can't read.'

His hands shook. 'Is this some kind of joke? Please tell me ...' Gary huffed and looked as if steam was about to pour from his ears. 'Please tell me you are being funny.'

'Did you actually think I was going to give my only surviving family over to you? You can burn in hell, Scumbag. I betrayed Josh once – I am never doing it again.'

From his pocket he withdrew a handgun and pointed it at my head. 'I should shoot you right here. You worthless, good for nothing son of a bitch!'

'Well, what are you waiting for?'

The hammer cocked. For several long seconds Gary pointed the gun with a tremulous hold. I waited for the bang and smell of gunpowder, the array of images to flash through my mind. If this was it, I'd leave this life proud.

'Turn around and get on your knees.' The cuffs wrapped around my wrists and brought a sense of déjà vu. Although I knew I faced years behind bars, this time was much more pleasant than the last. Like Josh, I would smile in my cell each day knowing I'd repaid him, and in some small way become the man Stevie had been.

From his car Gary withdrew a roll of silver duct tape. He pushed me face-first into the dusty ground and then bound my feet.

'Don't give two pairs of cuffs to undercover pigs, hey?'

A sharp sting splintered the back of my skull and blood trickled down my neck like sweat. I became tired. The graffiti on the wall of the warehouse blurred to white and then returned, blurred and returned.

The next thing I knew I was in the back seat of Gary Whitman's car, head tilting side to side like an out-of-rhythm pendulum. The raw rev of the old block motor sounded like a chainsaw inside my skull.

He planted his foot, and my head crashed against the headrest. My face slid over the slimy, bloody vinyl. A deep calm flowed through my body and my eyes closed. Stones crunched and curses rang shrilly, but I was elsewhere. I felt like I was dozing off on the sofa to the nightly news with Kayla, still privy to Dan Rather's soothing voice.

My father, the monster. My mother, the beautiful martyr. My brothers, strong, sure willed, engraved as a part of me. My baby, Kayla, the most beautiful woman I'd ever come to know. How warm she felt. Then Stevie's car, the EH wagon with blue racing stripes and surfboards on the roof rack. Josh's black four-wheel-drive.

That black four-wheel-drive pulling up to our childhood house, cruising down the highway to Bells Beach. That black four-wheel-drive, coming toward me …

Tyres screeched, glass shattered, metal crunched, screams.

Burning petrol stung my sinuses. Warmth came from flames lapping at the car's rear. Slumped forward on the steering wheel, unconscious, with blood streaming from his forehead was Gary Whitman, a glassy look in the one beady eye I could see, his jaw limp.

The door opened. I felt a hand slap my face. 'Dane, wake up. I've got ya.'

Josh unbuckled my seat belt and carried me to his car, the front now banged up, bull bar detached on one side. In the backseat he lay me down and placed a blanket under my head.

Inside, the car was cool and quiet. Light waves of soothing air seeped from the vents. The pain in the back of my head throbbed.

Josh disappeared and in the next blink he was undoing the handcuffs. 'Stay with me, Man. It's going to be all right.' The car doors shut and he started the engine.

Saliva dripped over my bottom lip, blood seeped from my skull, and a salty residue burned my eyes. An explosion sounded off in the distance, and then I was gone.

∗ ∗ ∗

A burst of cool air flowed over my burning cheek. 'Dane, we're here. Are you still with me? Come on, say something.'

The sky was now dark and sprinkled with bright white stars. Behind Josh's head the Southern Cross shone. My mouth was dry, my tongue scaly as I slid it over the front of my teeth.

'I'm here.'

We were at the docks, but not Port Phillip. This waterfront was smaller, only a few ships docked and odd containers parked at the front of a grassy parking lot.

'Where are we?'

'Western Port.'

Over a short hanging chain fence we stepped, Josh bearing much of my weight.

'What … what are we …?'

'We're getting outta here, Brother.'

Now we were on the gangway, limping along creaky planks in the direction of a ship.

Then I was gone again.

DIARY 24

January 11 1984

La Mont was empty.

We checked Mr Ignatius's home. We waited, we stalked, and eventually we knocked on the front door.

The young lady who answered the door had never heard of him. We didn't bother to spoil her dream home with news of what had happened behind those walls.

His cabin was vacated, but gave us a clue: a half-eaten, moldy sandwich on the kitchen bench, clothes spread across the floor and dried mud footprints. He'd fled the cabin and La Mont, and us.

We burned part of the cabin – not the room where he left his video player and tapes – and called the fire brigade before we slinked off down tracks in the overgrown woods.

The last place we looked for monsters in La Mont was the place where it had begun for me.

I had hoped to never see those walls I once thought were made of ice, but we had to check. I shuddered as we walked up the path I'd walked a million times before, and I remembered everything except his face.

'You sure you want to check here? He's gone, Shorty; fled the hell outta here.'

'I know. But ...'

A wreath hung on the front door. I knocked, and a man answered. His son ran to him and tackled his leg as he appeared in front of me with a huge, happy-holidays smile on his face.

'Hello, how can I help you?'

'Does ...? I'm sorry, I must have the wrong house.'

'That's okay. Who were you looking for?'

I was walking down the step. I looked back up to the second-story window where a child's dream catcher hung.

'No one.'

Wherever she is, I hope she is okay. I hope she feels regret every day. I hope she has experienced enough agony to last her a lifetime. I hope she is happy.

We set off after the next in line. Policeman. It took three calls to get an officer to let slip where he had been transferred to.

'Seattle, Ms Collins. Seattle PD.'

'Thank you.'

'Best of luck.'

Leaving La Mont before the December snow had started to fall, the car was like a library most of the way to Seattle. I was frustrated. Disappointed.

∗ ∗ ∗

We haven't made the papers here in Emerald City, yet. The Green River Killer takes most of the murder headlines. I kind of fit his victim profile. I wander out by myself, I have no home, no connections ... That'd be funny, wouldn't it?

I'm nearly sixteen, and I don't know how old I'll be when this ends.

Nights when we don't search, plan or investigate, I go to music gigs and work on my art. On days off I take my work down to Pike Place and hope that if I sell enough Oscar will stop dealing drugs.

I want to imagine that this will all be a bad memory one day. I want this all to be something these teenagers we once knew committed. I kind of want to be normal.

Some days I sell a painting or two. Usually I don't.

LETTER 10

February 14 1994

Dane,

With my lone birthday present I'm locked in the bedroom. I've seen it, and felt everything about it. I know it's on the floor at the end of the bed, out of vision from where I sit on the carpet and lean on your bedside table.

I wonder about my birthday. While many kids were no doubt conceived on Valentine's Day, I was brought into the world by a slut who I doubt ever told, that is if she knew, my father. I concluded a long time ago that concerning myself with who inseminated my mother is pointless, as is any thought of the woman whose womb I came from.

It's my own fault, but I'm worried. I don't know what's gone into my body. I'm weak and I don't know how I'll protect myself.

I've complied with the injections on top of chemotherapy he's administered. Whenever I feel pain he pumps me with something. A lot of the time I don't even have the energy to disagree. It's an uncontrolled joy like when a child bounces on a trampoline. With each landing the next jump gets higher and higher until what was fun becomes scary, and soon the black rectangle is out of sight and they forget they were even grounded at all.

The injections have increased, and now have been daily. I fly higher with each dose.

I've listened to him, because stupidly, I've trusted him. The spinning has ceased right now from the injection, but the world around still turns. If I see the half-unwrapped present, I'll be thrown into a hurricane.

I wish you were here to stop this. I still don't know how it's true.

The truth is always better, unless of course you have the luxury of ignorance and innocence on hand, which unfortunately I lost a long time ago on my ten-year-old knees.

I sat at the kitchen table this morning, woozy and disorientated from another injection.

'Fr, French toast, orange juice, freshly squeezed, and a grapefruit,' he said, waiting at the table with the ridiculous apron on you used to wear – again I was reminded of you.

The present lay on the far side of the table. I rubbed my hand over the lump on my thigh. I should have stayed in hospital.

'You didn't have to do this, but thank you.'

'You eat, eat first, yes, and then cake, and then present, yes.'

I ate. It was horrible: burnt toast, off-tasting juice and unripe grapefruit, but I ate it all. I told myself that it's the thought that counts.

'Now cake, yes.' He brought it out from the refrigerator, still dressed in that ridiculous apron – 'Cooking with Love', come on.

He put down the frosted carrot cake on the table in front of me. The sight and smell of it made my stomach flip upside down. Hardened, shiny white frosting on top of an orange-colored cake the consistency of dried vomit, a kind of sweet, kind of rotten scent.

I fucking hate carrot cake.

He adorned it with candles until he ran out at seventeen. With the long, shiny blade he sliced two pieces of cake, and then, after hesitating, a third. The mind doesn't work on such big projects often, so I didn't bother to even question …

He inhaled his piece and I played with the crumbled cake for prolonged minutes in an effort to not be rude. I ate one bite before I excused myself, claiming stomach cramp – you know, chemo crap.

His breathing intensified with excitement, as he reached for the present. I think he may have even tried to smile – it's always hard to tell with people who can't actually curl their lips up.

'Now, now is time for your present, yes, it is time.' He handed it to me. 'I-I hope you like it.'

I ripped at the wrapping the way a child might do.

My brain wasn't quite up to date with what my eyes saw. It was still fluffy, but old and dulled, an eye gone. It smelled musky and stale. My brain caught up to what I saw.

It was my past, plain and simple.

The chair flew back as I fled to the bedroom. I locked the door, threw Leroy on the floor and crawled under the sheets.

He's still here, I figure, as I haven't heard him leave. I picture him at the kitchen table with an undrunk cold black coffee, staring blankly at the wall.

Maybe in some way I'm scared this demon has come back to haunt me, that it is right in my kitchen, but I've lived too long and seen too much to be truly scared of anything, Dane. There was a time when the thought of Mr Ignatius sent shivers down my spine and made me weep inside and out, but he isn't Mr Ignatius anymore. He is Nurse Cameron, and I'm too tired to be frightened of a demon I believed to be exorcized long ago.

There are too many ways for me to feel stupid about this, and trust me, I do. His face and most about him was blocked out a long time ago. But why did it not come back? How did I not realize? Those lifeless gray eyes. The raw throat of a smoker. Carrot cake.

Kayla

DIARY 25

April 29 1984

We're on the run. Well, the Castrators are.

We messed up in Seattle.

I should have just taken charge for once and slashed the whiny creep's throat from behind.

We had Policeman.

He was bound to a chair, gagged, blindfolded, and beaten about the head. He was still in his dirty pajama bottoms – children's pajama bottoms. His whimpers sounded like a mouse's peeps.

'You got the faintest hope of not being cut up if you follow every word I tell you. If you don't, I'll kill you, and make the pain twice as bad.' Oscar leaned into Policeman's ear. 'Right, I'm gone take off the gag. Scream and your throat goes.'

He was lying, of course. Regardless of what he told us, we were going to cut him up.

I passed Oscar a machete. He ran the dull edge of the metal along the side of Policeman's neck. 'You got it?'

Policeman nodded, and Oscar slid off the gag.

Oscar pulled a chair around in front of Policeman. I stood behind Oscar and held his shoulders. Behind every crazy man...

'There's only one way you not getting killed today and that's if you give up the one person we need more than you. We need to know where Ignatius is.'

His lips shook. 'He's gone south, to California. I don't know where.'

'What do you mean you don't know where? Surely you sick fucks exchanged addresses and numbers before you left La Mont.'

'No, I swear, we didn't. The only thing he left me was a note saying he was going to California to get some sun and hide away. No address, no number: I swear.'

I took the machete from Oscar and walked to the back of Policemen. I ran the machete around his neck, firm enough to break skin, but light enough not to kill.

'I swear!'

'Shut up!' Oscar stood and squeezed the incision. 'You're going to have to think real damn hard if you wanna keep your nuts.'

It went back and forth like this. Maybe hours. I have no damn clue. It's hard to guess time when you're killing someone. Oscar stood and then sat, threatened and cut a little more. I jabbed, breathed down his neck and then followed with the cold steel of a blade.

Each time, a tiny piece of information came back to Policeman's mind. We needed that information. But I realized that the trickling of his memory wasn't an act. He would've given up Mr Ignatius if he'd known. These creeps don't have loyalty.

I took Oscar aside. 'It's time to cut him loose. He really has nothing.'

Maybe Oscar had become worn down. It went on too long. My big brother, tall as a tree, dark as tar, messed this up, and I messed it up, too, because I didn't insist. I let him go on, and on, and on, until ...

There was a knock at the door.

'Leonard!' a woman called.

Oscar stood. And then suddenly Policeman started to scream at the top of his lungs.

The woman fumbled with a set of keys as we rushed out of the room. We fled through the back door and into the reserve behind his house. I'd never run so fast and leaped so high in my life.

We stopped and hid behind a large oak. I felt my heart beat as if it was racing to reach its last. I peeped out and down the hill to Policeman's yard. The lady surveyed the area. I ducked back behind the tree and gasped for air.

When I peered around again, she was walking back into the house. The police would be on their way.

We left our apartment as soon as we had collected our things. On the way out I picked up a morning newspaper from the ground. The headlines had taken a break from the Green River killer to focus on the *now believed to be two perpetrators in the Castrator killings.'*

The word was out.

The Castrators are an African-American male between eighteen and thirty, and a shorter accomplice. I thought we were chasing, but we'd started running again.

LETTER 11

February 16 1994

Dane,

I spent the night holed up in the bedroom waiting for him to move. If I ever slept, I woke up gasping and remembered what had clawed back into my life.

With the break of dawn I rose and crept into the kitchen.

He glanced up from the usual undrunk cup of black coffee. 'G-g-good morning, Kayla.'

I felt sick, but not from chemo.

He sat there like a prune. A powerful monster, now shriveled. I could tell from his red eyes he hadn't slept. I doubt he had moved anything more than his chest to breathe. But even that I doubted. It would take a deep cut to find a human heart beneath his pasty white skin.

My lips trembled as I spoke, but the words felt like shiny razor blades. 'You're a fucking piece of shit.'

I stood at the end of the carpet and glared.

'How has this happened?' I asked. 'Tell me how!'

He glanced up. 'I hid here from the men who were killing us.'

Men? I thought, and then realized. He doesn't know it was me.

'I went, went to jail for seven years, and after I was let out, out last year I had my, my registration re, reinstated. I wanted to find you, and make, make things right. I looked from the, the time I got out.'

If I had had more strength I would have hit him. It hurts to know that he tracked me down. I've been running all along.

'Then I saw you in the, the newspaper. Your, your art gallery. I went into your, your studio one day and was going to … but then you came into the hospital. I couldn't believe my eyes. I got transferred to, to Oncology, so I could care for you. It was fate.'

Frustrated tears pressed at my eyes. But I gripped my jaw tight. I wasn't going to let him see me cry. 'Spare me your born-again, rehabilitated bullshit. I don't need your fucking care. And this isn't fate. It's a cruel coincidence. You tortured me … Why can't I recognize you?'

Again, he glanced up from his coffee, and I saw his face. Still, I didn't remember it properly.

'I, I was assaulted in jail, and they, they had to reconstruct my face. When, when I got out I changed it more with plastic surgery. I didn't want to look like me.'

'You can't change the pain you brought me …'

He interrupted me in desperation. 'I changed, everything. My name. My face. I want to, to do good …'

'Don't interrupt me.' I stood and pointed in his face. My legs were rubber. 'You can never make up for what you did.'

It was silent for a long time before I thought of something. 'If you want to do good, take me to see her,' I said.

∗ ∗ ∗

It was placid and still: neutral cream walls, wooden floorboards and white flowers. The receptionist greeted me with a warm smile that was all lips, and after I'd disclosed who I was, summoned a nurse, who greeted me with much the same smile.

A glare let him know to wait in the car.

'She's outside, sitting on the bench,' the nurse said, stopping at a set of white doors with cross-hatched window frames. 'She sometimes has trouble with her memories; her condition you see.'

Through a pane of glass, I gazed out to the garden and the bench.

She was seated straight and stiff, as if her spine was incapable of bending, with her hands on her knees. I couldn't see her eyes, just the gray and white striped hair running past her shoulders, textured like frayed rope.

I pressed down the handle and the door clicked open to the garden outside. It was as if I walked through a time portal. I choked momentarily before the breeze got me and I released a balloon of anxious, pent-up air.

She didn't look up, even when I stood in front of her.

We were alone, together. She wasn't aware I was there, and I couldn't see the person who had brought me into this world. It was as if someone had gutted every part of her. She was a shell.

'Mom,' I said.

She brought her head up from the grass at my feet and met my eyes with a bloodshot glance. It had been over a decade since I'd seen her and longer since she'd seen me.

'It's me, Mom. It's Kayla.'

Her mouth moved to mime my name, and seconds later as she comprehended, her mouth began to twitch and her eyes darted side to side. She strangled her thighs with bony fingers, digging into skin to form white circles around red.

I sat beside her.

'I've always thought of you as a paradox,' I said. 'You gave me life and then took it away. You let it happen. I've hated you for as long as I've known what it is to hate someone, and I've wanted to love you for even longer, and there came a time when I accepted that neither can ever be right.'

She gawked at me with a look that would've broken anyone else's heart. I couldn't hear the words any louder than those raspy breaths through chattering teeth, but I knew what she said.

I think she's probably said it a million times before, if she's been in the right frame of mind. She'll probably say it a million more.

She cried. I pitied her, while at the same time cursed myself for it.

Her lips wobbled the start of innumerable questions, '*Wh-wh-wh…*'

'I know you'd probably do things differently if you had the chance.' I was calmer than I ever could've imagined to be in this moment. 'I don't blame you, Mom, but I can't forget that you let it happen.'

I stood and peered down at her. Her jaw trembled as she mumbled under her breath. I leaned over and in my hands brought her head up gently. I looked into her pale, frightened eyes, and saw the epitome of hopelessness.

With sweet, poisonous lips I kissed her forehead and offered every part of my heart I've wished for so long to give to a mother.

'Goodbye, Mom.'

I'll never see her again.

I don't know what to do, Dane. He's helping keep me alive, but I want him dead. He doesn't know it was me, and I'm not sure if I can hide this from him. I'm worried that I'll see the police one day, that I'll do something to bring them around. Most of all, I'm worried that I won't have the strength to finish this.

Kayla

DIARY 26

September 13 1984

California. One word, one state, one miserly clue to follow.

Sacramento has been useless, and I've begun to wonder about Oscar's commitment. He has been the driver for so long. Is he tired? Or, is he stuck?

In Dee's apartment I have enough space to paint and sculpt, but I'm hidden. My hope of finding Mr Ignatius seems to drop every day. At night Oscar is out on a street corner selling crack for his cousin, while he seldom helps me search for clues. We barely even talk about it.

'Your fashion sense is getting worse,' I said to Oscar as he flashed past my open door.

He back-pedaled. 'I got new kicks, Shorty, you don't like?'

'I'm talking about that ugly red thing hanging out of your pocket.'

'Oh.' He stopped. 'Round here I'm protected if I wear it. If I got this, you ain't gotta worry about me getting hurt.'

I raised my brow, sarcastically. 'That's a funny view of things.'

He came into the room and sat on the end of my bed. 'You know,' he said, as he began to pull the ends of my socks out, knowing how much it annoys me. 'You're getting pretty damn good at this artwork.'

'Don't try and change the subject, Asshole.'

Oscar laughed. 'Kay-Kay, is all good. We're safe and settled.'

'What if I don't want to be settled? We haven't found him yet. Forget about the policeman, we haven't found the man.' I lowered my voice to a hiss. 'We found your monster, but how the hell do you think I'm going to sleep properly when I know mine is still out there? My nightmares haven't stopped.'

I fixed my socks. Oscar lay down on the bed and gazed at the ceiling. The cracked plaster was like clouds across the sky.

'You remember what I promised you when we set out on this mission? I promised we would find and destroy these men.' He patted my leg and stood. He pulled my sock off again before he walked to the door.

'That promise still stands, Shorty.' He held up his hand and pinkie-clapped three times. I scowled at him, and crossed my arms. He stayed in the doorway and grinned, the way someone does when they know something you don't.

'Blueberry pancakes,' he said and then poked his tongue out. He got me, but I didn't let it show. I shook my head.

'Come on, Shorty.'

'All right!' I held my hand up and pinkie-clapped three times.

I can feel what I love being dragged away from me. The sun shines but this is the grayest place in California. We've chased, run from, hunted and hidden for three-and-a-half years. I want this to end, but I want it to end right. I can't chase this demon forever, and I can't run from him, either.

CHAPTER 19

I blinked. Things went from black to a blue and then back again. Someone sat down on the bed beside me.

'Are you awake, Dane?' It was Josh.

I opened my eyes. 'Yeah.' I rolled my head over and looked out the small circular window to the endless ocean outside. 'What happened?'

'We're safe. Will be in Burma soon.' He patted my hand. 'Rest up, Mate. You'll need your energy.'

Josh blurred and I started to fade again. He went to stand and I gripped onto his hand. 'Don't go.'

He chuckled. 'How about I lie down too? Sleep if you're tired and we'll talk if you're awake.'

He lay on the bunk across from mine. I slept most of the time on the boat, but when I woke, dazed and delirious, Josh was there, sometimes with food and drink. He watched over me and we chatted. It was like we were children again, sharing a room, and wondering about the future.

* * *

The port was small and decrepit, filled mostly with rusted fishing boats and dinghies. Josh was on the deck of the *Pinafore IV*, the ship that had housed us for three days, chatting with the captain. I waited on the dock and gazed at a plastic bag, floating in the water like a dead jellyfish. Below the moss-covered beams, water lapped against supporting pillars that plunged far down into the seabed, *whoosh, wosh, whoosh, wosh.* A burst of cool sea breeze raised goose bumps on the back of my neck.

Josh descended the gangway carrying a backpack, and joined me.

'So what happens now?' I asked.

'Well, the ship will be going back to Oz, but on the way it'll stop off in Hong Kong. That's where I'll meet Kerry and from there, I don't know. The boats to America go from the main port in Yangon to the west. Once you get there, this'll be enough cash to get you a ride to the States.'

He handed me the backpack, and an envelope with a wad of American hundred-dollar bills. 'Supplies and some pocket money.'

'So this is it?'

Josh dropped his head. 'Yeah, I guess it is.

He lit up and I coughed, not from the second-hand smoke but from our impending goodbye.

'I need to know,' I said. 'Did you ever want to give up and run away like I did?'

'I don't see what you did as giving up.'

'I don't know … I missed out on seven years with you. I gave up on us. It's hard if I think about it.'

'The past is a lesson and it can be baggage. Stevie taught us that baggage will only weigh you down until you break, or you learn to relinquish it. I chose to relinquish it. Regret shouldn't affect the future.'

'But when do we settle down and stop running from everything?' I said.

Josh butted out his cigarette and tossed it into a puddle in the trough of a wooden beam. 'We've never run and never will. You can't run from something that's inside you.'

I mulled over what was happening, this goodbye, and I searched for more crap talk to put it off. 'I haven't figured out a lot, but I think life might be about balance. Not escaping the bad times or forgetting them, but creating enough good times to outweigh the bad. I guess it's how you see things.'

'That's it, hey.'

It was very possible that we would never see each other again. We both knew this.

Conversation stopped, the lapping water now the only sound.

A sailor called to Josh from the deck.

'That's my call.'

It was as if I'd finally conquered a mountain that I'd gazed at in the distance for so long, but at once needed to descend in preparation to climb another. As beautiful as the view on the next mountain would be, I still wished I could hold this view a little bit longer.

We clung to one another. Through the jumper's wool came the warmth and comfort of my brother's tears.

'If I don't see you again, Man ...' Josh stopped short, choking up. 'I hope everything turns out well with you and Kayla. I'm going to believe it does.'

'I love you, Brother.'

We released, nodded and then Josh walked away. With one foot on the gangway he stopped and turned. 'Next time I see you, Man, you better have trimmed that mullet.'

I laughed and released everything: tears of happiness and sadness, confusion and realisation. 'Fuck you, Short-arse.'

We smiled at each other once more, and then Josh climbed aboard. I stayed on the dock until the ship became a speck on the horizon.

Where he would go, I would wonder; what he would do, I would wonder; what he would feel, I would always know.

CHAPTER 20

I hitched a ride with a farmer to Yangon. It was late afternoon when I made my way through the marketplace. Rickety stalls and huts lined either side of the dirt walkway. Children with dirty faces in tattered rags played and laughed, while donkeys, chickens and dogs roamed freely, sniffing and searching for food on the ground. Merchants and locals hollered at each other, bartering for seafood and fresh produce.

The harbour beckoned ahead of me in the distance.

I passed a group of men playing poker and smoking cigars. Another group played blackjack. I grinned. At the conclusion of a hand a man stood and raised his arms. He squawked in Burmese and pointed to a donkey on top of which a man lay, bound by his arms and legs. I stopped short of the group and watched.

The men put down their cards and passed around a bottle of liquor. One disappeared momentarily and then reappeared with a bag. Three of them untied the man on the donkey and then pinned his arms and legs. The man with the bag knelt and from it withdrew a needle, a spoon, rubber hose and a small bag of heroin. He heated the powder in the spoon with a match until it turned to tar. He wrapped the hose around the man's arm and when a vein popped he shoved the needle into it. The man's eyes rolled back in his head with the ecstasy of an H rush. They left him on the ground and kicked him around for a while before they retied him to the donkey. He sobbed into the ass's coat. The man who had won the hand took the donkey and the man from his previous owner and left the group.

They moved slowly, and in a few moments I was walking by their side. The owner stopped and jabbered with others. The man on the donkey looked across at me with junky eyes. 'Help me,' he said.

Although he appeared Asian, his accent was American. 'I'm trapped. Please.'

I didn't reply, but continued in time with them on the other side of the road. From my backpack I withdrew the envelope with cash in it. I took out half and stuffed it into my underwear.

At the front of a small tin hut they stopped again and the man settled on a seat beside another, while the prisoner drooled like a mental patient on the donkey's back. The two men at the table dealt cards and played blackjack against each other, one playing dealer, the other the punter.

I crossed the dirt road and approached the men.

'English?' I asked, and they looked up.

'Little,' the donkey owner replied.

'I'll play you. Blackjack. For the donkey and man.'

He thought it over. 'Money?'

I showed him the stack of American bills and his eyes lit up. 'Okay, okay, we play. One hand. I deal. You win, you take donkey and American. I win, I keep and get money.'

I agreed. He took the deck and shuffled, smiling at his friend. He dealt. I got an eight and six, totalling fourteen. The dealer's card that showed was a six, his other card was face down as usual. He asked hit or stay. I waved, palm down in front of me to signal no more cards.

The dealer revealed his other card to be a queen, which meant he was forced to hit. The next card he turned was a ten – he busted. He smacked the table in anger. I stood and was about to claim my prizes when he flipped the table and stepped up to me with a knife drawn.

I raised my hands and he yelled at me, mostly in Burmese. 'Cheat, cheat,' he said in English.

'No cheat,' I replied. 'Fair.'

He growled and kept the knife high. 'I not like cards.'

'I played the cards I was given. You want money?'

He raised his eyebrows, curiously.

'I take donkey and man. You take money.'

He thought it over and then lowered the knife, and held out his hand. I handed him the envelope of cash. He flicked through it and then nodded. 'Go.'

I backed away from the men, took the donkey's reins and made my way along the dirt road, glancing over my shoulder every so often. We didn't speak until we were at the wharf, when the man on the donkey reached out and took hold of my sleeve.

'Thank you,' he said, and started to cry. 'You have no idea ...' His drained eyes blinked twice and then closed.

I traded the donkey and some cash for a ride in a cargo hold of a boat headed for America. Inside the hold, I set the man down on a makeshift bed. Dozens of Asian men, women and children filled the room, lit only by the dull yellow glow of a gas lantern.

∗ ∗ ∗

The days on the open ocean would've been longer without Michael Lau, the man I'd picked up in Yangon. We were fed by the sailors – basic meals of rice and vegetables – and given plenty to drink.

For the first forty-eight hours his heroin withdrawals were bad. I held him down and kept him clean and hydrated. Caring for him kept me from my growing nerves.

I dreamed of Kayla when I slept and I woke with the excitement of a child at Christmas, hoping I would soon see her again. There were nightmares, too. An Australian jail cell. The ship sinking. A party of waiting authorities. Never seeing Kayla again.

On the third and last day of the journey Lau settled and slept well. When he rose, he reached for the cup of water and gulped it down.

He sat up on the makeshift bed. 'Thank you,' he said. 'I can't thank you enough.'

'I couldn't just leave you there,' I said. 'Sounded a long way from home.'

He sighed and nodded. 'That couldn't be truer.'

'How did you end up on the back of a donkey being pawned around by Burmese drug mules?'

'Long story. Let's just say I got burned.'

'We've got hours before we dock. I could do with a long story Mr Lau.'

'Well, I suppose the first thing you should know is that it's actually Special Agent Lau.'

'An agent of what?'

'CIA … Now since I've told you something I'm never meant to let slip, how about you tell me about you, and how you ended up in a Yangon market, buying donkeys and men from drug mules, and why you're on a boat to America.'

My stomach dropped a little. 'Well. That's kind of a long story, too.'

'We've got some hours.'

So I told Special Agent Michael Lau of the CIA my story and he told me his.

Along with his partner, he'd been dropped in Burma on an undercover mission to gain inroads into the operations of Khun Sa. Both he and Wang were of Burmese heritage and fitted in fine, until Wang fell in with the wrong team. He took bribes and made deals with the drug lords of the Triangle. When Lau found out and moved to report him to his superiors, he discovered that Wang had framed him for making the deals instead. Wang was rescued from Burma, while Lau was left to rot in prisons. Then he was sold, and re-sold and traded, and all the time injected with potent H to keep him subdued.

'At first the militants along the border thought they could ransom me. When they found out I was useless, they were going to shoot me. But then a farmer bought me with a donkey and made me work his farm in shackles. Once he had no use for me he sold me to mules and since then I've been tossed around and filled with dope. Think they've kept me around for a plaything more than anything else.'

'How long have you been away?'

'Three years since I was first dropped in, which makes it two years in captivity. I honestly don't know how to thank you. I'm in your debt.'

'Just won a hand of blackjack, that's all. I'm sure you'll pay me back one day. Anyway, what'll you do when you get home?' I asked.

The cargo hold jolted. The ship had come to a stop. 'I don't know, Pal. I guess the first thing is getting back to my family. What about you?'

The door to the hold opened and sunlight beamed in. We covered our eyes. 'Exactly the same,' I said, and gazed out at America.

DIARY 27

April 12 1985

It has taken a lot to adjust.

It probably started long before I read the article to Oscar, but when the newspaper found its way into Dee's shitty apartment it all came to a head.

Potential Castrator Victims Arrested

Two men have been arrested in relation to their involvement in a nationwide child pornography and trafficking ring. The men were taken into custody last week in two separate arrests made in Los Angeles and Seattle.

During interrogation, detectives from the FBI uncovered the connection between the two men and their links to three murdered males said to be victims of the notorious Castrator Serial Killers.

One suspect had previously been targeted by the killers, who remain at large and tried to obtain information from him before fleeing.

Just like that my demon was taken from me.

I should have been happy.

We sat in Dee's living room: the funky-smelling, cluttered room with warped cream carpet.

'What do we do?' I asked.

Oscar held the article, though he couldn't read it. 'What can we do?'

'You know I hate it when you answer me with another question.'

He sighed. 'Well, we know it's them. I mean, what is there for us to do?'

I took the article from his hand and read over it again. What I felt in the living room was what I imagine breaking up feels like. And it was definitely something else, too. Failure.

'It's not over.' I was trying to convince myself. 'It can't be.'

Oscar stood. 'I think it has to be.'

I screamed at him.

* * *

For weeks after this we lived as normally as two teenage serial killers can. Oscar sold drugs and earned money. I painted and sculpted and earned much less. The portraits were the darkest I've painted, the sculptures the most distorted and disfigured. I went to the markets each day I could. In the afternoons I bought groceries and walked the city streets. Sometimes I imagined I'd find a creep on the streets who wasn't hidden safely behind prison bars. Or I'd imagine what might be happening to them in jail. I found some comfort, but it faded.

December came, and Christmas decorations adorned the streets of the ghetto. It was kind of like a kid's attempt at a birthday cake – shit covered in a bit of sweet. The shopping malls were filled with fake Santas, who invited children to sit on their knees. I nearly found my creep to kill. Dee even rummaged up a crappy plastic tree from somewhere in his putrid apartment.

It was the eleventh when Oscar knocked on my bedroom door.

I had adapted. I was content, at least on the outside. I had my art, and it was enough.

'Shorty!' he was cheerful and wore a Santa Claus hat. 'Get your bag packed. We going on an adventure.'

'What, we're moving? Why?'

'I found a nice place in Los Angeles. Santa Monica, Venice area. Through a contact. So we gonna live there for a while. Pack your stuff.'

I packed everything, which was next to nothing: a few clothes, my art supplies, my diary and a chewed-down pencil.

At first I was annoyed, but then on the drive I became excited with each passing mile of coastline, the golden beaches I've missed since San Francisco, and I got the feeling of starting over, again.

The apartment was on the border of Santa Monica and Venice. Not posh or fancy, but it was quiet and more than I could have ever imagined having. As soon as we arrived I threw my bags down in the bedroom and cornered Oscar in the kitchen as he sipped on a Coke. I wrapped my arms around his neck and clung to him. 'This is amazing,' I said, and he smiled.

Those next three December days were the happiest days of my life. Santa Monica and Venice don't know what winter is. Oscar and I walked down to the pier every day and sat for hours watching the waves glide in. Or we'd stroll the entire boardwalk several times, through the market stalls. We were in bare feet, arm in arm, talking about everything good and nothing in particular. There were no drug deals, no murders, nothing horrible. Oscar wore khaki shorts and a white tank top, and I sported a new light flowing dress. We were covered head to toe in sunshine. I forgot who I was and where I'd been. My mother could have been the most perfect person in the world, my father just a call away, my prom sorted with a great friend to dance me into the night. College could've been around the corner. There was no anger, no gravel lump in my throat, no sadness, no missing anybody.

I woke one morning to the sounds of Oscar rustling through the apartment.

He was dressed, his backpack on the sofa.

'What are you doing, Ozzy?' I rubbed my eyes.

'Sorry, Shorty, I didn't mean to wake you.'

'That's okay. What are you doing?'

When he dropped his head it dawned on me. He's my big brother, my best friend since I was ten, I can read him like a book. He'd only brought a backpack ...

'Oscar, what are you doing?'

He sat down and patted the sofa. At first I stayed put and glared. I didn't want to sit. If I didn't sit then he couldn't start to talk. If I ran into the bathroom and covered my ears and yelled LALALALA at the top of my lungs he couldn't tell me anything.

I sat.

'Shorty ...'

'Fuck you.' I tried to yell, but through my sobs I only squeaked. 'Why?'

He went to cover my hands with his but I tore them away and crossed my arms.

'You're the most beautiful person I've ever met, Kayla. You're gonna do great things. You got talent. You gonna paint, you gonna sculpt and do all that arty stuff. I ain't special.'

It was the first time I'd cried since I was a scared little girl alone in my bedroom, dreading to hear the second, fourth and ninth stairs creak. Oscar ignored my meager protest and pulled me close. 'You deserve better than what I can offer you. You my baby sis. You deserve to live happily and without crack heads and drugs dealers and gangbangers. The life I fell into, it ain't for you.'

'You don't get it.' I sniffled and wiped my nose on my wrist. 'I'd rather sleep in that stinking apartment with all of that crap as long as it has you in it.'

He kissed my forehead and cupped the back of my head in his huge palm. 'I know, and if there was any other ... this is how it has to be. You ain't safe up in Sacramento. I'm in this deep, Shorty. It's only going to get worse.'

'But, what will I do? I'll be alone – where will I go?'

Oscar reached across and brought the backpack to his lap. He opened it. There were no clothes inside.

'This apartment is paid for. There's enough cash in here to last years. I want you to do what you should be doing. I want you to be an artist. Buy a studio and sell your work. I ain't a smart man, Shorty, but one thing I know is you got talent. This is everything I've earned from dealing, and everything we took from those creeps. This money is for you, so you can have the life you deserve. You'll meet new friends, hell maybe even meet a nice guy one day who treats you right, and you'll be happy. In time you'll be happy here.'

'But ...' I didn't know what else to say. He wasn't adamant like he could be when he had a knife. He spoke calmly, and was sure, even if I wasn't.

We lay on the sofa for some time as I tried to accept it. At last I asked for one thing from him.

Along the beach we strolled, and talked about everything good and nothing in particular, the way we had done the days before. We laughed about what I might be doing when I turned twenty-five and all the fun times we'd had together. We wrestled – I won of course – and Oscar piggy-backed me around the shoreline and into the waves.

It was afternoon when we stopped on the sand. I knew it was time.

The biggest lump stuck in my throat, while at the same time I felt that feel of new beginnings. For everything we'd experienced together, our time had come to an end. It had been coming for a long time.

'Well,' I said, 'I guess this it.'

He nodded.

'I'm going to miss you, and you know I'm probably going to barge into the apartment in Sacramento in about a week.'

'I know ... I'm going to send you a Christmas present, and you can send one to Dee's if you like.'

'Yeah, right. Now you're just being silly.'

Oscar smiled a smile I'd first seen on a little Negro boy, tall and skinny, now ginormous and muscular, in an alleyway in La Mont. A smile that told me everything was okay, you're safe. The smile now told me the very same thing. Beside me was the tiny boy who'd grown into a man in front of my eyes, as I grew into some sort of woman. I saw everything precious I'd salvaged from childhood. I saw my brother, my best friend, my hero.

'We'll be moving from that joint in the new year ... and once I'm gone from there ...'

'I know. You're gone.'

'It's how it's gotta be. I'm sorry.'

I reached up, brought his head down and kissed his forehead and then hugged him. Not too tight. I knew I had to let go.

'Don't you ever say sorry to me,' I said into his ear. 'I love you, and I always will.'

In his arms I felt invincible.

'I love you too, Shorty. Forever.'

We let go of each other. Moments like this don't come around very often.

'Maybe I'll see you out in the world sometime,' he said. 'I dunno, in the news for your art, or maybe in the distance at an exhibition of yours. We'll smile ... and we'll hold our hands up, and we'll pinkie-clap.'

'I'd like that.'

He took my hand and opened it. In my palm he placed a silver necklace.

'It was my mother's. I want you to keep it.'

I closed my palm and hugged him once more, trying to savor everything.

'Goodbye, Ozzy,' I said.

'Goodbye, Shorty.' He started toward the car.

He opened the door.

'Hey,' I called.

Oscar turned. I held up my hand and pinkie-clapped three times.

Oscar smiled and pinkie-clapped back. 'Maybe when I see you next, you will be able to reach the top shelf.'

'Maybe you won't need a haircut.'

He blew me a kiss and climbed into the driver's seat. Once the car disappeared around the block it all hit me.

∗ ∗ ∗

I struggle sometimes to come to terms with this part of my life. Trying not to miss my brother, and trying to forget that my monster is still alive.

'There comes a time to hang on, a time to fight, and a time to let go. There comes a time for everything to start and everything to end.' It was written in a public toilet above the toilet-roll dispenser, a fancy way of saying 'Shit happens.'

He sent me a Christmas present. I cut the picture of us into a heart and placed it inside the necklace he'd given me. I didn't send a present back, yet.

LETTER 12

February 21 1994

Dane,

I have little time.

I woke early, as has become my habit. I need to be awake before anyone else is: before the newspaper trucks drop off their hauls to the stands on Eighth Street and before the surfers have donned their wetsuits to ride the first breaks. Before he is awake, crawling and creeping about the living room, or going into work, or washing dishes.

This morning I needed him. It was the start of a new cycle of chemo, but it wasn't this I needed him for.

I needed to finish it.

He plodded into the kitchen, rubbing his eyes. I was at the table with Leroy in front of me. Knots of dirt, clumps stained with semen, missing patches of fur.

When it began, I always imagined Leroy had the power to turn into a real lion at the sound of trouble. I dreamed he would transform the halitosis, breathing sickly into my face as Mr Ignatius kneeled in front of me. I always thought Leroy would protect me. But he was just a toy.

I needed to clean Leroy.

'Sit down,' I said, firmly, though I labored to keep my hands from shaking. 'We are going to talk.'

He sat across the table from me.

I took time to gather myself. I sat eye to eye with the man who had torn apart my childhood. 'There's something that you don't know,' I said.

'Are, are you okay?'

I smiled. 'I'm fine. But you might not be.'

'What, what do you mean?'

'Shut the fuck up and listen. You are going to prepare my medication. After that you are going to lie down on the bed in my bedroom. Don't ask any questions.'

He didn't. He prepared the chemo and then walked to my bedroom and lay on the bed.

'Just stay still.'

I tied the bed sheets around his wrists and ankles as hard as I could, the way Oscar showed me. He flinched as the binds became painful and his extremities started to swell.

Standing on a chair, I reached high into the wardrobe and removed the sheet of wood covering the hidden compartment – one you never found. I took down the shoebox filled with newspaper clippings.

Man Found Dead With Testicles Removed.
Killings across the Country Could be linked.
Serial Killer on the Loose.
Man Hunt: Castrator Targets Mature-aged Men

I flicked through them and smiled. I'm twisted, I know, but I found joy reliving the places Oscar and I had traveled, the sights we'd seen and all we'd accomplished together. I smiled at the thought of my big brother, a scruffy Negro from a broken home who loved me like only a big brother can.

I unfolded his letter, not read for some years now. '*Never write back,*' he wrote. '*I just wonted to say … I love you Shortee.*'

I'll read it again, I know; pore over every beautifully misspelled word and ill-formed sentence.

I stepped down from the chair with the shoebox. 'You never knew it was me, did you?'

'What, what do you mean?'

I sat on the bed and held the newspaper articles so he could see. 'It wasn't two men chasing you. I was the other Castrator.'

His face turned whiter than a wedding dress. 'You, you …'

'If you want to make things right, this is how you do it. Don't scream.'

I stuffed an old sock into his mouth and watched his eyes water. With the kitchen knife from the top drawer I popped off every button of his shitty cream shirt.

'I've wanted to do this to you for years.'

Down his stomach I smoothed the blade, trickles of blood emerging from shallow scrapes, and prepared for the first deep cut. I would brand him and then lower the blade to finish what I'd chased for most of my life. He quivered and made meager pleas for mercy. I relished every tiny nuance of helplessness. His pants came off and then his underwear.

I stopped, aghast.

His dick hung like a rotten, shriveled banana, and beneath where his testicles once were was a mound of darkened scars.

I took the gag from his mouth and he wept. 'It happened, ye-years ago, when I was assaulted in, in prison.'

I fell from the sadistic high of my revenge to now, to the happier times, the times after all of it was first over, the times with you, Dane, the times on the beach, and the times of this cancer.

I untied him and left the room. While I sat on the sofa, he emerged from the hallway and came and sat opposite me.

'K-Kayla,' he said, rubbing his hands nervously. 'I'm not going to tell anyone it was, it was you.'

'I don't care.'

'But, but please can you do something for me? Can you forgive me?'

My jaw clenched so tightly I thought my teeth might break. 'I'm not going to do anything for you.'

'Please, I need you to.'

My anger had started to boil, but now I calmed.

He edged forward in his seat. 'I need you …'

I brought up my forefinger and stopped him coming any closer. 'You did things to me that I wouldn't wish upon anyone. I can't forgive you and I'm never going to forget. But I'm going to move on.'

He went to talk but I cut him off. 'Get your things and leave and don't ever come back.'

I stood and pointed to the door. 'Get out.'

He collected his keys and wallet from the bench. He opened the door and turned to me. I started to feel nauseous, but hid it and stared him down, feeling stronger than I'd ever felt before.

This was goodbye to a man who'd infested me since I was ten years old. I'd been his puppet; he'd become mine; now it was time to cut the strings altogether.

'Goodbye Cameron Ignatius,' I said. 'You no longer exist.'

He left the apartment and closed the door.

I went to the kitchen table and retrieved the syringe. I sat down, leaned back against the cushion, relaxed and pushed the chemo medication into my arm via the catheter.

Right away I started to float a little. My sides hurt, a dull ache at first that became a strong throb. It hurt everywhere. I was high, up there somewhere.

I've found my feet, and still it hurts.

I'm worried, Dane. This doesn't feel good …

CHAPTER 21

Lau and I got the bus back to Los Angeles from the small nothing town on the west coast. When we said our goodbyes in Reseda, he gave me a number to contact him. I figured it couldn't hurt to have a special agent as a friend.

The taxi cruised south on the 405. Suburbs turned to valleys of green. We passed Getty View and as we got closer the freeway gathered lanes. At the LA National Cemetery the three-mile sign hung for Santa Monica Boulevard. I could barely sit still. When the driver turned right, it felt like the final leg of a race. I almost expected a finish-line tape to be there at the corner of Wilshire and Seventh when I got out of the cab.

I burst into the apartment and called for Kayla, only to find it empty. It took me three attempts at knocking on neighbours' doors to find out where she had gone. I ran through the streets faster than Carl Lewis, all the way to the front doors of the hospital.

'Kayla ...' I was out of breath. 'Kayla Manning.'

The receptionist on the ground floor entered Kayla's name into her system. 'Nephrology – second floor, Room 214.'

A doctor, security guard and several nurses asked me to slow as I sprinted through the hospital. I hurried up the stairs to the second floor and down the hall toward the ward. I slowed to a power walk at the ward clerk's station and turned left. I passed room 201, 202, 203, until I got to Room 214.

The curtain was drawn. I knocked, but when no answer came I entered.

She lay there, unconscious, heavy breaths clouding the oxygen mask. A tube came from her nose, and drips were attached to her forearm. From the window gentle sun glowed on her face, those forever-pert cheekbones were gaunt and grey. Even in her baldness she was the most beautiful thing I'd ever seen.

I fumbled for words. Frightened, I moved close and took her cold hand in mine. There was no response and I pleaded quietly for her to rise, still grasping for speech. Burying my head into her limp knuckles, two things came out: 'I'm sorry and I love you, Kayla. I love you, Rascal.'

Through the previous months, with the seesaw of hope and haplessness, the idea of seeing her had become more of a dream. And now I was here it did feel like a dream.

I tried, but failed, to hold in my tears. I pressed my eyes onto her knuckles and wept. Her hand moved. I brought my head up. With her free hand Kayla removed the oxygen mask. Her eyes remained closed. 'Stop crying you big sissy.'

'I'm sorry,' I replied, and dried my face.

'Dane? Oh my god ...' She turned her head. 'It's you, what the hell ... Am I dreaming?'

'No, Babe. I'm here.'

She worked her eyes open to thin slits. They were bright but worn down, like a candle nearing the end of its wick. She trembled but managed to raise her forearm. I leaned in, and she ran her hands over my face. She was drained, but started to laugh, and a thin river of happy-sad tears flowed down her cheek. I caressed her skin and wiped away the tears with my fingertips. I held the side of her neck and stared into her emerald eyes.

'I'm so sorry, Baby,' I said. 'I was ...'

With the little strength she had, she pulled me down by the collar. Our lips connected. We held that kiss for a long time, but when we broke it didn't feel long enough. I planted my lips on her again. Then she patted the bed for me to lie beside her. She couldn't move, but I found enough room and nestled in. I wrapped my arms around her frail body.

'Did you get my letter?'

She shook her head.

I went to tell her what had happened, but she stopped me.

'Shut up, Dane,' she wheezed, fading, her eyes on the ceiling, closing and then reopening. 'It doesn't matter right now.' She put the oxygen mask back on, drew some deep breaths and then took it off again. 'I'm just glad you're here now, Babe. I've missed you.'

'I've missed you more than I could ever miss eating. I love you more than every part of this life combined. I'm never leaving you again.'

Kayla faded off to sleep. I dozed on the hospital bed with my arms around her.

That evening I was woken by a nurse adjusting the intravenous drips. 'I'm sorry,' she said. 'I didn't mean to wake you.' She finished and then started from the room. I slid out of bed and followed her into the hallway.

'Excuse me, Nurse.'

She stopped and put down her folder.

'Can you tell me what happened?'

'Oh, you don't know?'

'No.'

'How do you know Kayla?'

'I'm her …' I looked into the room at the love of my life, slobbering. I had missed that drool. 'I'm her boyfriend, Dane. It's a long story.'

'It's good you're here now.' She sighed. 'Well, Kayla was originally admitted and treated for cancer. She was given a poor outlook but has battled on. She's still very sick, but as you would know she's a fighter.'

Damn right, I thought. The toughest little bitch I've ever met.

'And …' she stopped. Her eyes darted left and right before she ushered me to the chairs opposite the room. We sat and she continued. 'I'm not meant to say anything, I could get in trouble, but I think you have a right to know.

'One of her nurses offered to be her home carer. He administered morphine that was not prescribed and gave her increasingly greater doses, which wore her kidneys down until they failed. By the time she called the ambulance, she was in a very bad way. Only regained consciousness two days ago.'

'Shit. What happens now?'

'Well, the nurse has gone into hiding. And Kayla still has cancer, and now, with the poor state of her kidneys, she needs dialysis to filter her blood.'

I'd seen dialysis once before, when Teddy's father needed it, and we'd all chipped in so he could afford it. It was a horrible thing. I could picture it – tiny, bright-eyed Kayla so full of bounce and growling determination, shadowed by some skyscraper of a contraption. I grimaced at the thought. 'How long will she need it?'

She hesitated. 'Dialysis is something you need forever … unless a suitable transplant can be found.'

'Is she on a list for a transplant?'

Standing, the nurse peered into the room to check on Kayla again. 'She is, but I'll be honest with you, Dane, this list is awfully long.'

My lips trembled. 'Why her?' I screamed in my head. Life just isn't goddamn fair.

'What if I could give her a kidney?' I said.

The nurse raised her brow. 'It would make her life considerably easier, but it is a big thing to do.'

'If it will mean she doesn't need dialysis,' I lifted my T-shirt and pointed to my side, 'rip it from me now.'

She laughed. 'It's not quite that easy. We would need to run some tests to see if you're compatible – bloods and all that.'

* * *

I spent the rest of the day and night in Kayla's room. She woke twice and had little energy. I told her about the deportation. She struggled to speak, but we nestled in together and I held her until she fell back asleep. I dozed off in the chair beside the bed to the sight of Kayla bathed in moonlight. I woke constantly during the night to see her fogging her mask with hot breath and each time I prayed I would be compatible.

Compatibility testing took the entire next day. Needles, X-ray scans, lab tests. I barely slept that night. The day after, I had my psychological exam. That evening and the morning that followed I waited impatiently for the results of the evaluation, tapping my feet against the floor and fidgeting, head cluttered by anxiousness and another night of sleep punctuated by sharp gasps for air as I woke.

Kayla was out the entire time, occasionally sleep-talking about blueberry pancakes. I wanted to nudge her awake and see her eyes again, talk to her and tell her it was going to be okay. But I knew she needed rest and I told myself there would be plenty of time.

Kayla's nephrologist, Dr Marsh, entered her room late that afternoon. He stood at the end of her bed with a clipboard held to his chest. 'The test results have come back.'

I felt queasy. Kayla grumbled in her sleep. I sipped my coffee, stood and walked with him to the door.

'You're going to have to take it easy for a while, sacrifice some food, because you're donating a kidney to Kayla.'

Soon after I met with the anaesthesiologist, surgeon, nurses and social worker, and received my final instructions for the surgery, the most daunting of which was to fast after midnight.

Kayla flickered awake later that evening, while the sun set outside the window. I scurried from the windowsill to kneel beside her bed. 'I'm here, Babe,' I whispered. 'And you're getting a kidney.'

'Where from?' she said, barely strong enough to make a sound.

'From me.'

She worked her eyes open. 'I don't want your kidney, it'll smell.'

'Too bad. You can't do anything about it.'

She poked her tongue out and then faded off to sleep. I closed the curtains and crawled into bed with her. With her hand in mine, that night I slept deeply.

CHAPTER 22

The next morning, not long after dawn, I sat on a leather sofa in the cafeteria with a hollowed-out stomach. I felt an arse plonk down on the other end. 'Sorry, Pal; don't mind if I sit, do ya?'

'Go for it.'

He shuffled through the magazines on the coffee table, and I glanced over to see him take a copy of *Spin*. He flicked through it noisily. Soon after he had sneered at an article, he tossed the magazine onto the table and leaned back.

I was no longer interested in the news, but still I kept my eyes on the pages, my attention on the man to my right. I was certain, but the coincidence was almost unfathomable.

I slid the paper onto the sofa and prepared to sneak away.

'You waiting for someone, too?' he asked before I could stand.

I leaned forward with elbows bowed into my knees. 'I am.'

'My wife's up in oncology. Had this lump for weeks now and finally they tell her she's got lymphoma. I'm scared as hell, Pal.' He gazed out into the garden, so I took a moment to turn and examine his face. It *was* him. Agent Dean Ludwitz of the INS, the man who'd thrown me out of the country. He didn't know who I was. Not yet.

I followed his stare to the huge palm leaves spread like the open hand of a giant. 'So am I.'

'Who are you waiting for?' he asked.

'My girlfriend.'

'We're in the same boat then, hey. One day you're planning a vacation, well overdue, and the next you're coming into this place, finding out how long there is to live.'

'My girlfriend has had kidney failure, both of them. If she doesn't get a transplant then she's gotta be on dialysis for the rest of her life. She's twenty-six. That's just bullshit.'

He turned from the garden, and I felt his eyes scan me. 'Yeah, you're right,' he looked back to the palms, 'it ain't nothing but unfair. Life just ain't fair. So what happens now?'

My heart sped as if someone had shot a litre of adrenalin into my bloodstream. It was difficult to concentrate.

'I mean, what are you going to do?'

I released the breath pent up in my lungs.

'That's about the only simple part of this whole thing.' My heartbeat was still askew. 'I give her one of mine, and she gets a chance at a normal life ... Just wish I could take the cancer away, too.'

I asterisked this sentence in my head – Kayla and I were never going to be normal. We would both tear through time, not let it lead us. Our journey wasn't taken on foot – although I'd hitchhiked over more distance than I could measure – it was ridden on a fireball blasting through the days, weeks, months and years. Fuck normal, I thought. Safe, but boring.

'That's one helluva a thing to do. I'm sure she'll give you something nice for it.' He turned and winked. 'A massage some chocolates and I reckon some damn good loving, too.'

That pissed me off. I was scared as hell that I was going to lose her. 'Cancer, Mate. I'm not even thinking about bloody chocolates.'

'Point taken.' He crinkled his forehead. 'You know, you seem familiar.'

'Doesn't everybody? I'm the guy you talked to at the hospital in the cafeteria. The next time we meet I'll be familiar, or maybe I'll be a stranger.'

He chuckled. 'Deep as a puddle, Pal. I suppose you're right. Mind plays some funny old tricks on ya, huh. I'm probably going loopy.'

He was as sharp as a goddamn Wurundjeri spear. I was familiar.

'It does that, trust me; just this sterile shithole playing up to our fear.'

A grin lingered on his face for a while, and he stared into blank space. Then he stood, bid me goodbye and moseyed through the cafeteria.

When I entered the room Kayla was awake and beaming, though her eyes were open only a slither. I sat and gripped her hand.

'You never got milk,' she said.

I sniggered. 'You don't forget, do you?'

A knock came at door and a doctor leaned in. 'Just need to do some final things soon before the procedure this afternoon. I'll give you a minute.' He left us alone.

'You're taking that stinking kidney,' I said. 'Nothing you can do.'

She laughed. 'I know. Thank you. When I've got the energy, I will thank you properly.'

'Honey, if I could take away every bit of pain I would. You are everything to me, Kayla, and I would give everything for you. You never need to thank me.'

Her eyes welled. 'Dane, stop; you're going to make me gush, you jerk.' She cradled my left hand with both of hers. 'I've written so much stuff in my life, painted and sculpted, and said a lot, too. But I've never found the right way to express myself to you, so I'm just going to say it the simplest way.'

'I love you, Dane.'

It was the first time she'd ever told me. I wanted to run down the hospital corridor like a love-crazed teenager. But I stayed by her side and kissed her like a love-crazed man.

'I will see you after surgery,' I said after our lips disconnected.

The medicos entered as I left. I sat on the chairs in the hall, leaned my head back, my crown pressed into the bottom of the windowsill, and closed my eyes.

'Well I'll be damned.' It was Ludwitz.

It could've been a minute or an hour that I'd dozed off. The doctors were gone from Kayla's room.

'Didn't think we'd run into each other again,' he said. 'Big hospital.'

'Small world.'

He munched down on Skittles from the vending machine. Red, purple, green and orange, all of them whirled in his hand before he gorged them in one rainbow slobber.

'My Gwen is just three rooms down.' Although not unfriendly, he was not jovial, either. 'Is that your girlfriend in there?' he pointed toward Kayla.

'It is.'

For long seconds, maybe even a minute, he gazed through the patterned glass to Kayla in the bed. Silence clouded the corridor and made everything murky.

I stood. 'I might catch you later, I've just gotta ...'

He grabbed my arm. 'Hold on a second,' he said, and then spoke like a parent does to a small child when Benji goes to doggy heaven. 'You know, I figured out why you seem so familiar.' He took out his wallet from his coat pocket and let it fall open to show his ID badge. 'We need to talk, Dane.'

* * *

The motel room had that damp blend of cheap air freshener from countless affairs, hookers, transients and lacklustre unmarried men stained into the bubbled wall paint. The rain had poured down since we left the hospital – Californian rain like bathwater. The omnipresent motel Bible had been removed from the bottom drawer and lay open on the bedside table. The bed was loosely made – male made – and the windows were layered with several coats of dirt, an impression of transparency. A suitcase lay open beyond the foot of the bed, clothes strewn over the floor.

I was cuffed to the bed and near me in the lounge chair Agent Dean Ludwitz of the INS tapped his forefingers together. He had led me with a subtle gun to remind me not to run away.

'I don't know how the hell you got back here,' he said. 'Determined, I'd guess.'

I shrugged. 'Something like that.'

'I checked your name on the medical sheets, and I remembered it – the beating in Santa Monica. You did a real number on Agent Rogers. Still can't eat right. Started drinking, lost his job, wife. Everything.'

'I'm not overly sympathetic to women beaters.'

'He was undercover.' He sighed. 'Anyway, how *did* you get back here? False passport?'

I told him my story and he thought it over. 'You really love this girl, Kayla, don't you? The same way I love my Gwen.'

'I do. That is if you love your Gwen the way I love my Kayla.'

Ludwitz scratched his head. 'I guess if I'd somehow found myself in your situation then I might have done the same. But you still have to go home, Dane. You can't stay here. If I let you go, I have to let every single illegal immigrant go, and I can't make exceptions, even if you seem like the type of guy America would welcome.'

The best part of America already had. 'I'll die before I leave this country and my girl again.'

Ludwitz chuckled. 'That's about the only option you've got.

'Look, you don't have a choice here, Dane. You don't cooperate and your girl doesn't get the kidney. I could take you in right now and have you locked up. But this way you can give your girl the life she deserves. Once you are fine to fly you have to go home. For final this time, no sailing the seven seas.'

I don't think he believed half of what he said but he realised sometimes things are not black and white.

'Okay,' I said, spite forcing my teeth to grind. 'I'll go quietly after the operation.'

'Then we have a deal.'

I nodded. 'I won't run.'

'How long until you need to be back?'

'Half an hour.'

'We're going to stay here until then. You'll be under hospital arrest when we go back.'

Time moved slowly. I remained hostile to him and he stayed his distance. We understood each other's pain in some parts, but still I wondered, 'Why can't you just let me go?'

Mostly, I ploughed through ways I could escape but wound up at the same conclusion – he had me. I couldn't run. I needed to give Kayla the kidney. I just hoped he'd give me the time afterward to explain to her.

The second hand of the clock sounded like an axe chopping wood. I continued to run through hopeless scenarios of a happy ending. Ludwitz stood straight and crossed his arms. He glanced up to the clock. 'Time to get back to the hospital for your prep.'

'Before we go, do you mind if I make a call?'

He collected the telephone from the bedside table and brought it to me. 'Go for it.' He sat on the bed.

I turned the number on the archaic dial. 'Mind if I get some privacy. I'm calling my mum.'

'Yeah, no problem.' He stood. 'I'll get some fresh air. Two minutes, okay?' The motel door creaked behind him and clicked shut. I could see him through the white lace window shade, surveying the car park. With my cuffed left hand I slid the dial around to each number, one after the next.

The dial tone turned to a ring.

'Hello.'

'Good to be home?' I asked.

'It is, but I miss my donkey a little.'

I chuckled. 'I'm in a bit of trouble ...'

And I made my call.

* * *

I lay prone, my head planted into the hole of a donut cushion. The metal operating table cooled my skin through a thin sheet. The room was a clutter of surgeons, doctors, nurses and I'm sure somewhere a commentator, who conveyed the action. I couldn't see anyone, only the ground below me, from which tiny specks of glitter shimmered in light. Shadows passed over the floor: a man with a bucket, a kit of torturous instruments, a trolley, a machine, some legs, masked faces.

Ludwitz had returned me to the hospital, explained my arrest and cuffed me to the bed. He waited until I was in the Operating Room before he left me.

Conversation, instructions and checks floated through the air.

'Nurse ... Yes, that will be fine.'

'Two units ...'

'Marker please.'

'All set?'

'Okay, Dane, we are about to administer the gas. Just relax and count down from ten.'

'*Ten, nine, eight, Batman ... Goodnight.*'

CHAPTER 23

I woke in the hospital in a single room. Mouth dry, head just as dry. My left side was dull with pain. I was cuffed to the bed.

Ludwitz came in shortly after. 'It all went well,' he said. 'Your girl is doing fine.'

'I want to see her.' I tried to sit but was kept down by the restraints.

His eyes fell to the floor. 'I'm sorry. I can't let you leave the room. We'll be transporting you when the doctors give us the all clear.'

'You're fucking toying with me, aren't ya?' He turned and pushed open the door. 'Ludwitz!'

He ignored me and left the room.

I yelled until my throat hurt and banged my head into the pillow over and over. Eventually I broke down and cried myself to sleep. The night was peppered by broken sleep. I dreamed of walking along the beach with Kayla, not another soul around. Water cool against my ankles, sun warm on my cheek. Our hands felt like they could never be torn apart. We were free. Then I'd wake and fall back into the present. I was screwed. Australia. Jail. And never seeing Kayla again. When my eyes opened, the nightmare returned.

The next morning I woke to the dawn chorus of songbirds. Ludwitz sat by my bed reading a newspaper.

'How can you do this?' I was tired and weak, but ready to explode. 'I'm not asking to stay here, I just want to see her before you tear me away from her again.'

He looked up from his paper. 'I don't make the rules, Dane, but I have to abide by ...'

A knock at the door interrupted him. A man in a black suit and dark shades entered. 'Hello, Gentlemen. My name is Agent Mark Westway.' He flipped open his wallet. 'CIA.'

Ludwitz stood. 'What can I do for you, Agent Westway?'

'This man is of interest to the Agency. I will handle the matter from this point forward.'

'What is this about?'

'The case is classified. Thank you for your work, Agent Ludwitz.'

Ludwitz was astounded. 'You can't ...'

'I can. I have precedence.' Westway flashed his badge again. 'That'll be all, Agent. I'd rather not contact your superiors.'

Ludwitz was trying to catch flies in his mouth. Westway stood firm, with his hands held in front of him. The men stared at each other for another moment before Ludwitz dropped his eyes.

'Keys, Agent Ludwitz,' said Westway, holding out his hand.

Ludwitz passed him the keys for the cuffs. He unlocked the restraints and passed them back. Ludwitz looked at me in disbelief and then shuffled from the room.

Once he had gone, Westway closed the curtains and sat by my bed. 'Agent Lau apologises that he can't be here in person.' He removed an envelope from his jacket pocket. 'We are working on some things. He is doing well and will be fine in case you're wondering.'

He handed me the envelope. 'He hopes that this has sufficiently paid his debt. Agent Ludwitz won't bother you again. The rest is worked out.'

'Thank you,' I said. 'And please thank Lau for me.'

Westway nodded and left. I lay in bed, stunned, trying to comprehend what had just happened. I even slapped my thigh to make sure I wasn't dreaming.

Shortly after, some nurses came to check on me. They adjusted machines, took notes and then started to play with my bed.

'What are you doing?' I asked.

'Following doctor's orders,' one replied.

They wheeled me out of the room and down the hall. One held open the door to a room and two others pushed me in.

There was another bed already in there. Waiting in it was the most beautiful sight I'd ever seen.

I forgot about the pain and sat up as my bed was fixed into place beside Kayla's. She smirked up at me from the pillow, her eyes squinted and bloodshot. 'I was worried you'd gone for another adventure,' she said. 'But that man in the suit explained everything.'

Tears of joy built up and I tried to press them down, but one leaked free. I leaned to kiss Kayla's outstretched hand, thankful that I'd bothered to rescue a stranger from a donkey.

'I'm not going anywhere, Babe.'

* * *

For the next month I stayed in hospital with Kayla. No questions were asked, no bills given and we were left alone. I figured it was good to have a friend in the CIA.

At night I fell asleep with Kayla resting in my arms and each day I pushed her in a wheelchair around the courtyard. She smiled when she spoke about Burty and how he'd made hospital bearable. During these walks we unlocked the door to our pasts and let each other in.

'This one,' Kayla said, pointing ahead.

I parked her chair and helped her onto the bench. She cradled a toy lion in her arms.

'When we sat here, he always told me about this place just before heaven, where you can look in and see all the good that is still to come. Like Friday in the Sky.'

'He sounds like a wonderful man,' I said. 'I reckon he's probably found his Friday in the Sky.'

Kayla cuddled up to me. 'I'm sure he's on a ranch somewhere.' She hugged the lion tighter.

'Where'd the lion come from – was it a present?'

She sighed. 'Yeah, I guess. His name's Leroy. Had him when I was little.'

'You still are little.'

'Yeah.' Kayla laughed. 'And I've still got him.' She held Leroy out in front of her.

Until the sun faded to dusk, Kayla told me about her childhood, her teenage years and everything up until now. When she finished she was clutching Leroy like a protective blanket.

'What do you think?'

I ran my hand over her cheek and kissed her forehead. 'I think I love you enough to do this a hundred times over, and the more I find out about you, the only thing that changes is I love you more.'

She leaned over, kissed me and we wrapped each other up. 'I love you too, Dane.'

* * *

We returned to the apartment late in March with a care plan mapped out for Kayla.

I carried her luggage into the living room and she parked herself on the sofa. I went into the kitchen to make a coffee. I took the milk out of the refrigerator and rearranged the alphabet magnets into **KAYLR SU** … When I went to move the X, I noticed the picture stuck beneath it.

'Let's go,' I said as I sat down beside Kayla. 'I'll finish my coffee and let's just leave.'

She took the picture of the house in San Fran and gazed at me, wide eyed. 'Are you serious?'

'We'll figure out the money.'

Kayla bounced off the sofa and went into the bedroom. She returned with a backpack and tossed it to me. 'Open it.'

Inside were stacks upon stacks of hundred dollar bills. 'If you had let me finish that night on the beach, I could have told you that I've got the money.'

We sold the apartment in two days for well below market and packed up our lives.

Sunshine kept us company on the drive to San Francisco, warming the leather of the seats and making our palms stick together with sweat. We stopped on the outskirts of the city and bought a brand-new Stewart longboard for Kayla.

After a brief discussion, the estate agents accepted our offer for the house. The movers set up everything, and when it was done Kayla and I stood on the balcony overlooking the coast.

Kayla gazed into the distance. 'It's beautiful, isn't it?'

I wrapped an arm around her. 'Nothing like it.'

She looked over her shoulder into the house. I followed her eyes to the toy lion poking out from a box.

'I have to go do something,' she said and then kissed me. 'I won't be long.'

I hated to see her walk out the door, but I knew it was important.

DIARY 28

May 16 1986

It's been a year since Oscar brought me to Los Angeles and left me with a backpack of cash and an apartment.

I'm still haunted by our failed mission. It's an arm wrestle. I forget about it when the deep Californian sun shines on my skin. But the monsters have left claw marks deep in the tissue.

I've spent some cash and set myself up. I bought the '77 Cadillac Impala convertible, which had eyed me since it appeared in the used-car lot off Fourteenth, and I've rented a studio two blocks over in Venice.

Three months of planning and creation and I've been open for a week. During the day people browse as I work and I'm starting to earn something of an income. I go home each night to watch the news.

Normal is strange.

I'm trying.

I walk to and from the studio each day. Mondays I shop for groceries, and I top up on bananas most Thursdays. I visit the Fox on Lincoln to see a movie. I roam the boardwalk and foreshore, and soak up Venice Beach: I sit and laugh at the basketball players, I nod to the drum circles, and I buy random trinkets and jewelry from the market stalls, wave off offers from the smoke-sellers. I'm a normal part of Venice.

I take trips in the Impala to any reachable part of the coastline – down toward San Diego and up to San Francisco, where I gaze from the pier at the house on a cliff in the distance. I paint and sculpt and live how I choose. Mostly.

It's not easy to meet people. Most of them shit me. George and Jose from the corner store might be the only ones who don't.

I wish I could get rid of my fears. A creepy old man will make me jump in the studio, make me reach for the closest sculpture knife, even though he's just an old art connoisseur.

In the front of my mind I am a strong, confident woman, who could crush any man if he tried to hurt me. I've spilled the blood of those who tried. In the back of my mind I still quiver. Somewhere inside, I'm still the little girl dreading three creaks of the stairs.

I read that Oscar was arrested and confessed to the murders. The article didn't describe how the FBI were led to him, but spoke of revenge. It said he had acted alone.

After this I stopped reading the newspapers. By now the trial will have finished – open, shut.

To let him take the blame makes me feel like crap.

So why don't I just go and turn myself in?

Because to know someone loves you just for being you is the greatest feeling in the world.

He sent me a letter. Tears pushed into my eyes. He told me enough without saying too much.

'Do nothin. I'm fine. New plas to live, ain't bad. I think I be here for a long time, long leese you no. I can't tell you the address but just no I'm fine paying rent on my own – I would not have it any otha way. I like to think of you in your howse, and this is what makes this howse ok.'

He finished the letter simply: *'I love you, Shortee.'*

LETTER 13

March 23 1994

Dear Dane,

With the roof down on the Cadillac, I crossed the Golden Gate and cruised up the 101.

Leroy sat beside me in the passenger seat. When I glanced he looked back. He'd always be looking back.

I picked him up, kissed his forehead and then tossed him onto the highway. I didn't bother to check the rear-view mirror, but I imagined that instead of bouncing like a useless stuffed toy along the melted tar he transformed into the lion, ferocious and real, that I always knew he could be.

The many buzzers that sounded as I entered the visiting room in San Quentin reminded me of how monotonous beeps become in a hospital. Had things turned out slightly differently at one point some years ago, buzzers may have been beeps to me all this time.

I waited at the table, fiddling with my nails.

A huge, solid man with a shaved head in an orange prison uniform entered the room escorted by a guard. He ran his hand over his bald scalp where his afro used to be, his crystal-blue eyes wide in disbelief. With his hands and feet cuffed, he sat opposite me.

The guard left us.

'Lovely day,' I said.

He snickered and drew lines on the table, trying to hide his smile. 'I'd be out there enjoying the sunshine if you hadn't come.'

'You've got plenty of time to enjoy it.'

We locked eyes and all that was good about my childhood came back.

'I'm not surprised, ya know. I think my never and your never got different meanings.' Now he couldn't hide his smile. Never could. 'I've always wondered if you read …'

'I've read it a million times.' Warmth flowed through my insides. 'Perhaps I'll write back one day. Ambiguous and all. Or maybe I'll just tell them it was all me, and not let you take the credit.'

'You always been full of crap, Shorty.'

'And you still need a haircut.'

Oscar pretended to use an afro pick and smirked. Through the eyes of any other he might have looked like a vicious inmate, but he was the sweetest boy I'd ever met.

'I'm doing good, ya know. It ain't that bad in here. I never got to go on school camp, so I guess this is my version.'

I giggled about how I'd thought of hospital in the same way. We were family after all. 'I know what you mean. I just hope you have some friends to look out for you.'

'I've got plenty, Shorty. Don't you worry about me. Are you all good?'

'I'm the best I ever have been.'

'That's all I've ever wanted.'

The guard came over. 'One minute, Oscar.'

'They don't give me a whole lot a time for visitors these days.'

Sunshine glowed through the barred windows onto the table between us. 'I won't be coming up here again.'

He nodded. 'That's how it's gotta be.'

'Before I go …' It was hard to say something I had thought over and again for years, but not verbalized for just as long … I fell short. 'I just wanted to say thank you.'

Out came his infectious white-toothed smile, which had caught me by surprise in an alleyway in La Mont fifteen years before. 'You don't ever need to thank me.'

'Yes, I do. You gave your life for me. You sacrificed your freedom. I've always felt guilty knowing you are in here and I'm out there. It's never been fair.'

Oscar shook his head, still grinning. 'I've lived every day of my life from the time I met you until this moment right now, and I always will, thinking of you. You make me happy. I did bad shit on the streets, and I'll do my time in here and probably do more bad shit, but the one thing that has always made me go to bed with a smile is that I got to know you, Kay-Kay.'

He covered my hands with his. 'They might've put my big ole body in this joint, but my heart is right out there with you. They can't lock up our love, Lil Sis.'

We could've been running through woodland without a care in the world. There was no orange uniform, no prison walls, no metal cuffs. It was just Oscar and me, alone in our own little world.

Our hands entwined. His skin was warm, a warmth that has nothing at all to do with temperature.

'I love you, Ozzy. I always will.'

'I ain't never stopped, Shorty. Never will.'

The guard returned to Oscar's side. 'Time's up.' We stood and Oscar blew me a kiss. I caught it and pocketed it.

Oscar walked toward the prisoner's entrance with the guard at his heel. My eyes remained open, but the present disappeared. There were piggy-backs on a San Francisco shore. An awkward, drooling, teenage boy, sleep-talking about blueberry pancakes. A killer fashioned beautifully with cherry-red splatter on his chin. A gangbanger covered in bandanas with crack in his palm. A sacrifice for my life. An innocent. Most of all, I saw my big brother.

'Hey, Shorty!' Oscar called from the doorway.

He shrugged his arms away from the guard and held up his hands. With his pinkie finger he clapped three times against his thumb. I raised my hand and pinkie-clapped three times in return.

HOME

Kayla came through the front door with a bottle of milk. 'I figured I'd get it. We know what happens when you go out for milk.'

I stood up from the sofa and stopped her at the kitchen bench. I slid her bandana off and ran my hand over her scalp. 'You're beautiful like this.'

She perched on the kitchen bench and we kissed, and began to melt together. I carried her into the bedroom and lay her gently on the bed. Making love was slow. Intense. I felt things I didn't know I could feel.

Afterward, Kayla sprawled out on the bed, and broke into an open-mouthed snore.

On the balcony overlooking the coast I waxed the board – the one with orange and blue lines she'd bought me years before. Waves curled into the shore to form perfect barrels, while the break of dawn threw shimmers of white on the water's surface.

In the kitchen I finished a cup of coffee. Beside a vase of spring flowers sat a pad of Post-it notes.

'Just went out for a surf,' I wrote on a note, and stuck it with care on Kayla's cheek.

I went down the cliff-side path toward the water with board under arm, watching my feet imprint into the sand, and was startled by the flick of sand onto my leg.

'Last one into the water is a giant pile of crap!' Kayla called as she sprinted past me, holding the longboard above her head.

She made the water before I did. Side by side we paddled out into the surf and bypassed the breaker. On the calm behind the waves we sat up and faced each other. I held her hand. Water lapped against the board; my legs dangled in the sea.

Everyone was there with me. My mother. My brothers. And the girl I loved.

I was home.

DEAR READER

Firstly, thank you for taking the time to read *Just Went Out For Milk*.

Writing is my passion and bringing stories to people to entertain, educate and inspire is my aim in life. You are helping make this possible.

The story you just read was an adventure, not just to read, but to write. What started out as a completely different book transformed into the preceding novel. It was a gargantuan piece of work after its first draft, and much time has been spent editing and refining the story. What I hope remains is the best story.

I had several goals with the book. I wanted to deliver an adventure both physical and emotional for the reader to experience. I aimed to create real protagonists who had overcome a lot in their lives – I wanted them to be real, and not at all perfect, but loveable for their flaws. And I wanted a unique love story, where two people find their place in the world with each other.

I hope you enjoyed the story, and the journey. The next won't be too far away. Be sure to drop me a line with questions, comments or just to say hi.

Tommy